THE WARRIOR'S QUEEN

BORDER SERIES BOOK SIX

CECELIA MECCA

ALTIORA
PRESS

To Lisa and Tina, my friends forever.

est of Highgate End, Scotland, 1273

Graeme de Sowlis and his brother, Aidan, heard the scream at the same time. They exchanged a look, and he took off running.

"Graeme, no!" his brother shouted.

He skirted the wounded and hurtled toward the burning cottage. Unlike the other buildings, its thatched roof had not been unattached before the raid. Bright orange flames rose high into the night sky. Not realizing they were now secure from their enemy, the villagers ran in every direction, including away from the very structure Graeme now entered.

Smoke gushed out toward him when he opened the door, but he charged inside, ignoring the loud pop announcing the roof was near collapse. Smoke confronted him at every turn, rendering everyday objects—a bed, a stool—into invisible obstacles.

"Goddamn it, Graeme, get out of there," Aidan roared from the doorway.

He didn't need the warning to know he wouldn't last long in here. Graeme knelt and tried to ignore the smoke around him and the flames above him. He saw her boot first. Reaching for it,

Graeme pulled the child toward him. She didn't appear to be breathing.

Scooping her up, he stood and staggered toward the door. The acrid air would kill them both if he didn't hurry, but his brother's cries led them both to salvation. Once outside, he gasped for clean air, sucking greedily as the girl in his arms lay motionless. A crowd had gathered, and as he began to breathe normally again, unease welled inside him. Would the girl live?

No sooner had he laid her on the ground than an elderly woman shoved him aside and lifted the girl's head into her lap. His mind felt like it was stuffed with straw, but the murmured word "healer" finally penetrated. It seemed God had not forsaken them completely. When the peasant girl, no more than ten and two, began to cough, another woman fell on top of her sobbing. Graeme was about to tell the woman to back away to let her breathe when the healer did it for him. Pushed to the side, the woman then ran to him, threw her arms around him, and began to sob.

"Thank you," she murmured over and over again. "My daughter . . . thank you."

"Mistress, I must speak with this man."

At the sound of her chief's voice, the woman disengaged herself, bowed to them both, and ran to her daughter's side.

Graeme followed Ferguson MacDuff away from the crowd. As they walked, Aidan fell in beside them.

"By all that's holy, Graeme, you could have been killed," Aidan said. Though he was Graeme's junior by three years, his protective impulses were more akin to an older brother's. A situation, Aidan often said, born from his brother's predilection for danger.

They came to a stop a small distance from the gathering, somewhere they would not be overheard. "Chastise your brother all you'd like later, Aidan." MacDuff extended his arm. "I'm too grateful to him to join in."

Graeme wrapped his hand around it, a gesture of solidarity.

2

"All is secure?"

"Thanks to you and your brother, aye."

Graeme released the man's arm. "Bloody reivers," he said.

Earlier that evening, just as the three men had sat down in MacDuff's solar to discuss the problem of increased raids along the border, one of MacDuff's men had come running into his hall to report the attack. The laird had ordered Graeme and Aidan to remain behind, as if either would have done so.

"This is not your fight," he had said.

Perhaps not, but MacDuff was an ally to Clan Scott.

Brought back from his thoughts, Graeme turned to MacDuff. "The men were English?" he asked.

"Aye."

The three men watched as MacDuff's people began the task of regrouping after the second attack in a week.

"There's something different about this latest rash of raids," Graeme said, reiterating the words he'd spoken just before they'd received news of the attack. These raids were intended to rile the clans. "Will your men catch them?"

MacDuff shrugged, but he didn't look hopeful.

Graeme looked from his host's soot-streaked face to his brother's frown before turning back toward the still-burning remains of the destroyed home. The raiders had stolen enough livestock to devastate more than one family and nearly taken the life of a girl too young to understand the dangers of the border along which she lived.

"If we are to stop this escalation, we'll need their help."

Aidan spat. "The English. You mean the same ones who—"

"Our own countrymen are not above reproach in this dispute," Graeme reminded him. Reivers from both sides wreaked havoc on the borderlands, taking advantage of the growing instability at the expense of all.

The girl he'd rescued stood, and nearly fell. He rushed forward to grab her, loosing another round of gratitude from her mother.

"Where will you rest your head tonight?" he asked.

"My cousin lives just there," her mother said, pointing to a home not far from them.

"Your husband?"

"Dead."

"I'm sorry," Graeme murmured, knowing now why no one had detached the roof when the raiders were spotted.

He turned back to his brother and MacDuff.

"We'll help put this back in order," he said. "And then I leave directly for Kenshire Castle in the morn."

"And I with you," Aidan said.

"The attack was against my clan. I'll be coming as—"

"Nay, remain with your new babe," he said, aware he had no right to give MacDuff orders. "And you"—he turned to Aidan —"will ensure there's no repeat of this night at Highgate." He spoke not as a brother, but as the chief of Clan Scott. As such, Aidan had no recourse but to agree with him.

Graeme waited. His brother was only passably adept at following orders.

"You'll take the men with you?" Aidan said finally.

"I will," he agreed, picking the girl back up.

Though he had no desire to attend a celebration of any sort, let alone the May Day celebration he'd been invited to across the border, this attack could just as easily have been on Clan Scott land. A meeting with their southern neighbors was more imperative now than ever.

He would do what he must to keep his people and his allies safe.

Even if it meant seeing Emma, the woman who had rejected his proposal of marriage in favor of another.

"Emma, give the poor woman a moment to recover," Lady Sara said.

Gillian smiled at her old friend, the Countess of Kenshire, and reached behind her back. "Don't be silly. I'm happy to answer her questions. But first . . ." She extended her hand to Lady Emma and opened it. "Though it's already five months past, I wanted to offer congratulations on your wedding." This had been the longest she'd been away from Kenshire, but their dwindling funds made it difficult to travel.

Emma stared at the silver-plated comb for a moment and then clasped it between her fingers.

"'Tis lovely," she murmured.

Not quite as lovely as the woman who would wear it, but Gillian kept that thought to herself. Emma, the only sister of Sara's husband Geoffrey, was indeed a vision. More importantly, Sara loved her, which was the only recommendation she needed.

"Sara told me your hair was as black as your brother's, so I thought the amber stones would be perfect."

Emma threw her arms around her, and Gillian hugged her back, pleased by the artless show of affection.

"Thank you," Emma said, releasing her.

"So tell me," Sara interrupted, obviously forgetting her admonishment to Emma. "What is this about the Earl of Covington? It cannot be true."

Gillian reached down to lift the sides of her gown as she sat in a cushioned chair in the corner of the solar, where they'd retired after dinner to speak privately. The room had always been one of her favorites at Kenshire.

She looked at Sara and Emma's expectant faces. They had been in good spirits all day, preparing for the May Day celebration that had brought her family here. Gillian did not want to sour the mood and tried her best to appear pleased.

"It is indeed true, though the betrothal has not been formalized yet. You will have to tell me all you know about being a good countess."

Sara and Emma exchanged a glance.

Sara would pursue this. It wasn't in her nature to do otherwise. So be it. "And you—"

"Have no choice in the matter," she said with finality in her voice.

While her childhood friend's expression gave nothing away, Emma's scrunched-up nose conveyed her thoughts clearly. "Isn't he the one who gave support to—"

"Aye, he is the one." Gillian had expected their disdain. The Earl of Covington lent his support to a man that tried to steal Sara's claim to Kenshire. When that did not work, the man had tried to kill her. "He lacks honor and is loyal only to his title and coin."

"And he's old," Sara finished. "With poor judgment. The same man who supported Fitzwarren."

Gillian pushed aside the unease, as Sara was right. Unfortunately, an unwanted vision of the wrinkled earl was more difficult to get rid of. "There is nothing to recommend him," she said bluntly.

"Your father facilitated this match?" Sara asked, reaching out to squeeze her hand.

"Aye." She squeezed back and pulled away. "Just as he and Mother were married to forge an alliance between two powerful Northumbrian barons," she said, more for Emma's benefit than Sara's. Neighbors and friends since before they had memories, she and Sara knew everything about each other. In fact, this was the first time she'd ever held something back from her. But the matter was simply too embarrassing to discuss. And this was a celebration to welcome spring and Sara's baby son. She'd not seen her friend in some time, and she'd not dampen it with her troubles.

"It is a daughter's duty to marry according to her father's will. Unfortunately, my father wills this match."

Sara gave her a pointed look. "You've always done what was right. Acquiesced to your parents, your father, in all things. But this? Gillian, listen to me . . . you can say no. Your father is much like my own in many ways."

All three women crossed themselves in honor of Sara's father, the late Richard Caiser.

"He will listen. How could he even think to marry you to such a man? Covington is—"

"'Tis done," she said, her voice firm.

Even though she'd agreed just the day before and the earl had not yet been notified, it mattered not. This wedding would take place. It had to take place.

Otherwise, her father—her family—would be ruined, something she couldn't bear to contemplate.

"We can talk about the old earl another time. I'd much prefer to hear about you and how you came to be with Garrick," she said to Emma. Turning to Sara, she added, "And the babe. Tell me everything. What is it like? Was childbirth awfully painful? Did you—"

"You're as impatient as Emma," Sara said. "I will tell you everything. As long as you promise to discuss Covington tomorrow. Do not think the matter is settled."

Gillian knew that tone, which had become even more inflexible since Sara's ascension to countess. She would not let the matter go, which ensured she would face another discussion about her unwanted future husband the next day.

"Very well," she relented. "Tomorrow. But only happy thoughts today."

Which meant no more talk of her upcoming nuptials.

"Spring may be coming, but it certainly feels more like winter today." Gillian had escaped her father's watchful eye by accompanying Lady Emma on an early-morning ride. Sara and her sister had remained behind in order to greet the guests who'd begun to stream in through the gates of the heavily fortified Kenshire Castle. Back home, she could walk from one end of Lyndwood to the other while singing *The Song of Roland*. Not so here.

They'd just returned and given their horses to a groom when a gust of wind forced Gillian to pull her cloak more tightly around her.

"If the sun comes out, there'll be no need of those," Emma said.

Both women looked up at the sky, which gave no indication of its intentions for the day. "So tell me, what does Sara have planned for the next few days?"

Emma rubbed her hands together. "Never mind Sara. Cook has been preparing a feast like 'none along the border have ever seen.' She adores Hayden, as we all do, and says he deserves a king's welcome."

Sara's newborn son was a lucky boy indeed. "Your brother is so gentle with him."

Emma smiled. "Geoffrey is the proudest father in all of England. But I suppose all fathers are that way."

Not all.

"I'm so very happy for them, Geoffrey and Sara, and for you as well, Emma. Sara has told me so much about you in her letters, it feels as if I know you already."

Two young boys ran past them, apparently chasing something, or someone. The open joy on their faces made her grin along with them. This was one of the reasons she'd always loved coming to Kenshire. Its occupants were pleased to serve Sara, just as they'd gladly served Richard before her. Her father was not a cruel man, but neither was he as nurturing as Sara's father.

"Everyone is so happy here," she said.

Emma nodded to one of the two boys who'd just run past them. His friend held a squirming rabbit in his hands. Apparently that was the prize they'd sought. The other lad now had tears in his eyes, and Gillian didn't hesitate to go to him.

"Is something amiss?"

The boy pointed to his friend. "He catches 'em every time."

"I see."

The boy's friend bent down and released the poor creature, which scampered away.

Gillian resisted the urge to wipe away the boy's tears. Instead, she leaned down to whisper in his ear. "Do you entice him with apples or clovers?"

When he shook his head, Gillian smiled.

"Next time, offer your wild hare a treat. It's still cold enough." At his puzzled expression, she clarified. "He'll be hungry, so feed him. Even if your friend is faster, he'll come to you instead."

She stood, not sure if encouraging the boy to catch wild rabbits was wise, but they'd likely do so no matter what she advised.

"I bid you a good day, sirs."

"We ain't—"

"You very well may be someday."

The boys glanced at one another and then fled, likely engaged in further pursuit of their poor prey.

"What did you say to him?" Emma asked as she returned to the path.

"I just gave him an advantage he didn't have before today. You were telling me about the plans for this May Day celebration?"

"Oh! I nearly forgot. Aye, tonight, a feast in honor of the youngest Waryn. Tomorrow, a wagonful of flowers will be brought to make the wreaths and the May Day Queen will be crowned at dinner."

"Have you been to a May Day celebration before?" she asked Emma.

"Nay, have you?"

"Oh aye, many times. The earl held one most years here at Kenshire, some larger than others. I've not always attended though. Some years, my father would not allow us to travel. But in times of peace . . ."

"Peace. Along the border. Could there ever be such a thing?"

"I believe so. As long as there are more who wish for it than those who seek to take advantage of instability. Look at what the last years have brought. Who would have thought the Waryns would form an alliance with Clan Kerr?"

"I certainly never thought such a thing was possible."

When Clan Kerr took Bristol Manor, the Waryns' holding, the two families had become bitter enemies, even more so because the Waryns' parents had been killed in the raid. But Bryce Waryn had since married the clan chief's sister.

"May I ask—" Nay. She should not have said anything.

But Emma's open expression encouraged her, as did her words. "Of course you may. Ask."

"Well . . ." Gillian's curiosity would surely be her downfall.

Why had she opened her mouth at all? "It's just . . . Sara says you and your siblings truly harbor no ill feelings toward the Kerrs. But . . ."

Oh, Gillian, what have you started?

"'Tis fine." Emma stopped just before the huge oak door that marked the keep's entrance. "I suppose it does seem curious that we could befriend the very clan responsible for our parents' death."

"And the loss of your home."

Gillian!

"Aye, and that. But"—Emma shrugged—"we are family now. And neither Toren nor Alex Kerr is responsible for what happened. They'd been ordered to take Bristol by their king. If you knew them, you would more easily understand. Aye, I hated them once. But not anymore. Nothing good can come from hate."

That answer made her like Emma even more. If only the men who perpetually sought battle along the border felt the same way.

"I hope I would be as forgiving."

Emma looked as if she wanted to ask her something, but the words didn't come. Though she could very well let it lie, Gillian had been blunt with her new friend—she owed her the opportunity to do the same.

"If you're thinking of my father, there is nothing to forgive. He is not forcing me." They both knew she spoke of her marriage to Covington.

"But certainly you could not *want* to marry such a man."

"Want? Heavens, no. But it is my duty."

Emma opened her mouth and then promptly closed it. And when she offered no more discussion on the topic, Gillian was glad for it.

"PARDON ME SAYING SO, my lord. But you are really tall."

"So I've been told." Right now, Graeme just wanted a meal. Unfortunately, though he'd ridden straight through the day, he'd missed the opening festivities and, more importantly, dinner.

The serving boy, who seemed to finally remember his duties, ushered him into the entranceway, where he was greeted by Kenshire's steward. He'd met Peter on his last visit, to see *her*. "My lord, we're so glad you could make it. Would you care to join the others in the hall, or shall I have you shown to your chamber?"

Though he couldn't see the great hall from where he stood, the sound of voices and laughter, along with the gentle lilt of a harp, made its way to them. If he could avoid Emma for the night, he'd gladly take the opportunity.

"It's been a long day. My chamber, if you please."

"And I will of course have a meal sent to you."

Thank Saint Andrew for that. "Will you please share my greetings with the host and convey—"

"You may convey them yourself."

Graeme turned at the sound of the familiar voice. He bowed. "My lord."

Geoffrey Waryn, Earl of Kenshire, extended his hand. "There'll be no formalities between us, de Sowlis. An ally of Garrick's is one of mine."

He shook the earl's hand before turning to greet the man's companion. The Earl of Clave. Emma's new husband. He'd detected their feelings for each other on their brief visit to Highgate before they were wed. Ignoring the thoughts, he nodded and said, "Garrick."

"Graeme."

These two men, the Earl of Kenshire and the Earl of Clave, were in a position to help him improve the conditions along the border. He would do best to set aside old grudges in favor of their shared cause. Which meant he ought to do the neighborly thing and ask after their wives. Both of them.

"How fares Lady Emma?"

Though he asked her husband, Geoffrey answered, likely still protective of his younger sister. "Very well. Though I do miss her scheming ways every day. Luckily, Clave is but a day's ride from here."

"And Lady Sara?"

Geoffrey smiled, his fondness for his wife no less apparent now than it had been on Graeme's visit five months earlier.

"Both she and my son are well. This celebration . . . I'll admit, when Sara first approached me with the idea, I thought it appalling. With an increase in raids . . . so much strife. But of course, she was right. This is exactly what we need."

He wouldn't ruin the evening with talk of politics, but those raids were the reason he was here. "Perhaps you can spare a moment tomorrow to discuss such issues?"

Geoffrey looked at Clave and then glanced back into the hall. "Of course. Will you come with us—"

"He's asked for a meal to be sent." Peter, who stood off to the side waiting, saved him.

"I rode through the night and day," he explained, not wanting to offend.

Geoffrey's eyes darkened. "Has something happened?"

Graeme should have realized he would make the connection. No one would go to such trouble for a mere celebration. "Nothing that cannot wait until morning. Go, enjoy your evening."

The earl was astute. He paused, looked him in the eye, and only then nodded. "Please try to do the same."

Just as Geoffrey and Clave walked away, a serving girl bounded from the hall and stopped in front of him. The look she gave him, all wide eyes and parted lips, was an invitation. She lowered the tankard in her hands and thrust her chest out, giving him a tantalizing peek at her offerings. She was pretty—as pretty as any of the others—and clearly willing.

Mayhap he should enjoy his evening.

As he walked by, following the steward, who was either oblivious or exceptionally good at his job, Graeme leaned toward her. "Where?"

She didn't hesitate. "Later. There's a garden out back, my lord."

He winked and walked away, following Peter through so many corridors it would be a wonder if he could indeed find the exit, and the garden, later.

THOUGH GILLIAN HAD BEEN COMING to Kenshire since she was a child, its splendor continued to delight her, even as an adult. Five years earlier, when she was but ten and eight, she'd been allowed to visit during the annual May Day celebration again. So much had changed since then. The border had become more dangerous, Sara's father had passed away, and her own family, unbeknownst to most, was now on the brink of destitution.

"Gillian?"

She stood between Sara and Emma as they watched the dancers from the side of the hall. The meal and trestle tables had been cleared, and the first night was proving to be a resounding success. More than one hundred and fifty men and women crowded the hall, which could easily fit a hundred more—which reminded her of one that was missing.

"Neill will not be joining us?" Gillian asked Emma. She'd not yet met the lady's twin brother, but she'd heard plenty about him of late.

Emma sighed. "Nay. He's lucky to still be alive, praise every saint who will listen to my pleas."

"My brother-in-law is indeed making quite a name for himself," Sara said.

Neither Emma nor Sara seemed pleased by the prospect.

"Everyone is so happy to tell me of his success. 'Lady Emma, your brother was crowned the tournament champion,' or 'Lady Emma, have you heard? Your brother bested last year's champion.'" She scrunched her nose. "I understand he hones his skills. I've been told many, many times the importance of that type of training. But does he need to enter every bloody tournament in England?"

Sara chuckled. "To answer your question," she said to Gillian, "Neill is doing quite well, though we do miss him."

As they spoke, Gillian's father and her sister, Allie, appeared at the opposite end of the hall. He swept the room with his gaze, looking for her, no doubt. She'd tried to get Allie's attention but failed.

"What is it?" Sara followed Gillian's gaze and then immediately turned to her sister-in-law. "Emma, will you excuse us? If Lord Lyndwood inquires after his daughter, tell him she is with me, that I needed a private word."

"Of course," Emma responded as Sara tugged Gillian away.

"Where are we going?"

"To have a private word."

But as they made their way through the hall, that feat seemed nearly impossible. People surrounded them on all sides.

"Come," Sara said, guiding her through a side door. She pulled her into a corridor and then out another door and into the warm night air.

"It seems your celebration did indeed bring spring along with it." While the morning had been chilly, tonight was everything an evening in May should be. Inhaling the not-so-distant sea air, Gillian followed her friend, grateful for the respite that would not last much longer.

Sara meant to know what was going on, and this time she'd not be waylaid.

They walked to the edge of the small garden just behind the keep. A much larger garden provided Kenshire with herbs for their meals, but this was the one Sara had always favored. Filled with flowers that had just begun to bloom, it was one of two private places in Kenshire where it was possible to hold a private meeting during festivities such as this one. The other was down by the water.

"Out with it."

They sat on a stone bench just at the edge of the tall trellis, which hid the inner garden.

"Sara, this is your celebration. A time for—"

"Rubbish."

"I really did not intend to trouble you—"

"Gillian."

Her shoulders sank. When Sara used that tone, she was in trouble. There was no help for it—she would need to tell her part of the truth.

"He needs the funds desperately," she blurted.

"Your father?"

"Aye. And, of course, the Earl of Covington has them."

"But he's not the only—"

"He has been asking for my hand in marriage for years. Since his first wife died. It will be good for Covington . . . and Lynd-wood," she said.

"Nay," Sara countered. "It will be good for your father. You know Covington's history. The men he chooses to ally with. I cannot, will not, see you with such a man."

Gillian sighed. "Sara, 'tis as I told you. I have no choice. My father wills it."

"But—"

"I'm not like you," she blurted.

Though she could elaborate, there was no need. Her friend had defied a distant cousin's claim to Kenshire while wearing boys' breeches. She'd ended her betrothal to marry a reformed reiver. She did what she wanted. Fought for her people so fearlessly that sometimes Gillian thought she must not be human.

But she was not like that, however much she might wish otherwise. She'd been raised to fall in line. "My parents' marriage was arranged."

"And are they so happy?"

"Of sorts."

"Was your father an old man when they wed?"

"Nay, but—" Gillian sighed.

"If you do this, you'll never know the love and passion that you deserve. I know your father is a strong and powerful man. You've been taught, as I was, to obey your parents in all things. But will you please just *consider* that you can, by rights, say no?"

Knowing her friend would accept no other answer, she nodded. "Aye. I will consider it."

Sara didn't appear convinced. But she finally stood and attempted to pull Gillian up with her. "I must be getting back."

"Go," she said. "I will be right along."

Sara glanced back to the keep. "You're certain?"

"Aye. 'Tis a beautiful night, and if you don't mind—"

"Stay as long as you'd like. And don't worry about your father. I will take care of him. And will keep Allie company."

Though it had been some time since she'd seen her friend, so much remained the same. Sara knew she kept her little sister close, protected her at all costs. Although . . . she was not so little anymore.

"I know you will. Thank you, Sara."

With a smile, her dearest friend walked away. Gillian sagged back against the bench, drained by the thought of what was to come, but a noise behind her caused her to freeze. Should she call Sara back? Was there an intruder?

Nay, once her heart stopped racing, she realized there was no threat. It was a sound of pleasure, not pursuit—lovers meeting in the garden. As she stood up, intent on leaving, a moan reached her ears.

She should return to the hall.

Instead, she moved closer and peered around the edge of the trellis.

She barely managed to contain a gasp.

A blond girl in a servant's dress had her back to Gillian. She couldn't see the man yet, but the couple shifted a moment later, and moonlight shone on his face, making the features she could see plainly visible. High cheekbones and hair somewhere between blond and brown.

And it was short. At least on the sides.

But it was what he was doing to the woman that made her feet feel as if they were molded to the ground. When she tossed her head back, he ravished her neck with open-mouthed kisses. Supporting her with his hands, the man, a nobleman to be sure, turned his head just slightly and . . .

He saw her!

Gillian backed away and froze, unsure of what to do. Would he alert the girl to her presence? Would he come after her?

It seemed he'd do neither, for the sounds resumed. And Gillian took the opportunity to run away from the lovers. She only stopped when she arrived at the same door they'd emerged from earlier.

Leaning against it, Gillian closed her eyes and imagined the couple again. He'd been so tall and handsome, and yet there'd been something gentle about him. And the serving girl had clearly liked what he was doing to her.

Gillian had never so much as kissed a man under the watchful eyes of her father. She'd been courted, aye, but never left alone with a suitor.

And now it seemed she never would kiss a man. Well, with the exception of her future husband, but that thought was not a thought she wished to dwell upon. Better to go back inside, find Sara, and act like she'd never witnessed that embrace.

And try to pretend she didn't want that for herself.

3

"*A*n unlikely place for a meeting. But since you're here—" Geoffrey stood next to him, crossing his arms and looking at the spectacle before them.

"I'd say this is the perfect place," Graeme answered.

The midday sun shone down on a courtyard filled with people . . . and flowers. Lots and lots of flowers.

"What will we do with all of these wreaths?" the earl said, shaking his head.

Graeme looked at the pile that was becoming larger every moment. Though he'd been to a May Day celebration before and was as glad for spring as anyone, he couldn't answer Geoffrey's question. It did seem like an overabundance of floral wreaths. "You English do have strange customs."

But Geoffrey wasn't listening. Graeme followed his gaze and spied Lady Sara on her knees, laughing over a pile of orchids.

"Everyone deserves this," the earl said.

"This?"

Geoffrey spread his arms to indicate the courtyard. "The security we enjoy here."

He was about to answer—it seemed the perfect segue to a conversation about the border—when he saw her.

Lady Emma ran up to Sara, knelt down beside her, and joined her in laughter. He'd avoided her thus far, but it seemed the fates would not be kind to him today. She was even lovelier than she'd been at their last meeting. And the reason for it stood behind her. The Earl of Clave knelt down to give her something. She took it and beamed up at him as he stood and walked away.

Seeing her reminded him of the other woman he'd almost married . . . "Where is Catrina? And Bryce? I'm surprised to not see them here."

"She is with child," Geoffrey answered. "And unable to travel."

He looked at his host, considering Geoffrey's casual reference that Catrina was with babe. Eventually, Graeme turned to watch Sara and Emma once again.

"Congratulations to your family," he said. "Brigid has been kind to them."

"Damara here in England," Geoffrey said. "Though I doubt either goddess is responsible. My brother and his wife—" He cut himself off abruptly. "My apologies. I'd forgotten for a moment."

"As I said when I courted your sister, Catrina and I were promised to each other as children. We loved . . . love . . . each other as brother and sister. I'm glad that she's found love, and happiness, with Bryce. She deserves no less." He mostly meant it.

Geoffrey looked at him. "Catrina. Emma. You've not had much luck with the women in our family." Blunter than most men would be, but Graeme appreciated him more for it.

"I've not had much luck with women."

Geoffrey laughed, loud enough to cause notice. "That, my friend, is simply untrue. Every maid here is either looking at you now or has done so already."

And he enjoyed looking back at them.

"I should have said, 'with marriageable women.'" He turned to the earl. "Though I came to talk of war, not women."

The men moved to the side, allowing a group of young girls to pass.

"Tell me."

"An ally of ours was attacked by English reivers."

Geoffrey ran his hand through his hair. "Not so unusual. You have many allies, and attacks occur every day."

"This was different." He tried to explain. "In the last year, there have been many such attacks. But the reivers grow bolder. Their unwritten code, not to kill unnecessarily, no longer seems to matter. In the last month alone, I've been called to three separate incidents. A young girl was almost killed at this last one."

"What does Douglas say?"

"As Lord Warden of Scotland, he's been to every Day of Truce for ten years. And he agrees. These attacks we've seen lately are different. We both believe they'll continue to get worse if something isn't done."

"I agree."

Graeme had never been happier to hear those two words. He hadn't dared hope it would be this easy to convince him.

"There's been more talk of bribes," Geoffrey continued, "which undermines the process. Many believed that electing Matthew Hedford as the new Lord Warden of England would calm the tensions. And while I agree it was a strong choice, his appointment does not seem to have made a difference."

"Then we are in agreement?"

"We are. Consider Kenshire an ally to Clan Scott. And to peace. From what I've heard about you, Kenshire could not have a more loyal ally in the north."

It was enough, for now. Though soon they'd be forced to move beyond talk.

Graeme put out his hand, and Geoffrey shook it. No sooner had their hands dropped than he saw her.

The girl from the garden last night. The one who'd watched him.

But this was no girl. She was all woman. Approaching Sara and Emma with another woman, she knelt beside them, her hair a shade lighter than Emma's raven black. Her face was perfectly proportioned and sweet, much too innocent to have been watching him with such frank interest from the shadows.

"Who is that?" he asked Geoffrey.

His host looked at the women holding court among a bed of flowers.

"Lady Gillian, daughter of John Bowman, Lord Lyndwood. Or do you mean her sister Allie standing behind them? And a dear friend of my wife's."

Lady Gillian.

"A *marriageable* sort," Geoffrey warned, as if reading his thoughts. "As is her sister standing behind them."

Which meant she wasn't for him.

"And soon to be married herself, I believe."

"To?" He didn't care. Or shouldn't care. But he found himself asking anyway.

Geoffrey hesitated. "The Earl of Covington."

He didn't bother to hide his shock. "The Earl of—"

"Aye. And I do believe my wife is attempting to talk her out of the match. But it was, or soon will be, arranged by her father. I don't believe Sara will win this battle."

The Earl of Covington. Graeme didn't know much about him, but none of what he'd heard was good. And he must be . . . "How old is he?"

Geoffrey shrugged. "I've not asked the man, but at least Peter's age."

He watched Lady Gillian hand Emma a flower and tried to imagine such a woman paired with the decrepit old earl. What could her father possibly be thinking?

Just then, all four women looked up. Directly at him.

Sara smiled. Emma winked, the little minx.

And Lady Gillian simply stared. Did she recognize him? She

clearly did for she looked down just as quickly as she'd glanced his way.

So she was shy today? That had certainly not been the case last eve when she'd watched him pleasure the girl he'd walked away from moments later.

Had Lady Gillian been in his arms instead, he had a feeling he may have just stayed.

"ut with it." Sara knew her too well.

"I don't believe I—"

"Your cheeks are as red as that dress you wore that one year when—"

"Is he still looking?" There was no use denying anything was amiss, so she might as well enlist her friend's aid in escaping.

"Who?" Sara looked back up while Gillian handed Allie a flower, pretending to finish the wreath in front of her. "Graeme?"

Graeme. So that was his name.

"The one talking to Geoffrey."

When all four of them immediately glanced at the men, Gillian whispered, "Don't look," and put her head back down.

"Emma, did you just wink at him?" Sara asked.

"Indeed. I had thought it might be awkward to see him again, but his smile is just as charming as I remember it. I thought mayhap it would ease the tension."

"Tension?" Allie asked.

The women resumed their ministrations as Emma told them of her encounters with the Scotsman. Gillian listened with interest.

She loved weaving flowers onto the wreaths that would decorate the hall for this evening's feast. Everything about May Day at Kenshire made her happy, and despite the bleak future that awaited her when they returned home, she was determined to enjoy herself.

"He's watching you," Emma said in a hushed tone, as if the men could hear them clear across the courtyard.

She would not look up. She would not look up. She would . . . And yet she did. "My . . . he's tall," she blurted.

She'd thought Geoffrey impressively tall, but Graeme outstripped him. He looked even more handsome in daylight, if possible, but it was his unflinching gaze she noticed now. Directed at her.

Gillian turned to Sara. "So who exactly is he?"

"You never answered my question. Why did you look as if you saw the Monk of Byland's spirit when you spotted him?"

Should I say such a thing aloud? Will Emma think poorly of me?

"Gillian . . . ," Sara prodded.

"Please don't think ill of me," she said, turning plaintively toward Emma. The other woman looked the picture of innocence with a primrose in her hand.

"I suppose you don't care what I think of you?" Sara teased.

Gillian turned away from both Emma and Allie, and blurted, "I saw him last eve."

"That is quite scandalous." Emma smiled at her.

"Indeed, sister," Allie agreed.

"I saw him . . . kissing a woman."

Now she had their attention.

"After you left, in the garden," she said to Sara. "I heard a noise and, well, I followed it."

"Let me guess." Sara tossed a finished wreath into the growing pile. "The noise was our very own Graeme de Sowlis."

Gillian didn't recognize the name. Was he English?

"And so you," Emma continued, "immediately walked away

when you came upon them. Giving them privacy to conduct . . . wait, were they just kissing? Or something else?"

"Emma Waryn!" Though Sara admonished her sister-in-law, she looked as if she'd burst into laughter at any moment.

Gillian felt her cheeks grow hotter. "Unlike the two of you, I've never even kissed a man," she said in an undertone.

Sara already knew as much, but Emma was clearly surprised. "Never? Not so much as a—"

"Not even." Allie giggled.

When some of the other women who'd gathered in the court-yard looked up from their ministrations, Sara stood from her work. "Perhaps we should continue this discussion somewhere more private."

Gillian followed, barely resisting the urge to look back at *him* as they walked from the courtyard.

"I understand the garden is quite lovely this time of year," Emma said, falling in beside her.

Although Sara made a face at her sister-in-law, Gillian couldn't help but laugh. She very much liked Emma, who was even less reserved than Sara. She'd never imagined such a thing were possible.

Just before they came upon the keep's entrance, Sara's maid, Faye, stopped her. The kindly, plump woman had been a part of Gillian's life for as long as Sara had been, and she spared her a smile before speaking. "My lady, Mary would like to begin bringing the flowers and wreaths inside. We fear it will take hours to get them all hung before tonight. All else is ready. The musicians are preparin' already, in the hall."

"Very good, Faye. And can you please see if Cook needs additional help in the kitchen? She tossed me out this morning before I could speak with her."

Faye tsked. "She tossed me out as well. Of course, I am not the countess. Of all the impertinent—"

"'Tis Cook," Sara said, dismissing Faye's concerns.

"Pardon, my lady." With a quick bow, Faye left them.

"I'm so very happy for her," Gillian said. She'd learned through their correspondence that Faye had remarried, and not just to anyone—to Geoffrey's uncle. She needn't have continued on as Sara's maid, but she'd insisted on it, claiming it wouldn't feel right to leave the job to anyone else.

"Aye, she deserves every joy," agreed Sara.

"Oh yes, she is married to your uncle," Allie said to Emma.

"I never thought Uncle Hugh would marry again," Emma said. "They're ever so happy together."

Sara turned serious, and Gillian knew what she was going to say next.

"You deserve the same happiness, Gill. Have you thought about what I said?"

The nickname reminded Gillian of her sister. If only Allie could have joined her here. She looked at Allie who would likely join Sara in her protestations of the match.

Gillian looked from Sara to Emma, both women who were deeply in love with their husbands. Though she was glad for them, she was convinced her story would not end equally well. She'd told Sara but part of the tale.

"I promise," she vowed. "We will speak more about this tomorrow. But for now, there's a May Day Queen to choose, a feast to eat."

Sara didn't look convinced.

"Tomorrow."

It would be soon enough to face the cold reality that a love match was not always possible.

"Nothing will change between now and then," she pressed. "Please, let me have this night?"

Sara wrapped her arms around her. "Of course." She let go. "Now let us prepare for a night to remember."

He had not planned to participate in the makeshift tournament.

When Geoffrey shoved him toward the lists, he could have resisted. He had been prepared to watch. Nothing more.

"He is unwed," his host shouted to the marshal in charge of the match.

"Geoffrey," he warned.

But his new ally did not back down.

"And reputably an expert swordsman. I wonder how he'll fare with the quarterstaff?"

Geoffrey shouted loud enough for all around them to hear, making his participation inevitable.

"I will repay you for this."

Geoffrey, smirking, crossed his arms. "I look forward to it."

He was one of few Scotsmen in attendance, making him an immediate target. Of course, his height and build did not help. After just a few rounds, he was marked as the one to beat, even though he'd not touched a quarterstaff for years—not since he'd accidentally knocked his brother out once in training. Graeme had feared the worst, and he'd refused to pick up the weapon for years.

He hadn't planned to enter the match, but now that he had, Graeme was determined to win.

Some wielded the staff passably well; others had not so much as picked one up before. Only two of the participants, both Kenshire knights, proved a challenge.

Not surprisingly, after four matches, only he and one of those challengers remained on the field.

"Not bad . . . for a Scot."

Graeme ignored the man's taunts. He picked up the staff and held it at his side, waiting.

"You know the rules by now," shouted the steward. "Begin!"

The Englishman was better than him. More practiced. Extremely skilled. More than twice, Graeme felt the staff sliding from his hand, the only recovery a brief respite from another hit.

He had one hope of winning: endurance, one of his greatest strengths. He met each hit with one of his own, avoiding most of his opponent's thrusts. Ignoring the pain in his thigh where he'd been hit, Graeme countered with a thrust of his own. Then finally, amidst cheers and shouts from the spectators, he ended the match with an upward thrust so powerful his opponent's staff flew into the air in the opposite direction of his body, which now lay prone on the ground.

"We have a victor," cried the marshal.

Oddly, the faces surrounding him were friendly. The men clapped him on the back, congratulated him, and asked who he would choose.

Damn.

Graeme had forgotten about that custom. Of course, the whole purpose for this fight among unmarried men was to choose a champion. One who would crown the queen at this evening's feast.

Geoffrey threw his arm around him. "Well done. For a Scotsman."

"Why are your men not more hostile toward me?" he asked bluntly as they made their way from the training yard toward the keep.

"Richard," he answered. "The late earl was a champion for peace, and his father before him. Neither tolerated hate, and as a former reiver, I know better than anyone that there are well-intentioned people on both sides of the border. And ill-intentioned too, of course."

The Waryns' story was known up and down the border. After Geoffrey's inheritance was stolen, he and his uncle had turned to reiving to support their family. And though he thought as Geoffrey did—that a person's actions defined them, not their country—there were plenty of men and women who did not.

"That's quite a legacy to uphold." Graeme stopped and looked Geoffrey in the eyes. "I will not allow brigands and lawless miscreants to reverse a thirty-year-old tradition. Richard's father facilitated the first Day of Truce, did he not?"

"His name was Spencer. And aye, he did."

"I mean to uphold the ideals of that truce, and any man, or clan, who believes otherwise is no ally of mine."

Geoffrey nodded. "Then it seems I truly do have another brother in the north."

"You do." And he meant it. Once Graeme committed himself, and his clan, he would honor that commitment.

"But more importantly," Geoffrey smiled, looking up at the keep. "You've a decision to make tonight."

"The queen."

"Aye, the queen. Any idea who you'll choose?"

The question wasn't who he would choose but how he'd forgo their required dance. Because, as Geoffrey had not so tactfully mentioned, Lady Gillian was not for him.

5

"*O*h, Gillian, look at you!"

Thank heavens for Sara. Not that she needed an escort. It was just . . . she'd only worn this gown once before. Just before his troubles, Gillian's father had welcomed a nobleman whom he'd been considering for an alliance. Her mother had commissioned this gown for the man's visit, but Gillian's suitor had been promptly thrown out of Lyndwood after making a crude comment about the amount of skin the lovely dress revealed.

She had not worn it since. It was her little sister who'd reminded her of it, and Gillian had anxiously packed it away for this night.

"Do you like it?"

Sara, a vision in pale blue and silver, reached for her hand and spun her around. "It's simply the most beautiful gown I've ever seen."

Lavender silk lay underneath a white, open-sided surcoat with tiny blue flowers embroidered in so many places that it appeared almost blue from far away. She suspected her mother had fancied Gillian might wear it as her wedding gown, despite its white color. An expensive garment, to be sure, and one her family could never afford now.

"Did Mary arrange your hair?"

Though it lay in waves around her shoulders, the maid had indeed twined the sides with gold ribbon, pulling it away from her face. Every time she reached up to move her hair, she touched a ribbon instead.

"She did."

Sara's smile fell. "I wish—"

"Nay, not tonight. Remember?"

"But you are too beautiful. And kind. To be—"

"Sara . . ."

"Tomorrow then." Sara reached for her hand. "Tonight, we celebrate. Will you allow Geoffrey to escort us both?"

"Allie and my parents—"

"Will not mind. I shall send Faye to tell them you're coming down with us."

Not long afterward, she followed Sara from the chamber. The countess's husband was waiting outside, and he bowed upon seeing them. "Lady Gillian."

"My lord," she said, the formality of the upcoming grand feast influencing her.

And so it was that she stepped onto the balcony overlooking Kenshire's hall with its lord and lady. When they appeared, the swelling crowd below cheered. All had been welcomed to feast with them this night, nobles and servants alike.

"There must be two hundred people," Gillian said.

"More like three," Sara whispered back, waving.

Flowers were strewn everywhere amidst warm lighting from hundreds of burning candles. The fruit of their labors that day had transformed Kenshire Hall into a fairy's delight.

Just then, Faye appeared with the heir to Kenshire, the sweetest babe Gillian had ever met. When Sara took him from the maid, the crowd below cheered even louder.

As she watched, one man came into view. One who stood taller than the others.

He leaned on the stone wall farthest from where she stood, so Gillian could hardly see his face. But she could tell he was looking directly at her.

"Put your hair back," Sara said.

Gillian hadn't even realized she'd fiddled with it again.

"You know . . . everyone can still see you even when you try to hide your face."

How many times over the years had Sara caught her trying to sweep her hair forward?

"I didn't even realize I'd done it," she said. "There are so many people."

Sara handed the babe back to Faye, and they all moved toward the stairs.

"I'll never understand how you could become accustomed to such a thing." They'd reached the bottom, and Gillian took the arm Geoffrey offered.

"You don't," Sara whispered back, smiling and nodding to the crowd. "But they don't know that."

When they arrived at the table just in front of the dais, Geoffrey released her arm.

Gillian's parents stood there with Allie, waiting for the hosts to be seated, and she took her place next to them.

"Mother. Father." She took her sister's hand. "Allie."

"Good evening, my dear," her very proper mother said. "Your gown is lovely. You look quite beautiful this evening."

"As do you, Mother."

Indeed, she looked more like an older sister than her mother. Her hair, a lighter shade of brown more like Allie's, was hidden under a filer and veil.

"Good eve," her father said in his typical gruff tone. Gillian had hoped her acquiescence on the matter of Covington would have put him in a better disposition, but it mattered not. She'd resolved herself to enjoy the day, and enjoy it she would.

"Father."

They sat when their hosts had done the same. She told her parents about her day, omitting everything about the Scot, of course, and the jittering in her stomach that refused to go away whenever she looked at him. She could not seem to stop thinking of what she'd seen in the garden last night and finally allowed Allie to take over the conversation.

He was seated not far from them. When he looked at her, the urge to look back warred with her instinct to turn away.

"Are you looking for someone?"

"Nay," she said, much too quickly.

Her father's eyes narrowed.

"Nay, I am simply in awe of how the hall has been transformed. Are you not as well, Father? It was quite enjoyable to help make the wreaths earlier."

He grunted and picked up a piece of meat off the trencher he shared with her mother.

"John," her mother said. "Your daughter asked . . . is it not lovely?"

"Aye," he mumbled, clearly distracted.

And so it was. A lifetime of her mother's wasted efforts.

"Dear," her mother said, wiping her hands on the linen cloth that was being passed down. Had she even eaten anything? Likely not. There was little dignity in consuming a meal. "Have you met the earl's sister? Her husband seems quite . . . zealous."

Gillian looked up to where Emma and Lord Clave sat on the raised platform in front of them. Under the guise of whispering something to her, it appeared as if the earl was actually kissing his wife's neck.

Scandalous.

"She is lovely," Gillian defended her. "Her husband loves her very much."

Her mother's tsk was not unexpected. "That is hardly relevant."

"Yes, Mother," she said obediently, feeling her heart sink in her chest.

Allie opened her mouth to argue with her mother but closed it again at Gillian's glance.

"They say Clave Castle can only be reached two times a day, at low tide. That it becomes an island all other times of the day," her mother said.

"You've not been there?"

Clave was only one day's ride south of Kenshire. And while she'd never been to the castle, she was surprised her mother had not visited it either.

"I have," her father said between bites. "The 5th Earl of Clave was quite a man."

He must have been for her father to speak on his behalf. He trusted few nobles and liked even fewer.

"And the son?" her mother asked.

As the conversation continued around her, ever so proper and ever so boring, Gillian attempted to divert herself by watching as course after course was delivered to their table. Cook had promised a feast like none other, and she had certainly delivered on her promise. Even Gillian's mother nibbled on *fritur emeles*, a rare sight indeed.

Finally, when Sara and Geoffrey stood, the excruciatingly long meal was officially ended. Gillian excused herself and her sister, eager to escape, and made her way to Sara and Emma.

"I'm sorry to have abandoned you," Sara said.

Seeing Emma's confused look, Gillian explained. "My parents can be . . ." She looked at them, still sitting, neither of them speaking.

"Polite," Sara finished.

"Quite so."

"Pardon me a moment," Sara said, leaving them and making her way to the musicians.

"This is so exciting." Allie strained her neck to see where Sara had gone.

"What . . . oh, the crowning of the queen. I'd nearly forgotten this part."

When the music stopped, conversation did as well. Eventually, with the hall as quiet as it could be given the remarkable attendance, Sara, her husband beside her, addressed the crowd.

"The Earl of Kenshire and I extend our fondest welcome to you on the fine first day of May." She waited until the sudden outburst of cheers faded away. "And we are grateful for any opportunity to celebrate. All of our guests have endured many hardships in this rugged, beautiful land. Sometimes your struggles go unnoticed, so we would notice them here and now."

This cheer, different than the other, was one of respect. For the woman who represented hope, as her father had done before her, for those living along the border.

"We celebrate life." She gestured toward the balcony, and everyone looked up to where Faye stood with Hayden in her arms. "We celebrate the rebirth of our land, the warmth of spring, which will envelope all of us in its glow, and each and every person who has made this day possible."

A chill ran through Gillian to see Sara this way. She was every bit the countess. Gillian had always known her friend was special, and now, so did everyone else who was here tonight. Some said Northumbria would never see a man like Richard Caiser again, but Gillian disagreed.

They saw tonight something even better.

"My lady," Geoffrey said. "A beautiful speech, but you're forgetting one thing."

Of course she was not, but it was customary for the lord to announce the winner of the May Day Match and the man who would crown its queen.

Geoffrey did so with a grin. "Our winner today is a son of

Scotland and friend to Kenshire, Graeme de Sowlis, chief of Clan Scott and second of that name."

Though some rumbles accompanied that announcement, most accepted it with the grace that would be expected of Kenshire's guests.

Gillian watched Graeme as he made his way through the crowd and came to stand next to the earl and countess, his posture implying he belonged there. He accepted the *chapeau de fleurs* that would soon adorn the head of one of the women in the crowd, which he then lifted into the air.

"My revered guest," Sara said to the Scot, "who is the fairest maiden in attendance? The one you will crown May Queen?"

"Oh my Saint Rosalina. He's looking at you," said Emma.

Indeed, he was.

"And she seems to be looking back," Allie whispered.

Gillian swallowed.

"Lady Gillian, if it pleases you?"

She'd not heard his voice before but wasn't surprised by it. He spoke every word as low and deliberately as the last. His deep, manly voice crawled into her chest and settled there.

Emma pushed her forward.

The crowd parted, and she reached him much too soon.

"My queen." He bowed as deeply as if she were truly the Queen of England. When he stood, towering over her, Gillian had to look up. "Will you accept?"

He looked straight into her eyes, and she willed herself to do the same.

"Aye, my lord."

She hardly had to bend her head for him to reach it. Though the light touch she felt was, of course, from the *chapeau*, she imagined instead it was his hand caressing her hair.

The dance!

It was only when the musicians began to play a lively tune and the crowd parted that Gillian remembered the tradition—the first dance was to be theirs. When he held out his arm, she had no choice but to rest her own arm, and hand, atop his.

Her father would most certainly be watching. But there was no help for it, and he could hardly complain of her behavior.

Despite her jumbled thoughts, her training had been such that she nonetheless glided effortlessly through the hall as people moved to allow them space.

"You're quite a dancer," she said. She'd never danced with a Scotsman before. He dressed much the same as his English counterparts except for the lack of a coat of arms on his surcoat.

"You're quite a woman."

She stumbled.

Gillian *never* stumbled. She could dance with her eyes closed. Had been trained to do so. But he made her feel as if she'd forgotten how to use her feet.

"Yet you know nothing of me."

They switched arms, and the other dancers finally joined them, breaking some but not all of the tension.

"Not true," he said.

Ah, so the man thought highly of himself. As well he should.

"I know you are the most beautiful woman here."

She stumbled again.

"Though your dancing skills are a wee bit lacking."

"Lacking? I—"

His grin, so easy and comfortable, told her not to be offended. It had been intended as a harmless jest, a way to calm her.

"I know you are a friend of Sara's. And that you've been coming here since you were a girl."

"Everyone knows that," she said. Her shoulders relaxed. Though he was large and undeniably handsome, the Scots chief was also surprisingly easy to talk to.

"But they don't all know how curious you are, do they?"

She would have stopped dancing had he not continued to lead.

The gentlemanly thing to do would be to pretend he'd not seen her—and she'd not seen . . .

She pinned her stare on the floor, refusing to meet his eye or to defend herself.

"Did you like what you saw, my queen?"

Gillian couldn't speak if she had wanted to.

The song found an opportune time to end.

"May I?" another man said, reaching for her hand. She gladly took it.

As May Queen, Gillian would not stop dancing for the remainder of the evening. Which suited her well. What better way to spend her last eve of freedom?

At least she had no time to think about *him*. How he looked at her. How his strong hand felt against her own. What he'd said to her.

That his eyes were green with specks of brown and not at all like she'd imagined. That he smelled of woodruff—a mixture of hay and honey.

Another dancing partner. Another dance.

No time at all to think of *him*.

6

*T*hough he had to get out of the hall, Graeme should have chosen a better refuge. He would have done better to avoid the garden where he'd first seen Lady Gillian if he'd cared to get the woman out of his mind.

What the hell is wrong with me?

Was it because she'd watched him? Was the idea of a very proper noblewoman spying on such an improper rendezvous that tantalizing?

Aye. It was.

His purpose served, Graeme would leave in the morn. And after the way she'd danced through the night—and likely still was —he doubted the lady would break her fast before he left.

A good thing. He'd resigned himself to romps with widows and serving maids whose virginity had long since been taken. Women like Catrina and Emma and Lady Gillian? Not for him.

He'd watched her sit with her parents at dinner, looking miserable for one so beautiful, and he no longer wondered where she'd learned to stand so straight. It was a wonder her mother deemed Kenshire Castle worthy of her presence.

And her father. Graeme shuddered. So that was the kind of

man who could give his daughter to the Earl of Covington. Little wonder. He had as much life in his body as the pheasant served at dinner.

"Oh!"

Lady Gillian herself had just entered the garden. With the folds of her gown flitting behind her in the soft breeze and the flowers in her hair glimmering in the moonlight, she fit the part of a May Queen perfectly.

Was God truly so cruel?

He bowed. "My queen." Though of course she couldn't be—he knew that. Just his luck that the only ladies who caught his eye were either betrothed to someone else or nearly so. "Pardon me, my lady."

He began to move past her, but a tentative hand on his arm stopped him.

"Nay, I will go." She turned to leave.

"Wait," he called, suddenly unsure of himself.

She stopped and turned, blinking and obviously nervous. "I just wanted a brief respite—"

"From the leagues of suitors clamoring for a dance?"

Lady Gillian raised her chin. "Not suitors. I am to be wed."

He looked beyond her and, seeing no one about, pursued the question he'd been most curious about since hearing that very same piece of news from Geoffrey. "To Covington. Why?"

She looked as if he'd asked her a difficult question, when it was anything but.

"Because my father wishes it, of course," she finally said.

So damn proper.

"Do you wish it?" The devil in him wanted to see the curious girl from last eve, the one who had thrown propriety to the wind, rather than the noblewoman who stood with him here now.

"It does not matter what I wish."

"Yet sometimes"—he took a step toward her—"it does."

When she licked her lips, Graeme's cock hardened, reminding

41

him, as if he needed reminding, of what he wished. Or, more precisely, what he wished to do with her.

She shook her head. "Mayhap for you it matters. But for me—"

"Tell me, my queen." He treaded in dangerous territory but, as usual, would not heed even his own warnings. "What do you wish?"

She opened her mouth, and from the look in her brown eyes, it was to argue with him.

"Nay, do not argue. You are a queen tonight. And a queen's wishes do come true." He took one more step toward her.

They stood much too close for propriety's sake, but he could not bring himself to care.

"What"—he lowered his voice—"do you wish?"

When she pulled her hair to the front, he reached up and pushed it back. He'd done so without thinking, but that simple, intimate touch could not be reversed.

Nor did he wish it to be.

"One wish."

He was a fool.

A fool who was being pulled into a spell stronger than his good sense.

He could see the battle in her eyes. She wanted to flee. She wanted to kiss him. It was no less intense than the war he had waged within himself, but he'd already succumbed. She had not.

He waited.

"I wish . . ."

In that moment, Graeme's life flashed before his eyes. His clan, his family. The responsibility heaped on his shoulders so young. The raids, the battles. Catrina, Emma. In that moment, all of it seemed so insignificant and small compared to the answer this one woman would give him. For if she turned away, he'd never see her again. He knew that.

"I wish . . . for you to kiss me."

Graeme grabbed her arm and pulled her away from the garden's entrance, intent on granting her wish . . . and his own.

He pulled her into his arms and lowered his head. When she placed her closed mouth against his lips, a desire unlike anything he'd ever felt swept through his body.

Her kiss was so innocent, so eager. She'd never kissed a man.

He cupped her head in his hands and used his lips to open her own. It took his very proper queen the briefest of moments to understand, and when she did, she opened for him like the petals on a flower eagerly awaiting spring. When he touched his tongue to hers, she gasped against him. But instead of giving her time to be shocked, he swept it inside and showed her what to do.

When she finally responded, Graeme released her face, put her hands behind his back and did the same to her, enveloping his May Queen against him.

He would not relent.

Instead, Graeme breathed in her sweetness and passion, pressing against her and wooing her mouth as gently, and firmly, as he could. Her soft moan encouraged him, and the creamy white mounds pressed against him proved too tempting to ignore. He slipped a hand between them and cupped her breast.

When he ran a trail of kisses from her mouth to her neck, and lower, Graeme thought for sure her innocence would stop him. He counted on it. Because, God help him, if he didn't step back from her soon, he'd take her right here in this garden.

"I . . . had no idea."

Breathless and unsure, his English queen arched her head back, exposing even more skin below. He lifted his head, took one look at her half-closed eyes, the flower wreath, now askew . . . and he lost it.

He kissed her neck, then lower, her moans encouraging him as he pulled the fabric down to give him even greater access to—

"What the devil?"

The man's voice behind him, so unexpected, put him immediately into a protective stance. Graeme pushed Gillian behind him and reached for his sword.

"No! 'Tis my father. No!"

A fact he had realized the moment before she spoke. When the man reached for Graeme, he allowed it. The sting that followed his punch was well deserved.

"Stop. Father, stop it," Gillian screamed behind him while voices yelled from the other direction.

Her father wasn't alone, it seemed. They had an audience. And a rather large one at that.

It was the last thing he remembered.

"FATHER, PLEASE . . ."

"Lord Lyndwood." Geoffrey continued to restrain her father, who refused to listen to reason.

"That bastard defiled my daughter. Unhand me, Waryn," her father yelled, the words spitting from his mouth like venom.

"I will not allow you to assault my guest."

"Assault your . . ." He tried to shrug out of Geoffrey's grip. She'd never seen her father this angry.

"Father," she tried again. "I've not been defiled. I—"

"Be quiet," he yelled at her.

Which was when Graeme opened his eyes and stood. His expression, venomous. And directed at her father.

"I deserved that," he spat. But she"—he nodded toward her —"does not."

"Unhand me," her father repeated, though Geoffrey continued to hold him back. Everyone, it seemed, was here. Her mother, Allie, Sara . . . how had they come to her so quickly? How could they have known? Her cheeks burned with shame. This exposure was her worst nightmare.

"You will not tell me how to handle my own daughter, Scottish scum."

"Father!"

The skin around the chief's eye was starting to swell. Not surprising since he'd not even defended himself. Gillian suspected if he had, her father would be the one with the burgeoning black eye instead.

"You would marry your daughter to an old man, one with a more than questionable reputation, and yet *I* am scum?"

If her father was furious before, he was downright livid now.

"Graeme," Geoffrey warned. And then he said to her father, "I am going to let you go, and you will not"—he emphasized the last few words—"lay another hand on a guest in our home."

Her father's grunt was the only answer he'd give, but he did remain still when the earl took his hands from him.

Geoffrey turned toward the garden's entrance.

"Go," he said, presumably to the Kenshire guards gathered there. Gillian didn't dare move—she barely dared to breathe. She caught Sara's wide eyes, and quickly looked away.

"I'm sorry, Father," she finally whispered. "Mother."

She bowed her head, unable to look at them. She had never disobeyed them before, in anything, and it felt exactly as shameful as she'd imagined it might. Gillian wished she could walk deeper in the garden and escape all of it. But of course, this was her doing —there'd be no escaping from it.

What Allie must think of her.

"How could you?" her father asked. "You've jeopardized everything."

She could not bring herself to look at him.

"I will marry her, of course."

Gillian did look up then. She'd feared it would come to this. And while her heart thumped painfully in her chest at the thought of marrying this tall, strapping man rather than her betrothed, she knew there could be only one answer.

"Nay, my lord."

His eyes narrowed as he looked from her to her father.

"'Tis not necessary. As you know, we but shared a kiss—"

"More than a kiss," he countered, "which was witnessed by half the castle's inhabitants. I would say it is a concern."

"Concern?" Her father didn't move, but she could tell by his stance he wanted to throttle Graeme. It would be a miracle if he didn't charge the clan chief again. "You call ruining my daughter's reputation a 'concern'?"

"Her reputation would not be at issue had fewer people witnessed the incident," Sara cut in. "Why is everyone here? Did you also receive a message?" Sara's last comment was addressed to Gillian's parents.

Gillian's mother, who'd stood by her father's side saying nothing, as usual, finally spoke up. "We did. A young girl said to come quickly, that Gillian was in trouble."

Sara was already nodding her head. "The same message we received. But why would she do that?"

Without intending to, Gillian shifted her gaze to Graeme. He did not appear at all pleased. "No matter how it happened. We are here, and the situation must be resolved," said Sara.

Gillian knew that tone. And something told her she'd not like what was coming next.

"My lord," Sara addressed Gillian's father. "Although it is deeply regrettable, it seems your daughter has been wronged by one of our guests, which makes this as much my problem as yours. Luckily"—Sara looked at Graeme—"I know Graeme de Sowlis to be a man of integrity and honor. And he has offered to do the honorable thing and marry your daughter. So it seems our May Day celebration will include a wedding."

Everyone spoke at once.

Her father protested as only a man poised to lose everything could. Geoffrey tried to console him, and Graeme shouted over both of them, insisting there was nothing else that could be done. Only Allie remained silent.

Gillian let the men argue and caught Sara's eyes over the fray. Her friend winked, and well she should—Sara thought she was doing her a favor. But she didn't know everything. She didn't know why Gillian *had* to marry Covington. As overlord to the man who'd attempted to ruin her father, he would be the only one who could truly ensure Lyndwood remained in the family.

"That's enough," she yelled.

They all stopped and looked at her. Gillian had never before raised her voice to her father, but she had to put an end to this. Immediately.

"Thank you," she said to Graeme, trying not to remember the feelings he stirred in her. Trying to extinguish the small spark of hope in her heart. "For doing the honorable thing. But I cannot accept your proposal. I am betrothed to—"

"Nay," Sara stopped her. "You are not betrothed yet."

"But she will be," her father said, the desperation in his voice evident.

"Nay, she will not," Gillian's mother said, breaking her silence again in a most unexpected manner.

"Mother?"

"You know as well as I do that everyone will be talking about this by the time we return to the castle."

"Which means," Sara finished, "Gillian will be ruined."

"Nay," her father protested. "The earl will understand. He—"

"Will not have her. And you know it as well as anyone here, Lyndwood."

"But this is not his first marriage," Gillian tried to reason. "Mayhap you would be right, if he'd not been wed before. But he's a widower. Surely—"

"'Twas not a chaste kiss, daughter," her mother insisted. "Too many witnessed it." Desperate to be heard, her voice carried through the garden as Gillian had never heard it before. What was her mother doing? She knew what was at stake, and still she took their side. Had she gone mad? Or did she know exactly what she was doing?

This could not be happening to her. Nay, it could not.

"Lyndwood." Geoffrey crossed his arms. "You would allow your daughter to be so disgraced? If she does not marry de Sowlis, and quickly, you know what people will say."

They didn't understand! Gillian tried to plead with Sara, but her friend avoided eye contact. So she looked at her would-be husband instead, but she'd get no quarter there. His mind had been made up as well.

Of course she'd chosen to dally with the most honorable man in two countries. 'Twas just her luck.

"If so many hadn't seen it with their own eyes . . ." her mother said, trailing off. Could it be true? Would Covington no longer have her?

Oh God, Father. Mother. Allie. I am so sorry. She pleaded with her eyes for him to understand. To forgive her. But instead, he looked to the man who'd just ruined their lives, however unintentionally, and said the words that sealed her fate.

"I accept your proposal," he said. And then much too quickly, "But I will demand a bride price."

Graeme did not hesitate. "Of course."

"And you will wed her immediately. She will not return to your country in shame."

Gillian didn't know what to think. Could her father get enough money from the chief to pay off his debts? Is that why he'd agreed? It hardly seemed possible.

She could refuse.

Aye, they could not force her to say the words that would bind her together with this man forever. And yet . . .

Gillian, do you really wish to be with the crusty Earl of Covington rather than in the arms of this man who made you feel those things? What is wrong with you?

Wrong with me? Our family will be ruined.

"I will speak to her," Sara declared boldly.

Gillian's mother looked as if she wanted to say something, but instead she closed her mouth and nodded, allowing Sara to take Gillian by the arm and pull her deeper into the garden.

Gillian followed, unsure of what else to do, baffled by the speed with which her life had changed.

Sara finally turned to face her, the grin on her face as wide as the chapel doors on a Sunday morning. "Gill, you don't have to marry him. That horrid old man." She shuddered. "To think of you with him. This worked out splendidly, don't you think? Better than any of my plans to free you."

"Splendidly?" she repeated. "This is the worst—"

She stopped.

The thought of pretending she wanted to marry Covington over Graeme de Sowlis was absurd, even to her. The Scots chief was gorgeous. And he'd defend her even though he didn't know her. If her only concern had been to avoid a match with Covington, she'd be thrilled as well.

But she still did not wish to tell Sara the fullness of her family's problems . . . and now there'd be little point. So she snapped her mouth shut.

"The worst?"

She sighed. "The worst night of my life. I've never been more mortified. And I am so, so sorry. To have ruined your—"

"Stop. Don't you dare utter another word." Sara took her hands and squeezed them, her eyes lively and delighted. "'Tis anything but ruined. In fact, this is the best May Day Kenshire has ever seen!"

"The best?" She'd embarrassed herself, her family, *and* her friend. How it could be called the best of anything, she wasn't sure.

"Of course, silly. This will be the very first time we've ever had a wedding. If only you didn't have to wait until tomorrow. Your

49

gown is simply perfect for it. And you do seem most anxious for a wedding night. But alas—"

"Sara!"

Her friend turned serious. "I *am* sorry it happened like this. But I cannot lie and say I'm sorry it happened."

Gillian couldn't blame her for that, not when she didn't know the whole truth, but she couldn't rejoice that she'd ruined her family because of her cursed curiosity. And she certainly couldn't be proud of the teeny, tiny part of her that *was* happy—no, overjoyed—that she would not have to marry Covington. She was a terrible daughter. When one wedding could ensure they would keep Lyndwood, ensure her sister would be free to marry whomever she liked.

What had she done?

$\mathscr{T}$he festive mood from the previous day did not extend to this particular feast.

While some seemed quite content with the arrangements—Sara, Emma, and, oddly enough, Gillian's mother—Gillian herself could not relax. Not when her father and her new husband looked apt to kill each other. Not when she couldn't forget what her change in circumstances might cost her family.

Worse, her father's men and Graeme's men were staring at one another with open distrust, or worse.

Sara had insisted they stay for the midday meal—a wedding feast, she'd said. And while the remaining guests enjoyed Cook's cherry tarts and custard, Gillian had spent the past few hours trying to reconcile the vast changes in her future.

She had barely even spoken to her parents or Allie alone. Her mother had helped her into her wedding gown earlier, the same one she'd worn for the May Day celebration, but she'd said precious little.

When the maids finally left them alone together, there was but a moment for Gillian to question her mother's odd behavior. To which her mother replied, "God is a mystery to us." And then promptly kissed her on the cheek and left. Her sister was acting just as unusual and seemed to be avoiding her.

The wedding itself had gone by in a blur. Sara's excitement had infected her briefly, especially since her husband looked handsome when they wed, but the scowls exchanged between him and her father had quickly dampened her mood. This was no way to begin a new life, albeit one with a man who made her forget how to walk straight. And yet, after Kenshire's priest announced them as husband and wife—imagine!—and he leaned down to kiss her, Gillian was reminded of their exchange in the garden. Of the passion she'd felt for him.

That push-pull between excitement and devastation had tugged at her all day.

"You've hardly eaten anything."

They sat, as honored guests, on the raised dais next to the lord and lady of Kenshire. Gillian had tried to remember that fact each time she looked out at the crowd. She'd not have her wedding day remembered as the one where the wife and groom appeared as if they wanted to kill each other.

"I'm not hungry, my lord."

"Graeme . . . if it pleases you, my queen."

"The last time you called me that, we were strangers."

He picked a cherry out of the tart in front of them and popped it into his mouth.

"And we're strangers still," he said with a grin.

"Indeed, we are. After we go back for my belongings, I—"

"Go back?" He appeared genuinely confused. "Lady Gillian, we will be leaving for Highgate End immediately after the meal."

"Leaving for . . . but my belongings? Surely you cannot believe—"

"I do apologize," he said. "But urgent matters require that we return immediately. Your parents have assured me your belongings will be sent to you. And Highgate End is but a few miles north of the border. We can visit as often as you'd like. But we must—"

What had made her think she'd have any choice in the matter? From father to husband. Perhaps she'd merely exchanged one man's rule for another.

"I believe you will like it there."

She looked at the clan chief who had been nothing but kind to her. How was it possible that they were now married? How could she help her family?

"I'm sure I will . . . Graeme." She finally put a cherry from the dessert into her own mouth, sucking in the sweet, tart taste.

Though he'd given her leave to call him by his given name, it sounded much too intimate to her own ears.

Intimate. They would share the intimacies of husband and wife. Tonight.

Several things happened at once. Her heart beat faster, a wave of heat washed over her, and she began to choke on the cherry.

"Are you unwell, my lady?"

"Gillian," she said, waving off his concern.

"Are you unwell, Lady Gillian?"

He'd deliberately misunderstood. So her husband had a sense of humor.

"Nay, it's just that . . ."

He leaned forward. "That what?"

Gillian could hardly be honest with him. That particular topic had gotten them into this mess.

"That I'm married," she blurted.

Graeme turned away, spoke to Sara briefly, and stood. The next moment, he extended a hand to her and she took it. He must have asked for permission to leave before the meal was over. Normally, the bride and groom leaving their first shared meal would be cause for celebration. But this was not an ordinary wedding. The feast . . . the music . . . they had been arranged to herald a new season, not a new union.

Before they slipped from the hall, Gillian caught her father's eye. Well, at least she had her answer. He was, indeed, still furious with her.

She followed Graeme into the corridor and up to a small alcove that overlooked the very place they'd gotten into trouble. When they sat, she still had to look up, though not quite as far, to meet his eyes.

Her husband's eyes. They were kind eyes. She'd not noticed that before.

"I am sorry for this," he said. And it appeared that he meant it.

"I am as much to blame as you," she said.

"Are you scared?"

What an odd question. "Nay," she said. But then thought better of it. In fact, she was scared, but not for herself.

"Good," he said. "There may be some in my clan who will question your—"

"That I am English?"

He seemed to regret his words. "Aye. But most feel as I do."

"Which is?"

The set of his jaw changed, and suddenly it was the clan chief she sat with, and not the man. "To live this close to the border, peace can only be achieved by forging alliances on both sides. To ignore our shared land, and history, is to ignore our future."

"My father . . ." She'd meant to tell him that her father thought much the same. She'd always admired his steadfast faithfulness to the borderlands. To peace. But some of the men he'd allied with recently were questionable. Instead, she spoke for herself.

"I believe that as well," she said.

"You were going to say something about your father?"

Her father who now hated her. Her father whose future she'd put in jeopardy . . .

"I need to speak to him." She stood so fast her foot nearly caught in the hem of her gown. "Pardon me, my lord."

And without a backward glance, Gillian left her husband to

have the conversation she'd dreaded all morning. Though she barely dared to hope, perhaps it would dispel the nagging suspicion that had plagued her.

That her father would never forgive her.

HIS WIFE.

Graeme sat back, watching her leave, trying to imagine what Aidan and the rest of his clan would say. They would accept her or find another clan. Most agreed with him about the English, but some of the elders had been pressuring him to strengthen their existing alliances through his choice of a wife. They would be less than pleased about this development. His brother harbored no hatred for their English neighbors, but he'd be surprised by the new development nonetheless. Graeme had confided in him that he no longer planned to marry. Not after Catrina . . . and then Emma.

Graeme did not regret the decision, for there had been none other to make. He'd dallied with the wrong woman, knowing it could get him into trouble, and now he'd pay for his weakness.

So be it.

But that didn't mean he enjoyed being fleeced for the most outrageous bride price anyone had likely ever paid. Had Gillian's father not been such an unabashed opportunist, he would have been happy for the alliance to the powerful border lord. As it was, he couldn't wait to get as far away from Lord Lyndwood as possible.

"Most men aren't quite so forlorn on their wedding day."

He hadn't noticed Emma's approach.

"May I?" She gestured to the seat beside him.

"Of course," he said, watching her.

She was a beautiful woman—always had been—but he was surprised to discover she no longer had the same hold on him. In

55

fact, he found himself thinking longingly of Gillian's faint freckles as he looked at Emma's clear complexion.

"So it seems you've joined our ranks in married bliss," she teased.

"Bliss?" He tried not to sound bitter. "I'm not sure I'd call a forced wedding 'blissful,' but you have the right of it. I am, indeed, a married man."

"Is it true you were deceived?"

Graeme hadn't given another thought to who could have alerted Gillian's parents and his hosts to their indiscretions. "Apparently, but it matters not."

It would be easy to blame someone else, but he knew it was no one's fault but his own.

"You're not angry?"

At himself? Aye. But that wasn't what she meant. "What cause would it serve?"

Emma looked up, as if considering the point. "I'm not sure when you ask that way."

"I don't mean to say that I wasn't angry. Or that I won't be so again in the future. But to remain so would only shift blame, and in truth, I should have known better."

"Graeme . . ."

For the short time he'd known Emma, she nearly always smiled, or laughed, or teased. But not now. Her expression was as serious as he'd ever seen it.

"Something is amiss with Gillian," she started. "I don't know her well, but I do know Sara. And she's worried for her. Please take good care of her." She took his hand. "Sara loves her like a sister, which means I do as well."

He squeezed her hand and released it.

"She is my wife," he said by way of explanation.

"And as such," Garrick finished, approaching them, "he will never hurt or betray her. You're looking at the most loyal of men."

Both he and Emma stood.

"Congratulations, Graeme," Garrick said, standing next to his wife, who smiled at him like he was a god and not a mere mortal.

"Thank you," he said, shaking Garrick's hand.

Garrick turned to Emma. "And so you've nothing to fear, my love."

"Men," Emma said, tugging her husband's hand. "Come, dance with me."

And the man who was reputed to have single-handedly helped Prince Edward emerge victorious in the Holy Land walked, hand in hand, with his wife to dance at a midday meal.

Graeme shook his head.

Married? Fine. But that? Never. To open oneself up for the kind of pain that inevitably came with rejection? He'd rather be dragged to Acre by his toes and placed at the feet of the blood-thirsty Saracens.

8

---

*G*raeme helped his wife mount his horse. They would ride together. She'd protested the arrangement—and his manhood would no doubt feel the strain of having his wife practically on his lap. But this was the best way to ensure her safety as they traveled. Graeme had been raised on the border and knew every pass, hill, and tree from here to Highgate End. If he and his men were outnumbered, she'd be safe with him.

"A word?" Geoffrey asked just as he prepared to mount behind her. He looked up at Gillian, a vision in her crimson riding gown, her hair pulled back into one long braid at her back. She took the reins from the groom and nodded, clearly able to handle herself.

He looked past Geoffrey to where Sara, Emma, and Garrick stood. They'd requested that he and Gillian stay the night at Clave, but he was anxious to get her well away from Kenshire.

Or, more precisely, from her father.

The bastard had not even shown up to see her off, and her mother had done so only briefly. Both were now conspicuously absent from their departure and only the sister remained now, consoling her after a meeting with her father that had apparently not gone well.

"You're a good man," Geoffrey said. "You've done the right thing."

Graeme turned to look at his wife. "She doesn't agree."

His queen appeared anything but pleased.

"Emma believes there is more to it than a surprise wedding," Garrick offered.

"As does Sara," Geoffrey agreed. "But nothing that has happened in the last day mitigates our alliance."

"I'm glad to hear it," Graeme said.

"Assure Douglas that Lord Hedford is committed to peace, as are we. And if you've word of any further upsets—"

"I'll let you know at once," he said. "I've a meeting with Douglas and Kerr before the next Day of Truce."

Toren Kerr, chief of Clan Kerr and Geoffrey's brother-in-law by marriage, was staunchly committed to keeping peace at the border.

Geoffrey nodded. "Godspeed then."

"And much luck to you," Garrick added.

Graeme shook both of their hands.

"This land is ours," he said, nodding. "We will have peace if enough of us press for it."

The English earls exchanged a glance.

"We wish you luck," Garrick said, "on your marriage."

And when both he and Geoffrey burst into laughter, Graeme glanced once again at his wife. Ahh, well. She was a different matter entirely. He had no idea how to be a husband or even how to gain her confidence. But it was a challenge he looked forward to.

When he was finally mounted, Graeme led his men from Kenshire's courtyard and onto the dirt road that would take them north.

They rode in silence until the castle disappeared behind them. Graeme tried to ignore the heat and pressure of Gillian's body in front of him. If they wanted to reach Highgate End by the following evening, they would need to ride hard both days. Emma and Garrick had been attacked on this very road just five months earlier, and with Gillian along, he'd not take any chances.

"Are you still angry?" he asked finally, hoping she would engage with him.

Silence.

"Gillian?"

"Aye," she answered. "But not at you. I kissed you too."

"And this is the price we must pay," he finished. Though she'd not said it, Gillian could not have made it clearer that, whatever her reasons, she would rather be married to the ancient Earl of Covington than him.

So be it.

He spent the remainder of the afternoon considering border tensions, alliances, and just about anything capable of distracting him from her movements. She was too innocent to realize her effect on him, but every time she shifted toward him . . .

They needed to stop.

"Up here," he yelled to the men in front of him. Normally, he would ride in the lead position, but not with Gillian sharing his mount.

The riders veered off the old Roman road and made their way through a thicket of trees to the stream he knew was just to their east. Sure enough, the sound of running water reached his ears moments later.

The weather, if not his wife, cooperated today. There was hardly a cloud in the sky.

"Come," he said to Gillian, knowing she'd need privacy to relieve her needs.

When the small river appeared in front of them, Graeme looked for an area with ample cover.

"There," he said, pointing, and his wife understood immediately.

She all but ran to the underbrush, paused, and called out to him. "Will you turn your back?"

"No."

She startled and made a face. "No?"

"I care more for your safety than your modesty," he said, softening his tone.

"Well, I can't . . . that is . . ."

"Gillian . . ." He took a deep breath. "We are husband and wife. I'll be seeing much more of you than—"

"Ugh!" She squatted.

He did look up at the sky, but though his gaze was averted, his other senses were not. He could feel her moving, hear every rustle of the bush. If danger lurked, he'd sense it before he saw it. Luckily, the only danger was of him being unable to ride as he thought of her naked calves, her gown being hiked up. Her legs, his hand running down—

"I'm done," she announced. A moment later, Gillian emerged and looked toward the river. He nodded and followed her.

Bending down, she leaned toward the water and cupped it in her hands.

"Be careful," he said, knowing the rock she leaned on was more slippery than it looked.

Gillian rolled her eyes. Surprising given her propensity for decorum. What would his wife be like when she dropped all of the trappings of propriety?

Actually, he'd gotten a glimpse of just that. A glimpse that had procured him a wife.

"I can manage to wash my face . . . oh!"

She'd bent down to the river bank—and plopped into it as quickly as an osprey swoops into the water to retrieve its prey.

Graeme ripped off his sword and dove into the river. The strong current carried her along as easily as it did the leaves and twigs floating alongside her. His heart lurched as he reached out for the fabric of her now-drenched gown.

Pulling her toward the bank, Graeme called out and his men instantly gathered on the banks.

"Malcolm, grab her."

The slippery rocks made it difficult for him to climb out to the bank. One moment, he struggled to keep her above water, the next, she was lifted from his arms.

Coughing and wet, Gillian appeared otherwise unharmed. He scrambled up after her and knelt by her side, looking for any signs of a gash. She hadn't been in the water for long, but one could never be too safe. Infection could spread from such a small accident.

"Someone get her saddlebag and my tartan."

"I'm fine," she said, attempting to stand.

Graeme helped her up, recognizing the futility of arguing. For a proper lady, she certainly had a stubborn streak. Something sparked in her eyes—there one moment, gone the next—the change so quick he thought for a moment he'd imagined it.

But it had been there, and he smiled at the implications.

"At least one of us is happy," she said, though her tone was more playful than her words.

"Chief." The same man who'd pulled Gillian from the river handed him both the saddlebag and the tartan.

"Thank you, Malcolm," he said, taking both. "We'll be along in a moment."

Dismissed, the men went back in the same direction from which they'd come. Alone once more, Graeme looked at his drenched wife.

"Here." Though the sun warmed them both, the river water had been cold enough to make Gillian shiver. He wrapped the wool cloth around her and put her bag on the ground. Opening it, he pulled out a surcoat and kirtle.

"You'll need to change," he said, handing them to her.

Gillian took the clothing.

"But you're wet too," she protested.

"I noticed," he said.

She didn't move.

"Do you need assistance?"

Her riding gown, ruined, stuck to her body in places Graeme couldn't help but notice. And why should he not? This Englishwoman, a stranger, was now his wife. But she was also a virgin, he reminded himself. He would need to be gentle with her. Patient.

"I do not." She began to turn away but stopped. "Thank you. For saving me."

He bowed. "You're most welcome, my queen."

Finally, a smile.

When she disappeared into the bushes this time, he did not turn his head. Though he could only see her shoulders and the bottoms of her calves, it was enough. The moment Gillian removed her gown, his cock reminded him of how sweet she had tasted last night.

Waiting, no longer able to see anything more than shadows, he removed his own tunic and undertunic, squeezing water from them both.

When she finally emerged, dry except for her hair, which she'd rebraided, Graeme had to remember to breathe. Yellow suited her. She was lovely, his wife.

Just as lovely as the other women who've spurned you. Maybe even more so.

He would be a fool to forget she had been forced to marry him. This beautiful creature was not here because she wanted him. Or cared for him. She was here because she had no other choice.

"Oh!" When she spotted him, Gillian stopped and stared. This was certainly not the shy maid who'd allowed him to place a crown of flowers atop her head. This was the woman who'd kissed him back with such fervor they'd had no choice but to wed.

"I trust all is well?" He watched her eyes as they widened, her lips as they parted.

So his wee wife desired him, did she?

Well, that made two of them. He supposed there were worse ways to start a marriage.

He reached her in a few short strides. "You've not seen a man like this before?"

She swallowed and nodded. "I have . . . on the lists. But . . ."

When her hand moved toward his chest and then dropped back down, he took the opportunity and seized it, placing her open palm on his bare chest. She didn't move her hand, but it mattered not. The innocent touch sent his blood flowing in every direction. When one of his men shouted for him, Graeme silently cursed.

He removed her hand, twined his fingers through hers as if they'd done it a thousand times before, and led his wife through the trees, back to the horses.

He hadn't even realized they walked hand in hand until Malcolm glanced down, ever so briefly, at their joining. Immediately releasing her, he stuffed their wet clothing into his own saddlebag and grabbed a linen shirt.

Tossing it over his head, Graeme then lifted his wife up and mounted behind her, remembering too late nothing protected him from her back pressing against his chest.

They were on their way once again.

It was only much later that he realized they'd forgotten to eat. They would just have to wait until they reached The Wild Boar. There, he'd share a feast with his new wife in more ways than one.

9

---

*H*e didn't stop her this time. When she ran her hand along the firm ridges of his chest down to his stomach, her husband simply watched her. They stood in an open field, and though she was no longer wet, droplets of water remained on her husband, dripping down his masculine chest, and suddenly . . . she wanted to kiss him there.

"Gillian."

So hard.

"Gillian."

He touched her, but it wasn't the soft touch of a lover. Instead, he shook her as if . . .

"Wake up, Gillian."

Her eyes popped open.

Graeme sat behind her on his horse. Not in an open field.

A dream. It had been a dream.

"I'm awake," she murmured, looking around them. "Where are we?"

She had fallen asleep after sunset, but it was much later now. The low murmur of crickets and men's distant voices punctuated the otherwise silent night.

"The Wild Boar," he said, dismounting.

A groom took the reins as Graeme lifted her to the ground.

"Where are your men?" She spied a two-story stone structure and a stable beside it, but other than the groom, no one stirred. The larger building boasted a wooden sign, which appeared to be new. Two crossed arrows above the likeness of a boar.

"Inside."

She began walking toward the entrance, but her husband's hand stopped her.

"The hall can be a bit . . ."

"Aye?"

"Overwhelming."

Though she'd very much like to know what precisely that looked like, she didn't dare ask. "What do you suggest?"

Graeme raised his brows. "That depends on how adventurous you're feeling."

A proper lady does not show emotion.

"Do I appear the adventurous sort to you?" she asked sarcastically.

Graeme's eyes narrowed as they tended to do when he was rattled. Though her husband was still very much a stranger, she'd learned at least that.

"Very well." He gestured for her to lead, and she did. When he opened the door from behind her, Graeme's arm brushed against her side. Pity he was no longer shirtless.

Gillian! What is wrong with you?

"About time you show yer face."

Though Gillian had never been to The Wild Boar, or any inn, she'd heard of the place before. And its owner. Everyone on both sides of the border knew it was the one inn they could rely on for neutrality. Somehow, even though she was widowed, the owner and her son managed to keep trouble from their door.

"And you've brought yerself a wife, the men tell me."

Graeme stepped aside to allow the innkeeper to get a full view of her.

"Mistress Magge, I'd like to present my wife, Lady Gillian, daughter of Lord Lyndwood. Gillian, Magge is the owner of this fine establishment."

"If I could reach yer handsome cheek to pinch it, I would," Magge said.

Gillian stared at the woman in awe, shocked that she would speak in such a way to Graeme, a chief and obviously a warrior, and the largest man she'd ever met. This small, plump woman didn't seem to care if he were a commoner or the King of England.

Fascinating.

A shout from deep within the inn took Magge's attention away from them.

"Is yer wife the sort who dines in the hall or in private?"

What did that mean?

"We'll take a meal in our room," Graeme answered for her. "The men have already—"

"They told me yer needing a room. Yer usual is available. But it's the stable for them. More and more men every day," she muttered, leaving them alone in the entranceway.

"What's that smell?" Though dark, the inn did not smell as poorly as she'd expected. In fact—

"Magge's famed meat pies," Graeme said. He took her by the hand and led her back out the door and around to another entrance.

"The private rooms are back here," he said, releasing her and popping a key into the lock.

"But"—she looked at his hands, baffled—"where did you get the key?"

He moved his hand, just slightly, and opened the door. The key disappeared before she could process what was happening.

"Wait, where did the key go?" Gillian turned his hand around. Empty. "But it was there just a moment ago."

He lifted his other hand, the one that had not moved at all. An iron keychain lay flat against his palm.

"But how—"

"I've quick hands," he said, his voice low and meaningful. She wasn't sure what that meant, exactly. But somehow Gillian didn't think he spoke only of his ability to hide keys.

"Where—"

"I took it from Magge. She was about to offer it to me."

Gillian looked from one hand to the other and shook her head.

"After you, my queen," he said, standing to the side.

Once they were both inside, he locked the door once more, tossed the keys to the floor and reached for her before she could even take in their surroundings.

Gillian breathed in deeply, taking in his drugging scent—fresh water and man, that was what he smelled like.

He brushed her lips with his thumb, and Gillian resisted the urge to open her mouth. She had no idea what they were doing. What *she* was doing. All she knew was that she forgot all her manners around this man. Her training. Everything save his touch.

"My lord," a voice called from the hallway. "I've got firewood and—"

"Come back later," Graeme growled.

After a moment, the shuffling ceased and Graeme tugged on her lip, forcing her mouth to open for him.

"You're angry," he accused, lifting his finger back toward her lips. "Even now."

"Aye," Gillian managed, opening her mouth. "I didn't plan for this. For you." Gillian tentatively touched her tongue to his finger.

"Nor I, for you." He licked her finger then, sending a shiver from her hand all the way down to her core.

"But 'tis done. We can rail against the injustice of it, but it matters naught."

"Neither of us asked for this," he said. "It may be just another alliance."

She swallowed.

"Except for in the bedchamber." And then he took her finger completely into his mouth, wrapped his lips around it and sucked, just once, but ever so slowly. "Do you understand?"

Did he actually want her to answer?

But then, as abruptly as he'd pulled her to him, her husband dropped her hand and walked away. Had she done something wrong?

"I understand, but . . ."

"Gillian." He turned back toward her, and the pained expression on his face gave her pause. "If we continue, I will make love to you."

She had expected he would. After all, she was his by right.

"And though I'd like nothing more"—he nodded toward the small bed—"this is no place for your first time."

And though I'd like nothing more.

If she were honest, she wanted it as well. Consummation of marriage was necessary. Breeding was the ultimate goal of any marriage, of course. But she hadn't expected to want her husband. After all, up until last eve, she'd thought she was doomed to marry Covington.

She licked her lips as she watched Graeme pick the keys up off the floor.

No, this *man* was entirely unexpected.

But she supposed he was right about their accommodations.

"I'll get us firewood. And some food." Then he left without another glance. Probably for the best, given that she was staring after him like a moony cow.

With nothing else to do, Gillian moved toward the unlit brazier. The room was a bit chilly, in truth, and she always favored a fire, even on warmer days. As soon as Graeme walked back into the room, he dropped a large armful of firewood next to the brazier, but Gillian's attention was directed at the door. A serving girl, petite and quite young, entered with a tray of food, which she set on the bed. When she turned to leave, Gillian thanked her, but the girl didn't respond. Or close the door. Instead, she returned a moment later with a pitcher and two mugs, which she placed on the small table by the bed, and then left and returned a third time, her arms now laden with sheets.

"Can you take that"—the girl pointed to the tray—"for just a moment?"

No one spoke as they worked, Graeme on the fire and the girl on their bed. Normally, she would at least attempt a conversation with the girl, but Gillian found herself staring mutely at the entire scene. It was all simply too much. The reversal in her future, her fortune, her marriage.

When the girl finished her task, she took the tray and placed it back on the bed. Gillian muttered her thanks but didn't move. She only noticed Graeme when he stood directly in front of her.

"Gillian?" He lifted her chin, forcing her to look at him. "What's wrong?"

When she didn't answer, he took her hand and guided her to sit beside him on the bed. Taking a bite of Magge's famous meat pie, he began to eat. Gillian did the same, though she could barely taste the food.

"I know very little about you," he said between bites. "Tell me of yourself. Your home and your family."

She pursed her lips.

He nodded. "Then start with yourself and save your family for later."

"There's not much to tell," she said, startlingly aware that it was true. She'd seen so very little of the world and experienced even less. "I grew up at Lyndwood with my father, mother, and sister."

"Allie, correct?"

"Aye," she answered.

"And you are close to the Countess of Kenshire?"

"I am." She relaxed. Sara was an easy subject to discuss. "Our fathers were friends and allies. They fought together for peace. Though they both refused the title of Lord Warden, saying it corrupted too many good men, both Richard and my father spent years ensuring peaceful truce days. Kenshire was the only place he'd allow me to visit when I was a girl."

"Surely you've been elsewhere besides your home and Kenshire."

She took a bite of bread. Rye, her least favorite. But eating was preferable to answering the question. Gillian hated that she'd been so sheltered. It embarrassed her.

"You haven't," he concluded. "And now you venture farther away from home than ever before, to Scotland, with a man you hardly know."

"Aye," she said between bites.

"Tell me more of your sister."

"Allie is lovely, of course. Everyone says so. She's also sweet and carefree. Though she tends to get herself into trouble, much like Sara's sister-in-law Emma."

"And unlike you," he finished.

"Aye." He'd said it with such conviction, Gillian didn't think to deny it. And of course, it was true. Until now.

Graeme made his way to the side table, where the serving girl had left the carafe, and poured them both wine. He handed one mug to her.

"I find it curious," he said, his expressive eyes matching his tone. "And can't quite reconcile this proper young lady with the one I encountered in the garden both nights."

Gillian had never been so mortified in her life. "I don't know what came over me. I—"

"That was not a criticism, Gillian."

She stopped talking.

"Just the opposite, in fact."

"So . . . so you enjoy kissing me?" Had she really just asked that question? Her cheeks heated most uncomfortably.

He replaced the goblet and sat opposite her, the tray between them.

"Very much. But more importantly—" He took a bite of bread. "Did you?"

Should we be discussing this so openly?

He must have sensed her hesitation.

"It's true, we are strangers. And neither of us intended to be sitting here right now. But we are man and wife. And while we may go our separate ways in most things, as I've told you, there is nothing to shy away from in the bedroom."

While we may go our separate ways in most things . . . What did that mean? Did he intend to abandon her?

"I did, Graeme. Enjoy it, that is."

"Good, because . . ." He abruptly stood, taking the tray with him. Placing it on the floor, for there was nowhere else to put it, he turned back toward the bed. "I'm of a mind to do it again."

This time, when he sat next to her, Gillian was not nervous at all. She knew what to expect. However, he didn't move toward her.

As they sat, the distant noises of the inn below punctuating the silence of the room, Gillian eventually heard other sounds. The crackling of the firewood. Graeme's steady breathing as he watched her with those brooding, expressive eyes.

She swallowed, waiting, feeling her anticipation grow every moment.

"We shall get to know each other," he said finally, his finger tracing the outline of her cheek. It moved to her neck, the touch so light it sent a shiver to her very core.

His finger dipped below the neckline of her gown. "And you've nothing to be afraid of," he finished, correctly guessing her thoughts. Gillian knew little of what happened between a husband and wife. "By the time we reach Highgate End," he said, dropping his hand, "you'll know my touch well."

He leaned forward, placing his lips on hers. If she thought they were warm, the touch of his tongue when she opened her mouth for him was even more so. It glided across her own, studying it as intently as any pupil studying its subject. He circled and tasted, and Gillian gave of herself freely.

Too freely.

She thought he would touch her then. In fact, she hoped for his hands to roam her chest as they'd done before, making the hairs on her arm stand up straight. Instead, his mouth alone made contact, and though her body screamed to get closer, Gillian wasn't so bold as to encourage him. Besides, this was quite lovely.

Oh!

When he turned his head to the side, fitting their mouths together just perfectly, she changed her mind. Gillian wanted . . . more.

But it wasn't to be. Graeme eventually pulled back, his lips still wet with the remnants of their kiss. He stared so intently at her lips. What did he see there? Did he wish to do it again?

"I'll sleep on the floor."

Apparently not.

"The floor?"

When he stood, the bed creaked in protest. "Do you need assistance preparing for sleep?"

Assistance? Oh dear. How could she have completely forgotten about her maid? Morgan had been ill, which had kept her from attending the May Day celebrations. She didn't know that her charge was now a married woman.

"I do not. But I had not even considered—"

"Your parents have assured me they will send her to meet us at Highgate."

"How did you know my thoughts?" she asked, genuinely curious.

The look he gave her—both puzzled and intense—made her wish she hadn't asked. "I honestly don't know." Graeme retrieved the tray and walked with it toward the door. "I will be downstairs. If you need anything—"

She blinked.

"You will likely be asleep when I return. So I bid you good night." And with a polite nod, the kind a knight would give to his squire, Graeme left.

What in the devil was he about?

One thing was for sure. Graeme de Sowlis was the most contradictory, confusing . . . albeit loyal and respectful . . . man in all of England. And Scotland. And beyond, for all she knew. Perhaps it was good he'd left her. Gillian had more important matters to consider than her traitorous body's reaction to her new husband. At least Morgan would be joining them at Highgate and could give her news of home.

What would it be like, Highgate End? She supposed she would soon find out.

*H*er new home reminded her of a fire-breathing dragon roused from a long slumber. It stood tall and proud on the horizon, alone but powerful nonetheless. Emerging from dense woodlands after a decline that had left her more than a bit shaken, Gillian stared down at the castle sprawled in front of her. From their vantage point, she could see everything clearly. Green-topped mountains surrounded a valley with its small village and long road, which led to the castle that Graeme had inherited from his father.

In three days, she'd learned precious little about the man to whom she was now married. Though he came to her each night, his kisses holding promises they never kept, he spoke to her during the day as he would one of his men. Polite, as he'd accused her of being. Detached. And he would leave each night after kissing her senseless. She would fall asleep before he returned to their room to sleep on the floor.

Graeme was everything she'd expected in a husband. A companion, one who admittedly treated her well, and nothing more. Exactly like her parents. If he didn't look at her the way Geoffrey looked at Sara, well, that was to be expected. After all, this was no love match. At least she found him pleasing—no, more than pleasing—company.

"What do you think?" Graeme asked from behind her.

"It's bigger than Lyndwood," she said. "And quite beautiful."

The sun had just begun its descent, giving the castle an eerie glow that made her think of the many tales of Scottish superstition foisted upon her by her very English tutor. She'd never liked the Londoner, brought to Lyndwood by her father, and apparently, he'd never quite taken to the borderlands either. Once both she and her sister could read and write passably well, he had moved back home, never to be seen or heard from again.

Graeme appeared pleased by her statement. He was clearly proud of Highgate End and his role in its survival. She'd learned from one of her husband's men that when Graeme had been named the new chief of Clan Scott four years earlier at only five and twenty, upon his father's death, some of the elders had worried he was too young. He was the youngest chief in their history, but he took his duty to protect his clan seriously. His leadership had impressed them all.

"You've nothing to fear," he said, slowing as they approached.

"I'm not . . ." Well, actually she was a mite nervous. "But an Englishwoman—"

He nodded. "'Tis as I said. Some will resent that, but most will not care. Like Lyndwood, Clan Scott recognizes the necessity of keeping the peace with our southern neighbors."

Quiet descended between them as their party skirted the village to the east and approached the castle from the west. Graeme opened his mouth to say something, but he was interrupted when two men on horseback bounded toward them, seemingly from nowhere, too quickly for it to be a simple welcome. Something was amiss.

Graeme halted, and all of the others followed his lead.

"Graeme," one of the men said, stopping in front of them.

"What is it?"

From the man's resemblance to Graeme, he could only be his brother, Aidan. He had the same deep-set eyes and fierce expression as her husband, though he was slightly shorter and had longer hair. Gillian had only learned Graeme had a brother that morning.

"An attack, yesterday." He shifted his gaze to her, then back to Graeme. The question hung in the air between them, forcing Graeme to introduce her.

"My wife," he said. "Lady Gillian, daughter of John Bowman, Lord Lyndwood. This is my brother, Aidan."

If Graeme's brother hadn't looked so serious just a moment ago, Gillian would have laughed at his expression. She hadn't realized a person could look so shocked.

"Your—"

"I will explain later," Graeme said, wresting his brother's attention away from her. "An attack?"

"English reivers, but well-organized ones. They took more than twenty sheep from old Donnan."

"And?" Graeme's voice was more barbed than his normal tone.

"His wife—"

"If they hurt Grace . . . ," Graeme roared.

His brother's expression told the tale.

"Goddamn bastards," he shouted.

Despite the vehemence in his voice and the rage that had clearly welled up inside him, Gillian wished she could go to him. The urge to comfort this decidedly dangerous man she hardly knew nearly overwhelmed her.

Gillian didn't know who Grace was, but that didn't matter. Graeme had cared for her, and she wished she could take Aidan's words back. Or stop the raid from happening. She wished she could comfort his pain.

"A slewe dogge followed their tracks across the border but lost their scent near Ettrick. We'd petition for a cold trod but don't know which reivers did it. Only that they were English."

Gillian pretended not to notice the stares.

"We'll find them," Graeme said, a bit more calmly. He looked at her as he helped her dismount. "I apologize this is such a sorry homecoming for you, but I must go—"

Gillian tried to smile. The last thing she wished to be was a burden.

"Malcolm," he called behind them. "Escort my wife to the castle. See that she is settled."

Both of the brothers glanced at her before they took off— Graeme with regret and his brother with open curiosity—away from the castle and toward the village.

"My lady." Malcolm gestured for her to mount up behind him. Once closer to the castle, they circled two of the four towers before arriving at the gatehouse. Both iron gates were opened to them. The inner ward, similar to her own at Lyndwood, was filled with people, mostly servants.

And chickens. Everywhere.

A pentice traveled the length of the entrance to the great hall and kitchens. The covered walkway connected to a small building she imagined was the chapel just next to the northward tower. Beyond that, the gatehouse and stable. Though much smaller than Kenshire, it reminded her of it in some ways. Heavily fortified, Highgate Castle was more assuredly a defensive structure first and foremost.

She dismounted without help. Though she had been sheltered, one thing her parents had always indulged her in was her love for horses. Malcolm took the reins and handed them to a stableboy who'd approached from behind them. The other men scattered, some to the stables and others to the gatehouse.

"So you found yerself a good woman finally?" An older woman, well-dressed but clearly a servant nonetheless, said to Malcolm. Where had she come from?

"Mistress Fiona," poor Malcolm said, his eyes shifting back and forth between them. "I'm pleased to introduce Lady Gillian

Bowman, daughter of Lord Lyndwood, as the new lady of Highgate."

Her shock could not have been more apparent. Though her hair was covered, Gillian could see strands of gray peeking out. The deep lines around her mouth disappeared when her lips turned up into a smile.

"Graeme got himself married in England, did he?" The woman grabbed Gillian's hand as if she were a long-lost daughter and pulled her toward the keep's entrance.

"Get on with you," she said to Malcolm. "They'll be needing you after what's happened to poor ol' Grace."

When Malcolm didn't move, she repeated. "Go on now. I'll take over from here."

Apparently Fiona's shock did not last long. She chattered all the way into the entrance and only stopped when she and Gillian walked into the great hall. Highgate Castle, though it appeared circular from far away, was really more of a square structure. Ten long trestle tables lined the space in front of them, and a large hearth against the opposite outside wall completed the simple design of the hall.

"That leads to the armorer's tower," Fiona explained, pointing to their right. "And that way," she said, waving her hand in the opposite direction, "to the buttery and, at the far end, the kitchens."

Since no meal was being served, the hall was mostly empty.

"'Tis well appointed," Gillian complimented. "And clean."

It was true. Although Highgate lacked the splendor of Kenshire, it was obviously tended to by competent servants.

Fiona beamed. "Those who've served Highgate have done so for many years."

"Such as yourself?"

The old woman tsked, as if to say she'd much prefer to speak about Highgate's glory than herself. A loyal servant, and one Gillian liked already.

"I was lady's maid to Graeme's grandmother for over fifty years."

The pain in her voice, immediately evident, prompted Gillian to ask, "When did she pass?"

Fiona looked up as if she could see her lady even now. "But two months back."

Though she knew Graeme's father had been killed in battle four years ago, and his mother had been taken by illness when he was young, she'd not heard anything about his grandmother. Of course, Gillian hardly knew anything of her new husband at all.

"I'm so very sorry to hear that," she said.

Fiona held her gaze, seemingly assessing her, and Gillian did not look away. She'd need allies here at Highgate, and she desperately wanted this woman to be one of them.

"She sent you to me," Fiona said, her tone daring Gillian to disagree.

Though she didn't believe the series of events that had brought her to Highgate could possibly have been caused by Graeme's grandmother, she would not disrespect Fiona by disagreeing.

"An Englishwoman too," she said, almost as an afterthought. But there was no malice behind the words. Only resignation. "I'll be showing you around Highgate. Or are ye wanting to rest?"

"I would love to see more," she said, knowing it was the answer Fiona hoped for.

"And I'd also love to know how ye came to be my Graeme's wife, if ye don't mind sharin'?"

Gillian didn't mind at all. In fact, she looked forward to getting to know Fiona. And the woman clearly felt the same way. If only her husband were equally interested in opening up to her. She was beginning to feel he'd purposefully closed himself off.

But that was a problem for another time.

"Fiona, where are my—"

A woman who'd entered the hall from the north tower stopped abruptly, looking at the two of them as if someone had stolen her favorite gown. Gillian knew immediately, without being told, who she was. Not that Graeme had mentioned he kept a mistress here at Highgate, but there was no other explanation for the way the woman was staring at her. Unfortunately, the woman was everything she was not. No freckles marred her cheeks. Instead, she was tall and blond. Really, really blond.

But not, it seemed, very nice. The tone she took with Fiona would only be used by a person who cared little about giving offense. "And who . . . is *that?*"

Gillian opened her mouth to answer but was not quick enough.

"This woman," Fiona said cheerily, "is the new lady of Highgate."

11

"They will be brought to justice." Graeme dismounted and handed his reins to the stableboy who had run out of the stables to meet his chief.

"Why would Lord Blackburn risk everything on a raid such as this? It makes no sense." Aidan followed him into the keep just as the sun began to set on Highgate.

"I don't know," Graeme said, still furious but in control. Though it appeared the sheepherder's death had not been intentional, she was nonetheless dead. She would not be there to help usher her daughter's babe into the world. The circumstances of Grace's death would have devastated his grandmother. Though everyone had loved the healer, she'd forged a special bond with his family during his mother's convalescence.

And now she was dead at the hand of English reivers, commissioned by a man as black as his name. Rumors of Lord Blackburn's collusion with those who would disrupt the tentative peace at the border had persisted for years. One of the witnesses to the raid had even been there when Blackburn was caught cheating at the last Tournament of the North two years earlier. Luckily, he'd recognized two of Blackburn's men, which meant they could be pursued.

Though some, like Clan Scott, understood the value of the March Law from which the Day of Truce originated, others, on both sides of the border, despised what they saw as further interference in their autonomy.

This time, they'd gone too far.

"We'll go to the Truce ourselves," Aidan said as they entered the main keep.

"Aye."

Each month, a Day of Truce brought English and Scottish together, allowing wardens on both sides to bring lawbreakers to justice. If the raid had been conducted by Scotsmen, they would already have mounted a counter-raid.

"Brother," Aidan said, leading the way into the great hall. "I do believe you—"

"Aww, shite."

The scene that greeted them in the great hall was not a pleasant one. They were met with glares that would have sent Blackburn's men back to England in fear.

What in God's name was Agnes doing here?

His wife, seated at the head table, gave him the kind of look any woman would level at her husband if his mistress sat just below her. For her part, his former mistress appeared entirely unapologetic, just as he would have expected. The men and their wives— more than two dozen of them ate regularly in the hall—watched Graeme and Aidan enter as if expecting a wee performance.

"What is she doing here?" Aidan whispered.

Graeme had explained the circumstances of his marriage to his brother, and now that his initial surprise had faded, Aidan seemed pleased by the arrangement. Highgate needed a woman's touch, and he had no inclination to marry. That Gillian filled that role meant he could continue enjoying the company of women, much like Graeme had been doing, without "committing to one bed partner," as Aidan liked to say.

"I don't know," he responded. Though the widowed merchant's daughter was quite beautiful and an entertaining mistress, her jealous ways had worn on him. Graeme had ended their relationship before leaving for Kenshire.

Her presence tonight did not bode well.

"She needs to leave." Graeme took one step into the hall, but Aidan stopped him.

"Not now, brother."

Though none of the guests were close enough to hear their conversation, they were all watching, likely trying to gauge Graeme's response to Agnes's presence.

"You'd have her dine in the same hall as my wife?"

"I'd have you not ignore said wife hours after you dumped her off in a strange keep with none but Fiona to keep her company."

Oddly, Fiona was nowhere to be seen.

"I need to find Malcolm. Save me something to eat, will you?" With that, Aidan turned and walked back in the direction they'd come.

Coward.

Graeme *did* regret the circumstances of Gillian's arrival at Highgate, but it could not have been helped. He'd needed to attend to the sheepherder, to learn what had happened to poor Grace.

He walked toward the raised dais at the back of the hall, intending to ignore Agnes until he could order her to leave.

Gillian sat alone.

Without taking the time to wash, he took a seat next to her.

"Good evening, Gillian," he said, not looking in Agnes's direction.

"Graeme," she said politely.

A vision of his wife assaulted him. Her head, thrown back in abandon as he kissed the sensitive flesh on her neck. Her hand, gripping his tunic. Had he imagined such things happening? The woman who sat next to him now, though as beautiful and intriguing as the one who'd returned his touch, seemed an entirely different sort of lady.

Of course, the fact that Agnes sat just below them may have something to do with her coolness. Nay, it was more than that. She'd acted the same way at Kenshire . . . until they were alone in the gardens. These were the two sides to his lady—the proper miss and the vixen.

"Did you learn anything?" she asked, picking up her pewter goblet. Though Highgate End was no match for Kenshire, its hall and furnishings enjoyed a rich history. Despite its proximity to the border, his clan had survived, and thrived, for many years.

"We know who was behind the attacks," he said, the regret in his voice real.

"I'm sorry," she said in a small voice.

He stole a glance at her. Perfection. His wife, with those light brown freckles, lush lips, and long dark lashes, had no equal. Even now, his hands itched to touch her, to stroke her soft skin.

"You've likely heard of Lord Blackburn, the scourge that he is to the borderlands."

She'd just lifted a morsel of rosemary-spiced rabbit to her mouth and therefore couldn't answer. Unfortunately, Agnes caught his attention then and refused to let go. She glared at him as if he'd done her wrong, when in fact Graeme had given her coin and escort to Edinburgh, where she'd always planned to go. He'd even ignored the fact that her greedy father had attempted to extort him. What the hell was the woman doing sitting in his hall?

"She has much to say about you. And us," Gillian said from next to him.

He'd expected her eyes to appear wounded, her voice to be tinged with jealousy. Instead, his lovely wife spoke of Agnes as casually as she might about the cook's choice of main dish for the evening.

Should he expect more from a woman forced to wed him?

"I'm sure she does," he said, ignoring Agnes as best he could.

"I am sorry for your loss." Gillian took another sip of wine.

It took him a moment to realize she spoke once again of Grace. Unaccustomed to speaking of such things with anyone other than Aidan, he murmured, "'Tis as much a loss to my clan as it is to me. All adored her."

"I trust Fiona showed you around Highgate?" he continued.

"She did."

When he looked at her, Graeme was struck silent. How did one interact with a wife? Or more precisely, one who seemed content with a marriage such as theirs. An alliance, forged out of necessity and lust.

So they ate in silence. Each time Graeme glanced at her, Gillian looked away. Her smiles came easily enough for her friends at Kenshire, but they were much rarer for him. Unwittingly, he looked down at the opening of her gown, his eyes drawn to the line that led to a place he planned to explore that evening. He'd feel her breasts beneath his fingertips, and more. For Gillian may be the proper English wife at other times, but he knew the passion that simmered beneath the surface.

Though it had nearly killed him, he'd held back during their travels, unwilling for her first time to be in an inn or abbey. But their marriage could finally be consummated, and he would fulfill the silent promise he'd made to her that night in the garden. The night he'd crowned her queen.

<hr />

GILLIAN SAT on the edge of her feather bed in a comfortable but drafty bower, which, according to Fiona, had been unused for years. She watched the door that led to the adjoining wardrobe, a room that connected the lady's and lord's chambers. Such a room

did not exist at Lyndwood. Instead, her parents dressed in their own chambers, and they slept separately.

Earlier in the day, after the shock of Agnes's appearance had worn off, Fiona had brought Gillian here to show her where she would be sleeping. Three maids had accompanied them, and they'd stayed to dust and sweep as she and Fiona continued in their exploration of Highgate's upper chambers.

She could not stop thinking of Agnes. Why should she care?

She could hardly expect to have a husband as devoted as Geoffrey. No, her marriage would be more like that of her parents. She and Graeme would come together for the purpose of having an heir and for meals. Otherwise, she expected to learn as much about Highgate as possible in order to manage the castle affairs. That, at least, she'd been trained to do.

This? The consummation of their marriage? Gillian had planned to ask Sara to tell her about it in more detail, but she'd never had the chance. Of course, she had thought at the time she'd be marrying a very different sort of man than Graeme. Had she been forced to lie with Covington, she would have merely stared up at the ceiling and waited for it to be over. Graeme was different.

When the door opened, Gillian looked up. Her husband stood in the doorway, dressed casually in nothing more than hose and a loose linen shirt that hung well past his waist. Her heart raced, knowing what was to come.

"She's leaving on the morrow," he said.

Graeme had stayed behind in the hall after dinner, apparently to speak to Agnes. The woman had spent the evening glaring at her, and Gillian, for her part, had not given her the satisfaction of a return glance. Instead, she'd done exactly what her mother had advocated in such a situation. Simply ignored the woman. And while her father had never openly flaunted his mistresses, neither did they typically dine in the castle's great hall. But Gillian was proud of her effort and knew her mother would have been too.

"Very good," she said, folding her hands in her lap.

By now she was more accustomed to being in the same room with Graeme in nothing but her shift. The first two nights, she'd hidden under the covers. But he would simply pull the coverlet away and admonish her not to be ashamed in front of him.

A difficult feat, to be sure.

Graeme looked around the room as if seeing it for the first time. The furnishings included only a bed, a circular brazier in the corner, a wooden trunk, and two wall torches that servants had lit while they were at dinner.

"I've not been in here in years," he said. By his tone, Gillian didn't think he wanted to be in here now either.

"'Twas your mother's?" she asked, already knowing the answer.

"Aye," he said. "She died the day after I turned two and ten. An illness none could identify turned her frail and weak in the end. I try not to remember her as the woman who lay in that bed for so long. I'd rather think of her as the mother who smiled as she admonished my brother and me to stop chasing each other through the corridors."

Lost in thought, Graeme fell silent. And then abruptly extended his hand to her. "Come with me," he said.

Mutely, she obeyed, taking his hand and allowing him to lead her through the darkened wardrobe, a room filled with trunks. Mostly empty ones, Fiona had said earlier, except for the ones that contained the jewels of the former lady of Highgate.

Wrapping one hand around hers, a familiar gesture she'd come to enjoy these past few days, Graeme used the other to push open a wooden door that led to the lord's chamber.

"Did Fiona bring you here?"

Gillian shook her head. Graeme's bedchamber was nearly as large as the one at Kenshire! Only once in her life had Gillian seen such a room.

A hearth nearly as large as the one in the hall took up a large portion of one wall. The bed, a canopied wooden one, looked as

fine as the king's. Well, her king. Gillian did not know much about Graeme's sovereign, but he must also have a bed that enormous. Topped with fur coverlets and pillows, it also looked quite comfortable.

Gillian looked away when she noticed Graeme watching her.

"I'm sorry," he said.

Gillian turned her attention back to her husband.

"For your homecoming today. For Agnes."

Gillian sensed he was sorry for more, but he'd stopped talking. He'd released her hand upon entering the room. Pity.

"None of that could be helped," she said.

Graeme's eyes narrowed. "You don't care that a woman who shared my bed sleeps just down the hall? Or that—"

"I didn't say that."

"You might as well have."

What did he want from her?

He continued to watch her, and the nervous, fluttering feeling in her stomach intensified. The one she'd had on the night they met and on nearly every occasion Graeme was in her presence.

"Your father kept other women," he said as if just realizing the fact.

"Of course he did."

Graeme took a step toward her, and Gillian didn't move. "I will not."

He said it with such force, Gillian believed him.

"We may not have been married under the best of circumstances." Graeme took her hands, both of them this time. "But I'd never dishonor you, Gillian."

Everything she'd heard about Graeme pointed to the truth of his statement. But then when she saw Agnes . . .

Graeme looked toward the bed and then back at her.

"Let me prove it to you."

He led her toward the bed and pulled down the coverlet. Then,

abruptly releasing her hand, he moved around to the other side and promptly began to undress. Gillian looked away.

"What are you doing?" Why had she asked when she already knew the answer?

"Going to sleep."

She whipped her head back around, but Graeme was already lying down. She barely caught a glimpse of his broad chest before he pulled the white fur to his shoulders and then closed his eyes as if he were already sleeping.

"Graeme?"

He opened one eye, looking very much unlike the great clan chief. Instead, he teased her like an impertinent boy. "Aye, lass?" And then he opened both eyes. "Are you not coming to bed?"

She did so hesitantly, still not understanding. Slipping under the covers, she laid her head upon the soft pillows below her.

Gillian took a deep breath. "I don't understand."

Graeme shifted to his side, propping his head on his hand. "The night I kissed you," he said, his voice low, "I knew it was wrong but did it anyway. Do you know why, my English queen?"

She thought she did, but she shook her head anyway.

"Because I desired you. And still do. Everything about you sets my body on fire. I've never wanted to be with a woman more than I want you. But Agnes should not be here at Highgate. And while she is still in this castle, I will not touch you. I want you to know my control is greater than any desire, even one this powerful."

She'd never been more aware of her husband than she was in this moment. The heat from his body . . . the unique scent that was Graeme. And, shamefully, she wanted him to touch her. To make her feel the way he had those other times.

But she also admired his will. And since he'd never been shy about his desire for her, Gillian believed his words. The night before, when he'd kissed her, Gillian had thought he'd break his own vow to wait until they were at Highgate.

"What are you wearing?" she burst out, the thought just now popping into her head.

"The same thing I wear each night to bed."

In other words, nothing.

She looked up toward the canopy above them, folding her hands in front of her.

Graeme chuckled and lay back down, his weight pulling her toward him.

"I will sleep here?" she asked the canopy.

"Aye."

"My parents do not sleep in the same bedchamber," she blurted. "Did yours?" Gillian peeked at him from the corner of her eye. Graeme was watching her.

"Sometimes," he said. "Most often my mother slept in there." He indicated the bower from which they'd come.

So why did he want her to share his bedchamber? Graeme had already made it clear theirs was not a love match.

Desire.

He'd said so himself. He desired her.

"She was loved by the people of Highgate," he said. "As you will be."

Gillian turned toward him then. "Fiona, perhaps. But the others . . . I'm not so sure."

"None are more difficult to impress than Fiona. And none have been here as long. I found her after the meal, finally. And do you know what she told me?"

Gillian shook her head.

"She refused to dine in the hall until Agnes was gone."

Gillian's eyes widened.

"Exactly." He reached out, his finger tracing the outline of her face. "You've all the allies you need here at Highgate. And will gain more, no doubt."

Her father was the one who needed allies, but Gillian

remained silent. She already felt like enough of a burden. He needn't know of her family's troubles just yet.

"Something is troubling you," he guessed.

"'Tis nothing," she said, mourning the loss of his hand when he pulled it back.

He knew she lied, but he did not press her. Nor did he turn away from her. He simply closed his eyes and said, "Good night, wife."

Gillian watched the firelight flicker and listened to her husband's steady breathing. How could he possibly go to sleep so easily? Was he so accustomed to doing so with another person in his bed? Well, she was not. But it seemed she'd best get used to the feeling as he'd made it clear they would be sleeping together.

Gillian smiled and closed her eyes.

12

*G*raeme had never had a more miserable night of sleep in his life.

He might prefer the cold, hard earth to lying next to a woman he couldn't touch, haunted by the memory of her lips on his. The feel of her bosom beneath his—

Stop!

Though it wasn't yet daybreak, he slipped out of the bed as quietly as possible and dressed in the dark. The shutters were closed on the only window in his chamber, and both wall torches had long since burned out.

What the hell was I thinking?

He'd been mortified to see Agnes here, but his attempt at rectifying the situation had been foolhardy. It had been difficult enough not to make Gillian his wife in truth on their journey here. But to actually have her in his bed . . .

He opened the door a crack, looked back to see her still sleeping peacefully, and strode from the torture chamber. Servants were just waking up, so there was little movement around him as Graeme made his way to the hall.

"Good morning, my lord," a servant greeted him.

"And to you." He sat in front of the fire, which had already been lit by one of the servants. He gripped the armrest of the high-backed wooden chair that had belonged to his grandfather and stared into the fire. Trestle tables were moved into place behind him, but he ignored all of it, thinking of Grace. The raid.

And *her.*

She may not ever love him. But Graeme was determined to unleash his wife's passion. Despite a stringent upbringing and an unfaithful father whose alliances were questionable at best, Gillian came alive at his touch. It was a trait he found quite endearing.

"This is most unusual." Aidan sat next to him, a mug of ale already in his hands.

"Brother."

"I've never seen you up this early outside of the training yard."

His own regime, slightly more stringent than his younger brother's, was indeed predictable.

But not today.

"I'm waiting for Agnes."

Aidan's brows lifted.

"To ensure she understands the meaning of 'being on her way in the morn.'"

Aidan crossed his legs in front of him. "I'm surprised at your foul mood."

The implication of why Graeme should be in a better mood hung in the air. He'd not discuss his relationship with Gillian, so he changed the subject instead.

"I worry over recent events," he said, which was true enough. Light began to peek through the closed shutters just next to the hearth on the outer wall.

"There have been more attacks recently, but none of them have had any fatalities since the attack on Lord Clave and Lady Emma. We know the man's uncle was responsible."

"Aye," Graeme said. Garrick was an earl in both England and

Scotland, and his uncle had become covetous of his Scottish earldom.

"Inverglen was punished for his involvement in that attack, proving once again the effectiveness of the current system. The offenders will be punished," Aidan continued.

"They will," Graeme said, crossing his arms, "especially since we have Kenshire on our side. "But it makes no sense. For Blackburn to be so careless . . ."

His brother said nothing.

Though Lord Blackburn's only loyalty was to his own coin, something did not make sense. He had never made such an outrageous raid before.

"Do you think he intends to start a clan war?"

Aidan looked up, his eyes sharp. "For what purpose?"

"If March Law falls apart and the Days of Truce become a thing of the past, who benefits?"

Aidan thought for a moment. "Those who would take advantage of the instability for their own gain. But March Law has held for thirty years, Graeme. Despite setbacks like this one."

"Grace is more than a setback."

Aidan took a long swig of ale.

Graeme should apologize for that. His brother had not meant to be unkind. He was not the only one who cared about Grace. But he couldn't get the words out.

"Chief?" The word was delivered in a quavering voice.

Both he and Aidan turned, and he immediately understood the source of the young man's concern. Agnes stood in the entranceway, her arms crossed.

"She refuses my escort."

His brother's smile was too much. Graeme stood so fast the heavy chair nearly toppled on its side. He strode to the woman who'd caused him a sleepless night and confronted her.

"Agnes. We discussed this. You will accept his escort, or you may go alone. But you will leave my hall. Immediately."

"Graeme," she pouted. How could he ever have thought this woman appealing? She was so different from Gillian . . .

"Now," he repeated. The servants were beginning to stare, but he ignored them.

"I—" Her lip quivered. "Can we not speak alone, just for one moment?"

He was about to say nay when she stopped him.

"After we talk, I will leave with your man."

Gillian would be down any moment. He just wanted Agnes gone.

"Very well."

When he strode toward the door leading to the inner courtyard, Agnes followed.

GILLIAN STOOD at the entrance to the great hall, watching her husband walk away with his former lover. So much for his promise . . . a promise she'd been foolish enough to believe. She tried to ignore the hardening in her stomach as she walked into the hall. Spying Graeme's brother in front of the hearth, she made her way toward him.

"Good morn, sir," she greeted him.

He stood.

"Aidan, my lady," he responded with a bow.

"Gillian," she returned, moving toward the unoccupied seat next to him.

He began to move toward her, but she sat too quickly for his assistance. Gillian looked toward the entrance of the hall.

"How have you been settling, my lady . . . Gillian," he corrected.

She could tell Aidan was attempting to distract her and immediately warmed to him because of it.

"I . . ." How to answer that?

"As well as can be expected after being forced to wed and

move to a foreign land, only to be abandoned by your new husband?"

Gillian smiled. "Exactly so."

Aidan took a swig of whatever he was drinking. "I am sorry for that," he said, and seemed sincere. "And my brother is as well."

She glanced toward the courtyard.

"Tell me." Aidan brought her attention back to him as the hall began to fill with people for the morning meal. "Of your family."

Gillian frowned.

"You're not close to them?"

"Oh, no. It's not that." She didn't want him to think ill of her family. "It's just—"

"Tell me," he prompted.

"I—" She took a deep breath. "I worry for them."

She could tell he didn't understand. What harm would it do to share her concerns? He appeared genuinely interested. And certainly Clan Scott would not feel the need to sacrifice themselves to save her family, not when Graeme so clearly loathed her father.

A bit of the truth would suffice. "I was to marry another," she said. By his expression, Gillian could tell Aidan already knew of Covington. "My father needed the coin, desperately. I worry what will happen to them now."

"From my understanding, your father is quite influential. I'm sure he will arrange for a way to recompense the loss."

Aye, and that was exactly what she was afraid of. "I'm sure he will."

Feeling rude, she asked Aidan to share as well.

"Tell me," she repeated, "a bit of your clan."

The corner of his mouth lifted, making him appear younger than his age.

"*Your* clan," he corrected.

Gillian shivered. "I suppose, but I know there are many who likely do not want me here."

"Nay, lass. There is no doubt of it. You are my brother's wife, the lady of Highgate End, and a member of Clan Scott. If anyone dares cast doubt on the fact, they'll have me . . . and Graeme . . . to face because of it."

Though they weren't close to the fire, Gillian's whole body felt warm. First Fiona had declared herself an ally, now Aidan. This was a much better reception than she'd expected.

Save Agnes.

"You sound very much like your brother," she said.

Aidan crossed his legs in front of him. "I suppose that's to be expected."

Aidan's gaze turned toward the door, and the expression on his face told her Graeme had already returned. When she turned to look behind her, sure enough, her husband made his way toward them. And he did not appear particularly happy.

13

"Gillian. Aidan." Graeme inclined his head to both of them, unable to stop staring at his wife. She sat perched on the edge of her seat, her back ramrod straight. It was as if she belonged there already, the lady of Highgate in truth.

If it weren't for that damned fool woman.

He should not have believed her when she'd claimed to only want a word. No sooner had they found a somewhat secluded spot than she'd tried to seduce him. It mattered not that he was now married, or that he'd ended their affair, to their mutual satisfaction, well before he'd left for England.

Aidan had warned him not to get involved with Agnes, but he hadn't heeded his advice. At the time, he'd believed it wouldn't matter. That he'd never marry. After all, he'd tried twice, first with Catrina Kerr and then with Emma.

"The men are waiting," he told his brother, who rightfully looked confused.

"Already? But we've not even broken our fast."

"Already," he answered. "My apologies, Gillian. It's been many days since I've trained with the men, so I asked them to assemble earlier than usual."

Aidan, in charge of their training, did not appear amused. "Why?"

Graeme couldn't very well tell the truth. That a sleepless night lying next to this beautiful woman had already tormented him into a foul mood. One that a bitter departure with Agnes had not helped. In the end, he'd simply walked away from her while she was in midspeech. He would not continue to dishonor his wife by speaking to her, and the groomsmen could very likely hear their conversation. The last thing he desired was to be the subject of gossip in his own home.

Aidan and Gillian both stood from their seats at the hearth.

When she reached down to smooth out the front of her deep green gown, a color that complemented her dark hair nicely, he could not take his gaze from her.

Aidan coughed, gaining his attention. "Lead the way, brother."

Gillian frowned.

"Apologies, my lady, for not breaking my fast with you. If it pleases you, I'd very much like to introduce you to some of the staff this afternoon."

She looked as if she wanted to say something, but if so, she thought better of it. Her only response was to raise the corners of her mouth ever so slightly.

Just then, Fiona appeared from nowhere and led his wife away.

"I will take care of her," she said, shooing him dismissively. "Go."

Sometimes he wondered who gave the orders at Highgate. He or his grandmother's maid? But he couldn't lament the fact that Fiona treated him more as an equal than as her master. His mother was gone. And now his grandmother too. Fiona was the only reminder of a time when he had been surrounded by women who loved him. Who cared for him. And while he certainly needed neither, it felt good to know she was still with them, taking care of both him and Aidan.

With a bow, he strode from the hall and into the courtyard, prepared to continue on the path that would lead to the lists.

Aidan reached out to stop him. "Graeme."

He ignored him, ducking his arm.

"Graeme," his brother said more loudly.

He stopped.

"What's gotten into you?" Aidan asked.

"Nothing." Even to him, it sounded like a lie.

"You could have stayed with your wife. The men would have been happy not to eat stale bread."

He referred to the meal that awaited them during their training.

"Fiona is with her. She—"

"Needs you."

"I hardly think—"

"I never imagined I would be in any position to lecture my older brother about women. But she is not just any woman, Graeme. She is your wife."

"You think I don't know that?"

"I think you don't know her."

He took a step toward Aidan, his hands balling into fists.

"She is scared. And you've done nothing—"

"Scared? Of what? Surely not of me?" If he'd given Gillian the impression . . .

"Nay, you fool. Of what will happen to her family now that she's been sent here. And likely of her place in this clan. And—"

"Enough," he stopped him. "How do you know all of this?"

"I spoke with her."

Graeme had spoken with her too. Had spent the past three days with her. But she hadn't mentioned any of that to him.

"All I'm saying is that she's no Agnes."

"Of course she's not." Gillian was so much more. Kind and curious. Passionate and—

"Go to her."

Only then did he realize why he'd held himself back. He'd opened himself up to Catrina . . . to Emma, and both had left him. Nay. He'd sooner not chance it.

"I will see her this afternoon. Now"—he continued walking —"if you've finished advising me how to conduct my marriage, we'd best be on our way. Suddenly, I'm itching for a match with my younger, much less competent brother."

He couldn't see his face as Aidan walked behind him, but he'd never known his brother to shy away from a challenge.

Sure enough, when Aidan caught up with him, he narrowed his eyes and issued a challenge of his own. One Graeme was eager to accept.

Taking out his frustrations of the past few days was the exact thing he needed to get his mind off of *her*.

"WHAT IS THAT WONDERFUL SMELL?" Gillian followed Graeme into a room that, once inside, she realized was the bakehouse.

As promised, he'd spent the afternoon introducing her to the staff and giving her a very different account of Highgate than Fiona had. Whereas Fiona's tour had been peppered with stories about the people, Graeme's was far more focused on the castle's defenses.

The first thing he'd said, upon finding her in the castle, was that her maid, Morgan, would be arriving in two days, something that had immediately buoyed her spirits. Finally, news from home. And then she could decide on her next course of action. There must be something she could do to help the others.

On the tour, he'd treated her much as he had on their trip. Polite. Cordial. Still, he'd occasionally give her a look that assured her that he did indeed still desire her. But the looks were so fleeting, she wondered if she'd imagined them.

Not once did he mention Agnes. Why had he gone with her

earlier in the day? Was she still here? And why did she care so much when both of them knew this marriage was not one born out of love?

And still . . . he'd vowed not to dishonor her.

"I do believe it's . . ." He stopped and looked around. The room appeared abandoned.

"Where is the baker?" she asked.

"He's likely brought his wares to the kitchen for this evening's meal."

Graeme picked up a discarded wooden bowl, stuck his finger inside, and then licked the white crème from his fingers. "*Crème boylede*, as I suspected."

She'd never heard of the dish.

"Is it possible you've never tasted *crème boylede* before?"

She shook her head.

"Come here," he said, sticking his finger back into the bowl.

She walked toward him and lifted her chin.

"Relax," he said, glancing around. "You're allowed at least one impropriety each day."

"Is that so?"

"That is so, lass. Now stop worrying and open your mouth."

She did as he asked.

But when he placed his finger on her tongue and she wrapped her lips around him to taste the sweet, everything changed.

No longer was he her guide, and she the wide-eyed English-woman getting to know her surroundings.

Instead, she was simply a woman. One who could not deny the pull this man had on her. That he'd always had on her.

He pulled his finger slowly from her mouth as his eyes darkened with lust.

Though his finger was fully withdrawn, he didn't move.

Her heart thudded in her chest. Was he going to kiss her?

"Did you like it?" he asked.

Gillian swallowed.

"Very much," she said, aware her words held a double meaning.

"There will be more this evening."

Still, he didn't move.

And then a thought occurred to her. "But won't I need to share?"

Gillian could have referred to the custom of sharing a bowl of custard with all seated at the high table, but that wasn't what she spoke of at all.

And Graeme knew it.

"Never," he said, his voice firm.

Agnes was gone.

Perhaps she was a fool to believe Graeme, especially after seeing him with Agnes in the morning. She'd rebuked the advances of many a married man at Lyndwood, had she not?

And then, of course, there was her father's infidelity.

But she believed Graeme meant what he had said.

"Just know, wife." Her husband's tone took on a hard edge. "Neither do I share"—his eyes narrowed—"my custard."

She should not be so saucy, but Gillian found herself reaching down and dipping her own finger into the bowl. She intended to tease him by licking the rather delightful sweet off herself, but she didn't move quickly enough.

Graeme grabbed her hand and lifted it toward his mouth. When he wrapped his lips around her finger, a fluttering at her very core threatened the self-composure she so diligently practiced.

And then he suckled her trembling finger, withdrawing ever so slowly. Just before it was completely free of his lips, his teeth, barely touching her skin, closed around her, softly nipping. By the time her finger was free, Gillian could barely stand.

There will be more this evening.

She had never looked forward to a meal, and to afterward, quite so much.

*G*raeme released his wife's hand.

He wanted to kiss her. Nay, he wanted to take her here and now. Make her his wife in truth. That they'd been married for almost a week and had yet to consummate the marriage. It was unthinkable . . . and yet he wanted it to be perfect for her. He'd never bedded a virgin before, but Graeme clearly remembered his first time. The serving girl, a pretty, buxom young woman, had been loose with her favors. And while he'd never admitted it aloud, he had been quite nervous. She was older, more experienced, and self-assured.

Graeme had decided that cold winter night in the stable loft he'd never bed a virgin, and he hadn't, no matter her station. He'd come to quite enjoy his time with the fairer sex, and the idea of his bedmate being uneasy or uncomfortable did not settle well. Which was why, he supposed, he wanted to make the experience special for Gillian.

Tonight . . .

The bakehouse was no place for her first time, and though he would very much enjoy tasting more than just the custard for this evening's meal, they needed to leave.

Now.

He grabbed her hand, the feel of her delicate fingers a pleasure he refused to deny himself despite the unconventionality of hand-holding. He looked at her, his hesitant bride, and wondered, not for the first time, what she was thinking.

Gillian spoke little and revealed even less.

"We should be getting back for the meal." Her smile nearly felled him.

"You're looking forward to it, then?" Graeme was of a mind to skip the damn meal and take his wife to their bedchamber—his bedchamber—now.

In fact, that was not such a bad plan.

"There you are." Aidan ran toward them.

"What is it?"

"The Day of Truce." His brother looked from him to Gillian and back again, his expression making Graeme uneasy. "'Tis tomorrow."

Graeme shook his head. "Nay, it's not for more than—"

"We've just received word. The date has been changed."

"But I don't understand. Each month—"

"Apparently Douglas and Hedford came to an agreement, because of Blackburn, to conduct it and put an immediate end to the proceedings. There is a consensus . . ."

"There may be trouble brewing." Graeme chanced a glance at Gillian. "I need to go. Immediately."

"Aye, you do," Aidan agreed. "I've already had your mounts prepared and the men readied. I'd come if—"

"You know I could never allow such a thing. I need my second here, especially now." Aidan understood. He'd not leave Gillian unprotected. Ever.

Aidan nodded—it was what he'd expected, of course—bowed to Gillian, and left.

"I'm sorry, lass," Graeme started. But his wife cut him off.

"'Tis not your fault. Go," she urged. "See the offenders of the raid brought to justice."

And he could tell she meant it. Activity whirled around them in the courtyard, but it felt as if the two of them were alone together. He brushed away a tug on his heart that had nothing to do with desire. For the briefest moment, he imagined this same scene, years from now, with bairns at their heels. Gillian had experienced the very worst of welcomes to Highgate, and yet, she genuinely seemed to understand.

They'd not have their wedding night yet, but he'd be damned if he'd leave her like this. So, in full view of everyone, he pulled her toward him.

And kissed her.

With every bit of pent-up desire . . . with the burgeoning feelings he didn't care to categorize . . . with every part of himself, Graeme kissed her. He held her face to him and did not hold back. She gave of herself freely, and he took her offering.

He stopped only when cheers erupted around them.

Graeme held her face still, his thumbs running against the smooth skin that felt so unlike any part of him. How had he gotten so lucky?

"I plan to do just that," he said. "And when I return"—his lips turned up ever so slightly—"we will finish . . . the custard."

Gillian's laugh, the sweetest sound he'd ever heard, followed him away from Highgate End.

SHE SAT next to Aidan at the evening meal, grateful for an ally. But not completely clear on why he was still here.

"You are Graeme's second," she started, picking at the figs in front of her.

"Aye, lass. That I am."

"And this particular Day of Truce is rather important given that the fiend Blackburn is on trial?"

She didn't understand his chuckle.

"My apologies, Lady Gillian. I'm just . . . pleased to hear of your assessment of Lord Blackburn on behalf of Highgate."

Gillian could not allow him to think that, exactly. "Of course, I am rather vexed on behalf of Clan Scott." She nodded to a servant, who filled her goblet with more wine. "But Lord Blackburn's underhanded tactics are well known in England as well."

He looked at her curiously.

"My father said he was actually caught cheating at the last Tournament of the North. And that he made an enemy of Clan Kerr ever since."

"Your father is correct."

"He did not have many kindly things to say about the man."

Aidan took a bite of the lamb in front of him. She was about to ask him a question about Graeme when two Scott clansmen entered the hall and waved Aidan toward them.

"Pardon," Aidan said, standing.

As she watched, they spoke for a moment and then looked at her. They were talking about her. Though Gillian had been generally pleased by her reception at Highgate, she knew the people did not trust her yet. Why would they? She was a stranger. And an Englishwoman. But this was her home now. And though she'd been sheltered, Gillian had at least been trained to run a household. She could do this.

So why were they looking at her so—

"Morgan!"

It had to be! Every head in the hall turned toward her. She hadn't meant to shout, but she was so pleased by the prospect of seeing her lady's maid, she'd momentarily lost control.

So very unlike her.

Gillian folded the linen napkin she held and placed it on the table. Rising, she made her way to the opposite end of the hall, where she could now see trunks being brought in from the outside. She recognized some of the men. They were from Lyndwood. Yes, Morgan was here!

The petite, brown-haired woman ran toward her. And although Gillian knew she should not embrace her in full view of everyone, she did so anyway. If Graeme could hold her hand and kiss her in front of his people, she could very well show affection to the only familiar face here at Highgate.

"I didn't expect you until tomorrow," she said.

"They were surprised I rode so well." Morgan motioned to her father's men, who nodded to her when she glanced their way.

Fiona appeared and introduced herself. "Welcome, Mistress Morgan. My lady has been looking forward to your arrival."

She smiled at Fiona. "Aye, very much. I'm pleased to introduce you to Mistress Fiona. She is . . ." Gillian stopped, not knowing how to introduce her. A lady's maid, without a lady to care for, would typically receive another less prominent position.

One look at the older woman's face and Gillian knew exactly what she had to do. She prayed for Morgan's understanding. "She was lady's maid to my husband's late grandmother."

Fiona's face fell. Aidan stopped talking to his companions.

"But I should be quite pleased if she shared your duties, Morgan, and would serve me as well." She rushed to finish, "Of course, only if Mistress Fiona—"

"I accept," Fiona said, her uneven smile telling Gillian she had done the right thing.

"As such," she said to the older woman, "if you could arrange for the remainder of my meal—"

"Done, my lady. I'll have one of the girls bring it up to you straightaway."

Gillian moved away from the hall and motioned for Morgan to follow. Greeting the men as she walked by, she excused herself to her brother-in-law and wound her way upstairs and toward the lady's chamber, ushering Morgan inside.

"This is quite lovely." Morgan placed the sack she carried at the foot of her bed. "Will a pallet be brought in here?"

She'd shared her bedchamber with Morgan since the girl had been assigned to her when she was but ten and one. Would Morgan stay here? Would Gillian? Or would she sleep in her husband's chamber every night as he'd alluded to the night before?

"'Tis a good question." She moved to the bed and motioned for Morgan to do the same. Her maid folded her hands in her lap, and though she'd seen her sit exactly the same way many times, something struck her about the properness of it, especially since Allie had told her it was a habit Morgan had picked up from *her*.

It had seemed quite normal at Lyndwood.

"Tell me . . . everything."

Morgan took a deep breath.

"So much to tell, my lady." Morgan tapped her fingers together.

Her maid was nervous.

"Morgan?"

"I can hardly believe yer married, my lady. And this is our new home. When you didn't return—"

"Morgan." She did not mean to sound so stern, but her chest felt tight in anticipation. "Is something amiss?"

Her maid's nod, so slight, confirmed Gillian's greatest fear. Her family would lose Lyndwood. If her father could not pay his debt to the Crown . . .

"'Tis Allie."

Gillian's throat went dry. "What is it?"

Morgan's already thin lips disappeared as she pursed them together. Whatever she had to say was not something that came easy for her. Gillian held her breath.

"Allie has been promised to Covington."

Nay, not that. Never that. She'd barely allowed herself to fear it.

"My lady, did you hear me?"

"There must be some mistake. She's much too young. Covington specifically asked—"

"For your hand in marriage, aye. My lord reminded him so. He said—"

"Wait, Father spoke to Covington?"

"Aye, my lady."

Morgan's hands were no longer folded neatly on her lap. Gillian could not stop looking at them.

"He arrived at nearly the same time as your father. He already knew of your wedding."

Morgan stopped, and Gillian looked her straight in the eyes.

"He was not pleased," Morgan said.

Gillian didn't ask how Morgan knew all of this. Her maid was well liked and resourceful. If any member of the household at Lyndwood knew something, Morgan knew it too.

"Oh, Allie." Her heart hurt to think of her lovely, perfect sister attached to such an old man. Though Gillian had said her sister was much too young to marry, she knew, of course, that was not exactly true. At ten and nine, the only reason she was not already promised to someone was because of her father's insistence that Gillian marry first, as was the custom.

This could not be happening.

"Your father and Covington argued something fierce," Morgan continued, warming to her topic. "And the very next day, the same day I left for Highgate, the betrothal was announced."

"When?" She had to stop it. Somehow she had to stop it. The thought of her sister married to that man . . .

"The first of June, my lady. 'Tis said the earl did not wish to wait so long, but he finally relented."

"And Allie?"

Morgan shrugged. "Lady Allie was, well, Lady Allie."

Which meant she had accepted the decree in public, as Gillian had done, and cried foul in private. Neither of them would dishonor their parents, but Allie was more likely to put up a fight. To what end? Her mother would certainly not approve of the betrothal, just as she had not wished for Gillian to wed Covington, which had become fully clear at Kenshire. Unfortunately, however, only one person's orders mattered in Lyndwood.

The baron's.

She and Allie and their mother obeyed him in all things, even if they disagreed.

Allie would eventually fall into line and do as she was told. Lyndwood would be saved, but at what cost?

Nay. I will not allow it.

"There is still time," she said, thinking aloud.

The door opened after a quick knock. Gillian waved the serving girl inside.

"Time for what?" Morgan asked, looking longingly at the wooden tray laden with food.

Gillian smiled at the serving girl, trying to remember her name.

"My lady? You've got that look about you," Morgan ventured.

She wasn't sure how Morgan recognized "that look." She had so rarely defied her father. For all his shortcomings, he was her father, a fact that nothing would change. And yet . . . she'd also spent plenty of time with Sara throughout the years and could hear her friend's voice now.

'Tis time your father sees what is in front of his face. Being perfect will not turn you into a son.

Perhaps Sara had been right. Perhaps it was time to break the rules a bit, as her friend had always encouraged her to do.

"And what look is that Morgan?" she asked, standing.

To which her maid mumbled, "The look of the Kenshire women."

*G*illian paced back and forth, glancing every so often at the guards stationed on each tower. The battlement, made for defense, was the perfect spot for her to look for any sign of Graeme. He'd been gone for two days, but according to Aidan, he would arrive imminently. Her brother-in-law had been in a closed-door meeting with a member of a neighboring clan for most of the morning, and Gillian could not have been more surprised when he'd sought her out in the hall.

"Our visitor says Graeme is just behind him," he'd told her.

Gillian had awaited this very news for two days.

"Thank you for letting me know," she said. And then she waited. Aidan obviously had more to say.

"If Ferguson is in a better mood later, I'll be sure to introduce you to him."

"Ferguson?"

"MacDuff. Of Clan Bourne."

But it was his next words that startled her.

"MacDuff didn't realize Graeme was just behind him until he met with two Scottish reivers on the road. The men apparently ran with Geoffrey Waryn years earlier, and they know my brother."

"I see," she said.

It was common knowledge Sara's husband still had allies in a community marked by odd allegiances. To each other first, and to country only occasionally.

But why had Aidan told her all this?

At her apparent confusion, Aidan shocked her by saying, "I thought you'd want to know. To be kept informed."

In all her years, Gillian couldn't remember one time . . . even one . . . when her father had deigned to tell her, let alone her mother, anything of import about their keeping. Was it so different here in Scotland?

Sara is as involved in the affairs of Kenshire as her husband. But that is most unusual. Is it not?

Now, standing on high, she looked out at the horizon. Beyond the castle walls, rolling hills extended into the distance, still green despite the chill that hung in the air. Though they'd passed a small village on their way to Highgate End, it was not visible from here. Gillian turned in the direction she thought the village might be, but only the activity in the courtyard and the castle's high walls were visible from this vantage point.

She'd spent the previous day fretting about what she'd say to Graeme, whether she'd tell him all. But the continued warmth she'd received from Aidan and Fiona had encouraged her. She could not protect her family, her sister, alone. This was her new home, and everyone had proved to be most understanding. She'd tell her husband everything and ask for his help.

In truth, she wished she'd been more forthright with Sara too. She'd scarcely let herself believe her family's position was this strained.

When a hand touched hers from behind, Gillian pulled it back and spun around.

114

"Graeme!" Though travel worn, he was as handsome as the day she'd first spied him at Kenshire.

She looked back over the parapet. Nothing.

"Where did you come from. I—"

He reached for her hand again, and this time she allowed it.

"I thank you for assisting the men." He nodded toward one of the guards in a nearby tower. "But I believe standing watch may not be the most suitable position for you."

She reached up with her free hand, before thinking, and brushed it along his cheek. No longer smooth, the few days' growth made him appear more fearsome. It tickled beneath her fingertips.

"How did you know—"

"I saw you up here," he said, capturing her hand with his own. "Even if it were not for this"—he gestured toward her gown, a bright blue which could likely be seen quite clearly from afar—"I'd not have missed the sight."

When he looked at her like that, Gillian felt her knees quake.

He took a step toward her.

She could feel the warmth of his body, and when he leaned in to kiss her, Gillian didn't hesitate. His lips slanted over hers, gently at first, but then more insistent. She was just becoming accustomed to the feel of him when Graeme suddenly tore himself away. Then, without preamble, he grabbed her hand and pulled her along. They walked toward the tower he'd pointed to earlier, and then beyond it.

"Graeme? Where are we going?"

He didn't look back. "Where we belong."

That made no sense.

They were headed to the main keep. She remembered Fiona telling her this was called the armorer's tower. She followed Graeme down the winding stairs, her heart beating harder and harder with each passing moment.

"Graeme, I need to tell you something," she started.

He stopped, and Gillian ran into him. It was like hitting a stone wall. He didn't budge. Instead, her husband caught her around the waist. Standing there, in the middle of the tower on a small platform with stairs above and below them, they didn't speak. Instead, he told her with his expression all she needed to know.

They would talk. But not now.

"'Tis midday," she said as he reached out to open a door. Once ajar, Gillian could see it was a secret passageway. Graeme ducked into it and Gillian followed. He closed the door, which was disguised as a part of wall, and continued to lead the way toward their chambers.

"The armorer's tower was built years after the keep. There are many secret passageways," he said, answering her silent question. "But this one was designed as a last defense for the lord . . . and now lady . . . of Highgate."

They'd arrived.

Graeme opened the door to the lord's chamber, pulled her inside, and closed it behind them. Except for the guards, they'd seen no one on their way here. Indeed, if that hidden passageway was one of many, one could move about the castle without notice. For some reason, the thought excited her.

"I've much to tell you," she repeated as he pulled her toward him.

"And I you," he said.

"Later."

He'd had no intention of ravishing his wife today.

In fact, after the hellish two days he'd spent being betrayed, by Gillian's father no less, Graeme had come home unsure of what he intended to do first. Speak with Aidan, assuredly. Formulate a new plan. Make his wife understand he did not blame her for the sins of her father.

But certainly not this. At least, not before he'd had a chance to announce his arrival.

And yet Graeme had found himself riding up to the gate at a more frantic pace than usual, and when he'd spied his wife on the ramparts, that flash of blue had instantly cheered his spirits.

And so he'd tossed all good sense aside and run to her like a lovesick squire. Not, of course, that he was in love with his wife. But he could not deny the urgent need that had only intensified each time they were together.

Their differences could wait. The fall of darkness could wait.

Graeme intended to make this woman his wife in truth.

As always, she responded to him so completely that it was a wonder he had not tossed aside his good intentions earlier. He wrapped his arms around her, and she did the same with him. When he lowered his lips this time, he felt the difference. This was the start of something he intended to finish.

"So soft," he murmured.

Graeme captured her tongue then and gave her no quarter. Mindful that this was indeed her first time, he wanted to distract her from any pain she might experience. So he circled and pressed until his wife's breathing became heavier.

He would seduce her, pleasure her, then make love to her.

Breaking contact with her lips, Graeme trailed a path of kisses to her ear.

"How are you feeling?" he whispered, lowering his mouth to her neck and not stopping there.

"I—"

Graeme smiled against her skin. His goal had been met.

"I don't want you to be able to talk." He kissed the valley between her breasts, thanking the unknown dressmaker for giving him such access. Cupping her with both hands, he squeezed gently as his mouth continued to deliver promises of what was to come.

Though Graeme had always relished the feeling of a woman's

pleasure, the jolt that came from his wife's soft moans shook him to the core. He'd do anything to please her, to make her forget everything save his hands, his lips.

"So much . . . to tell . . ." She did not stand a chance. He was able to dip so far below the fabric of her gown his tongue nearly touched the tip of her breast. She might want to tell him something, but that something would have to wait.

16

*H*e turned her around and began to unlace her gown at the back.

"Are you going to make love to me now?" Her traitorous body knew there were important matters to discuss. *Urgent* matters. But all she could think about was his lips . . . there. His hands like irons, scalding her and making her unable to form a coherent thought.

"I am."

Once untied, the gown dropped on its own, her arms easily emerging from the flowing sleeves. Why wasn't she the least bit nervous? Shouldn't she be?

"Do you know what that means?"

She stepped out of the gown and turned. He tossed it aside in a heap.

His tunic joined it on the floor a moment later.

"How did you manage that so quickly? You couldn't possibly—"

"I told you." He lifted his hands, so large and powerful they could probably kill a man. "They're quick."

Gillian almost asked if she could touch him. Surely she didn't need permission, but she suddenly felt quite shy as she stared at the ridges on his chest.

"You can . . . and should," he said before he captured her lips with his own, somehow understanding. Whether she'd said it aloud or he simply knew what was in her mind, it hardly mattered. She took the invitation, wrapping her arms around his naked back and allowing herself the pleasure of being pressed up against him. His mouth slanted against hers, his tongue insistent that she give him her own, which she did, gladly. The swirling and thrusting nearly tore her in two—Gillian found herself pulling her husband closer, wanting more of him.

This kiss was different. The very thin fabric that separated them was nothing like the thicker velvet of her gown. This defense was fragile, taunting. It would not hold up.

When he pulled away, the sense of loss was immediate.

"I'd see you, lass. All of you."

Gillian had never kissed a man before Graeme and had certainly never allowed one to see her naked. But oddly enough, she wanted to show herself to him. At her nod, Graeme lifted her shift and pulled it over her head in one quick motion.

The look in his eyes made her feel . . . proud. She did not attempt to cover herself.

"Beautiful," he said just before he removed his trewes and stood before her utterly and completely naked.

"Oh—" She should be terrified. Certainly there was no way that would fit inside her. But instead, she wanted to touch it. Touch him. His legs were thick and muscled like every other part of him.

Gillian tossed away any vestiges of shyness and allowed her curiosity free rein. This man was her husband, and as he had said, more than once, the bedroom was not the place for reservations.

Even so, I can't very well ask if I can touch it.

She opened her mouth, still staring, but before any words formed, he took her hand and guided it to him.

"Do you remember what I said?"

Aye, very well.

"In here, there are no secrets. No shyness. If you want something, take it."

He wrapped his hand around hers, curling her fingers around his thick column before letting go.

Graeme moaned, his head tilting back and eyes closing. Even more fascinating than the feel of him beneath her was the realization she had power over him. When she moved her hand, *she* was in control. His eyes whipped open, and he reached out so quickly it took a moment for her to realize his intent.

Graeme cupped both of her breasts and rubbed his thumbs over her nipples, making them peak. There were simply too many sensations. Her insides felt as if they'd melt away from her, the throbbing between her legs growing more insistent with every caress.

"What is happening?" she managed.

Graeme's low growl sounded like pain and pleasure all wrapped into one. He lifted her as if she were a feather pillow and carried her to the massive bed at the other end of the chamber. Once he'd lowered her to the mattress, Graeme moved over her, the muscles in his arms bulging as he held himself up.

"Your body is preparing for this," he answered.

When his mouth closed around her breast again, she reached around his back and attempted to hold on. To grasp and grab at anything to keep from falling under the spell that was Graeme de Sowlis.

He gave her breast the same attention as her mouth. And when he moved his hand down between them, Gillian pressed against him.

"You're ready," he murmured against her breast.

She could have told him as much.

When he nudged her legs apart, Gillian allowed it. Graeme

lifted his head then, his eyes saying that he was sorry as clearly as if he'd spoken it.

But what did he have to—

His manhood pressed against her, and with his hand guiding him, Gillian suddenly felt filled, if just a tad. Sure, that was pleasant enough. If this was lovemaking, then . . .

"Ouch!" she cried when he entered her completely.

He kissed her then, his lips moving over hers more gently, more reverently, than before. Gillian concentrated on the feeling of his lips. Proud that she already knew how to touch her tongue to his. They circled and swirled, tangled together—

And then he moved.

Oh yes, he moved and it was glorious.

"It doesn't hurt any longer," she said, pulling away to tell him that. To her surprise, she wanted more—she wanted to be even closer.

Still propped above her, Graeme moved slowly, entering and then retreating. But it was not his movement or the knowledge that he was inside her—inside her—that stilled her.

It was his expression.

His hooded eyes and set jaw sent a shiver through her entire body. Suddenly, she wanted to meet his every thrust with one of her own. His eyes bore into hers, the connection they'd shared in the garden still very much present.

"Good," he said, the tone like the lathering of soap, smooth and slick.

He moved against her, faster and faster, and Gillian, understanding, did the same.

"You're holding back," she said.

How do I know that?

"You are a virgin," he said, moving even slower now.

"Nay," she said, not allowing it. "Not any longer." Mimicking his own movements, she circled her hips and watched his mouth open. Though part of her wanted him to kiss her again, Gillian also enjoyed watching his face. Knowing she was affecting him this way.

"Faster," she instructed and didn't wait for him to comply.

"Gillian, you don't know what you—"

She was doing this to him. Giving him as much pleasure as he gave her. Finally, Graeme gave in to her silent plea. When he lowered his mouth to hers, she was lost in a haze of desire so strong she couldn't believe she'd waited so long to experience it.

He filled her, moved with her. Kissed her and made her want to let go.

And so she did.

Gillian's world exploded.

She gripped him with her fingers . . . her toes scrunched into balls as a wave of pleasure claimed her entire body. Pulsing and throbbing against him, she cried out again and heard him do the same. When he finally collapsed on top of her, she held on to him as tightly as possible.

For such a large man, he should have been crushing her. But he wasn't. Instead, it was a sweet pressure, his legs entangled with her own. Still inside her, Graeme was not separate but a part of her.

"So . . . that was lovemaking?" she asked stupidly.

He pulled himself up and gazed down at her, those eyes intense enough to ignite a flame.

"That . . . and more."

He pulled himself away, grabbing her at the same time and rolling her on top of him. She rather liked it here. Her husband's body was so hard, it was rather like lying on a table.

Though much more enjoyable.

"More?"

Her cheeks warmed as he glanced down between them. When he looked up, the resolve in his expression startled her.

"That was you becoming my wife in truth. And I, your husband."

"But we were married back at Kenshire." Was that really not even a week ago?

"Married, aye. But wedded in truth now."

She supposed he was correct.

"So we are stuck with each other?"

Though she said it in jest, a shadow crossed his face. So quickly, Gillian wondered if she imagined it.

"It seems so," he said.

The tender moment between them had been banished by that one simple statement. The chief had returned. The man whom Aidan called inflexible.

Surely he knew she jested? She was about to tell him just that when he spoke her name, his voice full of both hesitation and resolve as he pulled away from her and placed her on the bed next to him.

"Gillian—"

"Aye?" She sat up and pulled the coverlet toward her. Or tried to, at least. Graeme swatted it away. No shyness between them.

"We need to talk." He stood, the evidence of her innocence obvious on his manhood.

"Did it hurt?" he asked, looking down and moving to a small wooden washing stand. He dipped the waiting cloth into the bowl of water and wrung it out, the splash of water echoing in an otherwise quiet room.

"Not for long," she said, watching as he sat next to her on the bed. Gillian assumed he'd use the cloth on himself, but instead he brought it to her.

"I apologize; the water is cold."

He was right. But the cold didn't bother her. Gillian stared, fascinated that such a large man, a clan chief and renowned warrior, could manage such a gentle touch.

He washed her, and then himself.

"You said we needed to talk," she reminded him as he began to dress. This time, when she covered herself, he did not protest.

Instead, he sat beside her on the bed and looked at her as if he were about to offer news she'd prefer not to hear.

"Well?" she prodded.

Graeme frowned. "I'm going to kill your father."

Surely she had not heard him correctly.

He heaved a sigh. "I should say instead, I'd very much like to kill your father."

"What happened?"

He'd said he needed to speak to her, but Gillian had been so concerned for Allie that she'd nearly forgotten about the Day of Truce. And then . . . well . . . they had not spoken much about either topic.

Though she knew he would never hurt her, the expression on his face was frightening. He looked nothing like the lover who'd ministered to her every need moments earlier.

"They set him free."

She didn't understand. "My father?"

"Blackburn was declared innocent of all charges."

"Nay! 'Tis not possible. There were witnesses—"

"He evoked trial by local visnet," he said simply, waiting to see if she understood.

She did.

Trial by combat had been the customary approach for accused murderers since the inception of the Day of Truce. But in Blackburn's case, she'd assumed trial by hue and cry with witnesses to the crime would easily convict him. He'd been pursued and eventually turned in to the local sheriff, Graeme had said, which should have meant his conviction would be automatic.

But by invoking trial by local visnet, Blackburn had put the decision of his guilt or innocence in the hands of twelve men who would first hear a witness speak in his defense. And only if that witness was more respected and well received than the original accusers would the defendant be set free.

Which meant the man who defended Blackburn had to be—

"No." It could not have been.

"Aye," Graeme said, confirming her fear.

"But why?"

Her father held no affection for Blackburn. Would never have even associated with such a man before. And yet, this was the same person who'd promised her hand, and now her sister's, to another equally nefarious man.

"No one was sure," he said, looking at her for answers. As if she had any.

"Was it because of me?"

That unwelcome thought refused to budge once it entered her mind.

"Perhaps."

But he clearly didn't blame her. How could that be?

"I was not allowed close enough to him to ask," he said. "Although, since I was armed, illegally, that might have been a good thing."

Both sides were supposed to come to the Day of Truce unarmed, but very few did. Gillian was just glad Graeme had not gotten himself killed.

"Aye," she agreed. "A very good thing." She frowned. "I am so sorry."

Gillian wanted to reach out to him, but she didn't dare.

Graeme shook his head.

"This does not bode well for peace," he said. "Even if I wanted to let the matter pass, even if I could convince my clan to accept the outcome of the *trial*." He shook his head. "Our allies are many, and none pleased with recent events. The raid was not an isolated one, and I fear this is merely the beginning."

Gillian felt as if the bed would open up and claim her. Or perhaps she just wished it so. Her father had helped free the man who'd killed Grace.

"The people of Highgate will blame me," she said, thinking for the first time of the repercussions of her father's treachery.

126

But Graeme was already shaking his head. "I will not allow it."

Her heart lurched. His tone had been so fierce. So protective. If she wasn't careful, Gillian could lose her heart to this man.

Would that be such a bad thing?

Aye, if he did not return her affection. And how could he? After what her father had done?

Allie.

Gillian could feel the blood drain from her face. She looked past Graeme, not daring to meet his eyes. How could she ask for his help now? When the only recourse would be for her father to receive the funds he needed another way? A way that did not include selling her sister off to a wealthy, crooked earl?

"What is it?" Graeme cocked his head to the side as if remembering. "You wanted to tell me something."

Oh dear.

This would not do at all.

17

*G*raeme sat alone in the solar, waiting for Aidan to arrive. He'd sent word for him, and requested a tankard of ale, long enough ago for both to have arrived by now. Like the lord's chamber, the solar sat along an outside wall, which meant it also boasted a hearth. After a visit to Conisbrough Keep in England, his father had added a hearth to nearly every outside room at Highgate, including this one.

Graeme stared at the colored stones depicting his clan crest and the other emblems that dotted the drab stones around them with blue, red, and yellow. Never could he have imagined sitting here, chief of Clan Scott, without his father, at such an early age.

The transition had been a difficult one, even though he'd served as his father's tanist for more than a year before his abrupt death. None had expected the brawn, robust man to be felled in a battle that had started and ended in the same day.

"You're thinking of Father."

His brother always did have the ability to discern his thoughts and moods. Not that Graeme was particularly reticent with him.

"Aye."

Aidan sat in the cushioned seat opposite him. Two windows, their shutters wide open, gave evidence to the fast-approaching night. He hadn't realized how long he and Gillian had spent in his chamber—*their* chamber.

A servant approached with a tankard and two mugs, which she arranged on the table between the brothers.

"You're new?"

She bobbed a curtsy. "I am, my lord."

"What is your name?"

"Heather, my lord."

He glanced at Aidan. The girl, no more than ten and three, was poorly attired. He intended to find out why—and to help as need be.

"Well met, Heather. Thank you for the ale."

She curtsied again and scurried from the room.

"Where is she from?"

Aidan shook his head. "I will find out."

"And see that she—"

"Of course, brother. But more importantly—"

"Is anything more important than the well-being of Highgate's people?"

Aidan rubbed the back of his neck, a sure sign of his annoyance. "So prickly this eve. One would think you'd be in a better mood."

Graeme gave him a look that would wither a lesser man.

"Very well. That may indeed have been out of turn." Aidan took a swig of ale. "Though I am happy for you. And for Gillian. It's about time—"

"Aidan," he warned, and his brother thankfully stopped talking.

"What happened?"

It took him a moment to realize Aidan was talking about the Day of Truce.

"What did the men tell you?" Graeme drank deeply, cringing at the thought that the bastard Blackburn was walking free even now.

"That Lord Lyndwood, among others, spoke on behalf of Blackburn's character, allowing him to be declared innocent."

"Then you have most of it. None were surprised by the other men's testimony. But Lyndwood . . ."

Aidan took a long draw from his mug before responding. "Revenge?"

Graeme shrugged. "Perhaps."

"What will you do?"

He looked up, surprised by the question. "What would you have me do?"

Aidan's eyes narrowed. "This cannot stand. The man was responsible for a raid that

killed—"

"I know well what happened in the raid."

"Then surely you—"

"What? Am I to call our allies against Blackburn and all twelve men who spoke on his behalf, Lyndwood included? And then what, Aidan? We would start a war, and well you know it. We'd be back to the chaos of our grandfather's time, when murder and kidnapping occurred daily, on both sides of the border. Is that what we should do?"

Aidan's voice rose to match his own. "What is the alternative? To sit back and allow an English bastard like Blackburn to lead a raid on our land? To kill innocents and then walk away without so much as a lashing?"

"I don't know."

For some reason, Aidan's own tone softened. Perhaps it was because Graeme so rarely uttered those words. "Cross-border raids are becoming more common. Blackburn would never have attempted such a thing even a year ago."

"That we agree on, brother. I never suggested we do nothing. Just that we not—" he finished his ale and stood to fetch another, "—start a war."

"If not war, then what?"

Graeme sat back down and looked at the face so similar to his own. "If not war, then peace."

The elders would not like it, but if Aidan could be convinced, anything was possible.

"I'll start with the most likely adversary, the one whose daughter is now my wife."

"What exactly do you propose?"

He didn't like the idea but could see no other way. "To speak to Lyndwood."

"Speak to—" His brother stood, slammed his mug down, and began to pace. "Talk. That is your proposition? Talk to one of the men responsible for Blackburn walking free?"

Graeme smiled against the rim of his mug. "Aye. Talk."

"They will never agree. The men are mad for revenge. They—"

"Are not the chief. Come, sit back down."

Aidan, of course, did not.

"Do not speak to me as if we were still children, Graeme. Will the others see this as an acceptable path forward?"

"If you'd sit," he said, "I'd gladly explain myself."

Aidan finally heaved a sigh and returned to his chair.

"We cannot go against this ruling. To do so would court criticism from both sides of the border and put our allies in the untenable position of choosing between loyalty to us and loyalty to their commitment to peace. But we can ensure men like Blackburn are unable to wreak the havoc they so desire. I must understand how this happened so I can prevent it from happening again. To us or our allies. On *both* sides of the border."

From the white-fisted way Aidan clenched his mug, Graeme could tell he was unsatisfied. He understood, for he himself was still as angry as if the ruling had just occurred. But Graeme had vowed to protect Clan Scott against any outside threat. And right now, the biggest threat was the very real possibility the hard-fought peace that had kept them safe for decades would unravel around them.

Still, March Law needed to change, to be modified to fit the times in which they lived. Jurors from both England and Scotland must be included in trials. Sanctuary should be offered to those who confessed. He had said as much to the Lord Warden before returning home, and Douglas had agreed with him. Facts must be gathered first; then they would act.

He could have simply told Aidan that Douglas was on board with the plan to alter the law. But that would have been too easy. He'd wanted him to accept the outcome from his chief first.

"Very well."

And now, to convince the others.

"Come, we've much work to do."

Graeme lingered over the table to refill his mug. Perhaps just what he needed to forget the impending crisis. And his wife's question earlier that day.

So we are stuck with each other?

SHE'D NEVER SEEN her husband quite like this. When Fiona had informed Gillian her husband and his brother would be taking their evening meal in the solar, and they'd requested her company, she hadn't quite known what to think. She'd changed hastily and now stood at the door watching the two men as they turned toward her. Though Graeme wasn't smiling exactly; he had a strange, flushed look about him. He rather seemed like he was in his cups.

"Come in, my lady," Aidan said.

A long table, quite like a trestle table but not as long, was set for dinner. Both Graeme and Aidan moved from their seats, presumably to sit for the meal. When she didn't move, Graeme made his way toward her.

She'd wondered if this feeling—the insistent fluttering at her very core—would cease after what had transpired between them. If anything, though, it had intensified instead. Despite her worry for Allie and concern over her father's recent actions, all other thoughts fled when Graeme reached for her.

She looked down inadvertently, trying to imagine how his manhood, so long and thick earlier, could be so inconspicuous now. Her cheeks reddened when she looked back up and realized what she had done.

Graeme took her hand and leaned in toward her. "I thought we had agreed. No shyness between us."

His whispered words sent a shiver through her.

"I did not mean—"

"Pity if it was not intentional."

And then he very obviously looked down, directly at her chest. When he raised his eyes, they sparkled with merriment.

"That, I can assure you, was quite so."

Without further discussion, not that Gillian would have been able to manage it, Graeme led her to the table.

"Good evening," she managed to Aidan.

"I will apologize straightaway, Lady Gillian. My brother and I have been in discussion."

He began to fill his trencher with rabbit and meat-filled pastries.

"In discussion?" She couldn't help but smile. The mood was lighter than she'd have expected given the circumstances. No doubt they *had* been imbibing.

Graeme followed his brother's lead, filling his own trencher. "Of sorts."

Gillian looked between them, wondering which of the men would satisfy her curiosity about the private meal first.

Graeme took pity on her. "We thought it best not to appear in the hall as such. And though the circumstances surrounding the failed truce day are dire, we do, in fact, have a plan."

She could not resist teasing him. "As such? Whatever do you mean?"

She had, of course, witnessed men in their cups before. Including her father. Some became rowdy. Some became angry. But Graeme and his brother merely seemed cheerful. There was something quite endearing about that.

"Wine, my queen?" Graeme poured her wine himself. Aidan almost choked on his first large bite of bread and looked back and forth between them as his jaw worked on the food. "Queen," he finally repeated.

"Did your brother tell you how we met?"

Aidan took another bite. "Most," he said. "But I'd hear your version too."

Gillian smiled, remembering their dance.

"You currently dine with the May Queen herself," Graeme said ceremoniously.

"Ahh, I wonder who proposed such an honor?"

She glanced at Graeme, whose guilty expression gave him away.

"Well then." Aidan took one final drink, grabbed an apple, and stood. Without further comment, he walked toward the door more than a bit unsteadily and bowed. "Until tomorrow, fair queen."

She watched the door close behind him.

"I do believe your brother is drunk," she said, taking a sip of the red wine Graeme had poured her.

"I do believe you're right," Graeme replied with a smile.

They ate more slowly than Aidan, Gillian in no rush to finish. She'd considered all afternoon what to do next, torn between helping Allie and knowing Lyndwood was the last place in the world Graeme would desire to visit. Holding her tongue earlier had been the right thing to do, but she couldn't keep her concerns from her husband forever.

"Drink," he said, pointing to her wine.

"But I—"

"We've so many troubles ahead. Enough to match the ones we left behind at Kenshire. But tonight . . ." He frowned. "I would happily tell you all will be well. But I cannot do so and remain honest. Still, I would have you leave your worries for tomorrow."

Gillian did drink deeply then. His judgment was both bleak and accurate.

"But let us have tonight to enjoy each other."

His slight smirk reminded her of the first time he'd looked at her at Kenshire, at once charming, sensual, and kind. Graeme was all of these things. But tonight, he was also more relaxed than usual.

If only she could say the same for herself.

Should I tell him?

"To us." Graeme lifted his mug. "Then tomorrow, to Lyndwood."

Gillian froze. Could she have heard him correctly? "My lord?"

He put his mug back down. "We ride to Lyndwood tomorrow."

"We—"

Did he know about Allie? Who would have told him?

"The men want war, but Clan Scott is committed to peace, despite what transpired this week. I need to know why it happened. To assess the situation before discussing a course of action with the Lord Warden. So"—he raised his mug again—"we ride to Lyndwood tomorrow. To speak with your father."

"Speak?" Did she dare hope?

"Aye, to speak to him. I thought you would like to accompany me—"

"Of course!" She raised her goblet high. "I would be delighted to accompany you. More than that, I . . ."

Nay. I will tell him tomorrow.

As he said, they deserved a single night without worry, and if they were truly riding to Lyndwood, she would have a chance, however remote, to help Allie.

"To our wedding night," she said, toasting her husband gladly.

"*Y*ou're not drunk."

He'd never been accused of such a thing before. As Graeme opened the door to their bedchamber, he tried to gauge Gillian's mood.

A change had come over his wife upon learning they'd be leaving for Lyndwood tomorrow. Though he'd never describe her as carefree—she was much too thoughtful for such a designation —she smiled more easily than before. The news had pleased her.

"You say that as if you're disappointed."

Gillian sat on the bed, out of his reach.

But not for long.

"When I first joined you, I thought—"

He began to walk toward her. The soft glow of candlelight put him in mind of her gown on May Day, the one she'd also worn to their wedding. She looked radiant, ethereal, as if she was not from this world.

"I am very careful," he said. "Unlike my brother."

She smiled. "I do see what you mean. But I like him."

"As do I." He returned her smile, taking another step forward. "Why did you think I was in my cups, my fair English queen?"

He stood next to her now. And waited.

"You appeared more relaxed than normal. Which I thought was odd given the circumstances."

He raised his brows. "And which circumstances would those be?"

Graeme would not touch her. Not until she requested it. Even though he wanted nothing more than to slip her gown off and continue to explore every—

"Was that a knock?" he asked, certain he'd heard a sound coming from the wardrobe room.

"Oh, aye. I nearly forgot to tell you—"

But he had already crossed the room and was pulling the door open.

"Oh!" A young maidservant he didn't recognize stumbled into the chamber.

"Who are you?" he demanded. Gillian pulled on his arm, jolting his attention to her.

"I was just trying to tell you. This is Morgan. She arrived from Lyndwood after you left, and—"

"Ah, yes." He remembered being told her men had arrived with Gillian's belongings and her lady's maid. They had apparently stayed the night and returned to Lyndwood in the morning. A pity, he'd have liked to speak to them ahead of his own visit there.

"I thought I heard your voice, my lady. My apologies for—"

"'Tis nothing, Morgan. You may—"

"Return to the lady's chamber," Graeme finished.

Morgan looked from him to her lady. "But surely you need my assistance?"

"She does not," Graeme said firmly. If he could not remove his own wife's clothing, then he was a poor husband indeed.

Gillian made a face at him and then gave her attention to the maid. "You may return to the lady's chamber. It appears your assistance is not needed tonight. But thank you, Morgan."

The maid bobbed a courtesy, muttered, "My lord," and left.

Gillian crossed her arms over her chest, which only brought more attention to her ample breasts. "You scared her."

"Scared? I've done no such thing."

She did not appear convinced.

"I simply informed her—"

"In a tone well-suited to a battlefield. As you towered above the poor woman."

"Towered? Would you have me kneel before her?"

To illustrate, he lowered himself to one knee.

"Happily met, Mistress Morgan," he said, looking up at his wife as if she were the maid.

"It is indeed a pleasure to—"

"Stop," she said, laughing and trying to pull him up. "'Tis absurd."

When she reached for him, Graeme took advantage and pulled her onto his lap.

"The only absurd thing here . . ." He moved her dark hair to the side to give himself better access to her neck, "is that I find myself alone with my beautiful wife, and she's not yet unclothed."

He lowered his lips to the soft flesh behind her ear and kissed her there. Not stopping at one kiss, Graeme ran a trail of them down her neck and toward the front of her gown. He scooped her up into his arms, stood, and carried her toward the bed.

Rather than lay her down, he lowered her to her feet and spun her around.

"I've often wondered why a lady's gown should be laced at the back when she clearly cannot reach there."

He watched her shoulders rise and fall as he unlaced the ties, her breathing becoming heavier.

"What do they call this?" Finished with his task, Graeme reached around and ran his hand from her shoulders down the front of her gown, just barely brushing her breasts.

"Embossed cloth," she whispered.

He continued to allow his hands to wander, feeling the raised gold fabric beneath his fingers, less interested in the material than he was in the woman beneath it. He stepped toward her, so close they were touching, and reached for the linked gold circles around her waist, the belt clasp the final maddening barrier before he could rid her of the surcoat.

While he unfastened the belt, Graeme whispered, "And why do they make these so very difficult to remove?" He kissed her ear as the clasp finally came undone.

"I do believe," she said, her heart hammering below the hand he'd splayed across her chest, "'tis not meant to be unfastened from behind."

When the surcoat dropped to the floor beneath them, Graeme gave his attention to the plum-colored kirtle beneath it.

"Such fine fabric." He ran his hands along her arms and toward the front before bending down to grab the hem of the kirtle.

In one swift motion, he'd pulled both the kirtle and the cotton shift beneath it up and over her head, tossing them aside. Gillian began to turn, but he stopped her, removing his own shirt and trewes as quickly as his hands would allow.

Why did his heart hammer as if he were an untried lad? It was as if she were a queen in truth. As if she were an unobtainable beauty and not his wife, whom he'd enjoyed hours before.

His cock stood at full attention, begging for relief, but he was determined to wait. To hold out for *her* pleasure. To give her every pleasure she deserved in the bedchamber.

"Graeme?"

He'd been about to move his hands, but at the sound of her voice, they stayed in place instead. "Aye?"

"What are you doing?" She began to turn, and he stopped her once again.

"Seducing you, my queen."

Her head still turned, the adorable pert nose that he suddenly had the desire to kiss scrunched up. He watched her expression turn from confusion to understanding to . . . *that* was what he waited for.

Graeme moved closer, pulling his wife toward him. Encouraged by her gasp, and trying to ignore the feel of her buttocks against him, he reached around to tease her taut nipples.

"I need to know," he murmured against her neck, "what you enjoy."

Kissing her, Graeme lowered his hands until he found the curls that guarded her most precious treasure.

"Tell me," he said, slipping a finger inside, not surprised by the slick wetness there.

"All of it," she breathed out.

He moved his fingers at an increasingly fast tempo that soon had her panting. Not good enough. He wanted her out of control. Wild for him. With his free hand, he caressed her breast, his chest and manhood pressing against her from behind.

"That," she whispered.

"'Tis a climax you seek," he said, "and I will give you one. In the future, you can simply ask. For my touch, for release, for anything you want. In here, I am yours."

To prove it, Graeme brought her to the very edge.

"What do you want?" he asked.

"I—"

He slowed. Waited.

"I want you to—"

"Make me come," he helped.

"Aye," she said.

Had his own desire been any less fierce, Graeme might have chuckled. She couldn't say the word. But she would eventually. For now, it mattered not. As long as Gillian understood there was no need for pretense between them. In here, they were husband and wife in truth.

And then she cried out his name, the sweetest sound he'd ever heard.

When she came back down from that sweet place where time and place held no meaning, he finally turned her around to face him. Kissing her with all the pent-up passion he'd felt since their first meeting at Kenshire, Graeme guided his wife to the bed. He should wait, give her time to recover. But the feel of her against him, the strain of holding back . . .

He just couldn't do it.

Not bothering to pull down the coverlet, Graeme lowered himself over her. He traced a finger from her collarbone down the center of her chest, careful not to touch any sensitive parts.

Yet.

"How do you feel?"

She sighed. "Relaxed."

She glanced down.

"You've a habit of looking down there," he teased.

"Does it unsettle you?"

There were plenty of things about Gillian that unsettled him. The ease with which they came together. His constant thoughts of her when they were apart. The idea that, despite himself, he might be falling for his own wife, a woman who'd been forced to wed him. Aye, those thoughts unsettled him. Her habit of staring at him? Not at all.

"You can look." Graeme took her hand and placed it on him. "You can touch. I will say it every day until you believe me—in here, nothing stands between us."

"I can do . . . anything . . . I'd like?"

He'd been hard before, but now his arousal was almost painful. She stroked him, without knowing how, priming him for what was to come.

"Dear God, woman."

That only emboldened her.

Graeme wrapped his hand around hers, showing her, and didn't the minx give him the biggest smile he'd seen from her.

"This is fun."

No more.

Graeme took her hand, and the other one as well, and lifted them both above her head. Holding them in place, he guided himself into his wife, apparently much too slowly for her pleasure. With one pump of her hips, Gillian set the pace.

Well, if she wished for him to move more quickly, he'd not disappoint. He thrust faster and moved his hips to ensure her pleasure.

When she tried to pull her arms down, presumably to wrap them around him, Graeme held them in place.

"Do you want me to let you go?"

"No," she said. "I just want—" She met his every thrust. "More."

Graeme gave her everything he had to give, and when she peaked, he did so with her, the delicious release so powerful he nearly forgot to breathe. Gillian's face was no longer serene. No longer detached. She was not his English queen, so beautiful but so proper. In here, she was his wanton goddess.

19

"*Y*ou do that often, you know." Graeme reached for her hair and smoothed it behind her ear.

They had stopped to give the horses a rest, and she'd sought out a thicket of trees so she could relieve herself. After attending to nature's call, she righted herself and began to walk back to the clearing. He must have followed her to keep watch because he was leaning against a massive oak tree along her path, his arms crossed and casual, exuding confidence and sensuality. Knowing him now as she did, both of those traits were as obvious as the age of the tree he pushed away from to approach her.

She hadn't even realized she'd swept her hair forward until he reached out to right it.

"What are you trying to hide, my queen?"

The endearment filled her heart with joy. In fact, these past two days of travel had been two of the happiest of her life. She would finally see her sister today, and it heartened her to think that she had a plan to save her.

Granted, it was not the best of plans.

If her father could not be talked out of the betrothal, Gillian would simply convince Allie to come to Highgate with them. She could not be allowed to marry Covington. Aye, Gillian had been prepared to sacrifice herself for her family. To appease her father. Earn his respect. But the earl was a bad man. Though she understood his motivations, her father was cruel to contemplate giving her, and now her sister, up as a sacrifice.

After this past week with her husband, she had a new understanding of what he was asking of them. Of what her sister would be giving up if she were to wed herself to Covington. There could be more.

Sara and Geoffrey . . . Emma and Garrick . . . these were not rare instances of married couples who loved each other. Her parents were the anomaly.

Love was possible between husband and wife. Gillian knew it because she was falling in love with her husband. Why else would her heart thud out of its chest every time he was near? Or why would she crave his presence, seeking him out for all manner of reasons throughout the day?

Why would a simple touch move her so deeply, making her wish to know everything about this man? So that she could understand him, help him, love him.

"Hide. You've made it quite clear, my lord, there should be nothing hidden between us."

"In the bedchamber," he replied, taking another step toward her.

Though the day was just perfect—not too cold or too hot—and the sun had already begun its descent, Gillian's cheeks reddened.

"But not outside of it?"

She could have bitten her tongue. What could she be thinking, taunting him in such a way? There *were* secrets between them outside of the bedroom—hers. Gillian had not yet told him about her father's troubles or even Allie's betrothal. Though she knew it needed to be done, she couldn't stand the thought of further burdening him. Hadn't her father already done enough? If there was a chance, however small, she could convince her parents out of their hasty actions, it behooved her to try. She wasn't deluded enough to think it would work. But at least she could tell Graeme she'd done her part.

One thing she knew for sure—she would not leave Allie to her fate. Surely he would agree with her on that. Would he not?

He cleared his throat and retreated back into himself. When they were alone together, he gave all of himself to her. Pleased her beyond anything she could have imagined possible. At other times, he remained very much a stranger, as if he were purposefully holding himself back. The suspicion that her father was at fault was another reason she'd stayed silent.

"I believe we were discussing you," he said. He reached for her again, this time pulling her toward him. "Do not hide your face, or any other part of you."

"I wasn't hiding my face. I—"

Her words were cut off by a kiss. Not a gentle wooing one but a hard, insistent kiss that demanded an immediate response.

Which she gave him.

Gillian met his tongue with her own, clutching his tunic to keep her knees from buckling. How could she so quickly be pulled under his spell?

"My lord?"

When one of his men called to him from behind, Gillian attempted to pull away.

"Nay," he said, though he did take a moment to call back, "A moment."

They listened, heard nothing, and then Graeme laid his hand ever so gently on her cheek.

"So lovely . . ."

Gillian didn't know what to say. No one had ever spoken to her in such a way before. Sure, people had called her beautiful before. Allie and Sara and Morgan and even her mother. But they all adored her, and so she'd shrugged off their praise as the bias of loved ones.

But when Graeme said it...

She closed her eyes and concentrated on the feel of his hand against her.

Just as suddenly, his hand pulled back. Gillian's eyes flew open to see the chief, not the husband.

"What is it?"

Graeme sighed, a painful sound she was sure held more meaning than she could unlock standing here among the oaks and pines just a few short hours from Lyndwood. But unlock it she would.

"We'd best be getting back."

His hand dropped. For a moment, Gillian thought he'd kiss her again, but instead he took a step away from her, clearly intent on rejoining the men. With nothing else to do, she followed.

LYNDWOOD CASTLE, an old motte and bailey castle, its moat long since dry, was a modest holding for a man of Lord Lyndwood's reputation. Though Gillian rarely spoke of her father, changing the subject every time he raised it, Graeme had heard plenty of tales about the man.

There were few secrets along the border. Some of the borderers had scattered north, moving deeper into the bosom of Scotland. Others had fled south, where the English king still cared enough to intervene. The men and women who remained all had one thing in common: pride. None wanted to admit the rising tensions might eventually be their downfall.

For the rest of them, protected only by March Law and their own alliances, life had not gotten much easier. Raids continued, though they were less bloody than they'd been before the Days of Truce. Blackmail and bribes were part of their way of life. But despite it, those who continued, perhaps foolishly, to believe Scottish and English could live peaceably less than a half-day's ride apart—those like Clan Scott and Clan Kerr and Kenshire and Clave—would have to work together to survive.

And then there were traitors like Lyndwood.

"Allie!"

His wife dismounted more quickly than Aidan moved when he spotted a fallow buck.

He'd seen Gillian's sister at Kenshire but had not really noticed her then. He thought back to Gillian's description of her. She'd called her sister "sweet and lovely." And indeed, she was lovely, but the sisters did not share much of a likeness. Whereas his wife was beautiful and dark, proper and perfect, her sister's gold-kissed brown hair looked more like his own and her movements were far less reserved than Gillian's.

"Gill, oh how I've missed you."

He tore his gaze away from the women, allowing them their privacy, and concentrated instead on the rest of their greeting party. Namely, the man who'd betrayed him. Gillian's father stood with his wife at the entrance to the keep. Dismounting, Graeme didn't take his eyes off the baron who'd allowed Grace's murderer to walk free.

Graeme could understand why the man held a grudge against him after the events at Kenshire. But now he felt neither guilt, nor remorse, for what he'd done. Marrying Gillian had been an unexpected boon of the May Day celebration, and despite the circumstances, he didn't regret it for a moment.

Graeme dismounted and walked toward Gillian's father. Neither man smiled. Indeed, it took every bit of restraint left to him not to strike the bastard down where he stood.

"Scott."

Graeme stopped, surprised. He'd not have expected the man to acknowledge his position as chief of his clan. The greeting, though curt, was not without courtesy.

"Lord Lyndwood."

He turned toward Gillian's plain-looking mother, who resembled neither of her daughters. Where, indeed, had the women inherited their beauty, and each so different from the other? Certainly not from either parent.

"My lady."

He took her hand, kissed it, and stood. She looked past him, at Gillian, who'd suddenly appeared at his side. And then her mother did something remarkable. She held out her hand, took Gillian's, and squeezed it. No embrace. No words of welcome. Just a simple touch—the kind of greeting his mother would only have given him if he'd done something badly wrong.

As he listened to their exchanged greetings, Graeme studied the older woman's expression. There was love there, but it was tempered by restraint—so unlike the much more natural connection between the two sisters.

"Do come inside," her mother said, ushering the group into Lyndwood.

Everything about it was different than Highgate End. That both halls exuded cleanliness and order was about the only thing they had in common. The servants here moved slowly, deliberately, and none talked out of turn. And where Highgate had become a castle in just the last generation or so, Lyndwood's décor—coats of arms and elaborate tapestries reenacting the feats of various English kings—clearly announced to visitors the Lyndwood family was old, connected, and important.

"As you can see, preparations are underway for the evening meal. Daughter?" The lady of Lyndwood indicated for Gillian to accompany her, and Gillian followed. The woman who had so passionately embraced him in the forest was not in this hall.

Or so he thought. The sparkle in her eyes when she turned to offer a final glance made him smile.

English queen indeed.

"Shall we?" Lyndwood extended his hand. After nodding to his men, indicating they should follow the steward who'd introduced himself to them in the midst of the family greetings, he indicated for Graeme to follow.

Lyndwood ushered him into a small but well-lit room off the hall—a steward's office? He sat across from his host at a well-used desk, waiting for the man to speak.

"That business at the Day of Truce. It was regrettable."

"Regrettable?" Graeme's jaw twitched. He'd remain calm only because he had been trained to do so. And because this man was, unfortunately, Gillian's father.

"I had no choice but to speak on Blackburn's behalf." He said it with such conviction, Graeme almost believed him.

"Did you believe the words you spoke that day?"

Lyndwood's eyes narrowed. When last they'd met, the man had betrayed him at the Day of Truce. That the baron defended himself now told Graeme almost everything he needed to know.

Almost.

"No."

It was the only answer that offered hope for the future. But it angered him nonetheless.

"I'll remind you Clan Scott land was raided. People were killed. If you did not believe he was innocent, why did you do it?" He forced his hands to remain still. "Revenge?" he guessed. He'd thought long and hard on the matter, and it was the only answer he could come up with.

Lyndwood actually laughed.

"Tell me, my lord," Graeme asked. "What is so amusing to you? That the healer who'd spent her life saving others was killed?" His voice rose with each word.

"I am sorry for the loss of such a woman," Lyndwood said. "But the idea that I would let a bastard like Blackburn walk free, risk my reputation by aligning with such a man—"

"And Covington," Graeme reminded him.

"For revenge? Against my daughter's husband?" Lyndwood no longer looked amused.

Graeme leaned forward, impatient with the man's innuendos and pretty speeches. "Then why don't you tell me exactly why you did it."

"I did it . . ." Lyndwood leaned back in his high-backed chair and folded his arms. A defeated man. "To save my family."

Graeme waited, not so patiently.

"Two years ago, a distant relative of my father's"—he crossed himself—"thought to dredge up a tired old claim. He meant to take Lyndwood from us. So I paid two thousand marks to the Crown to resolve the dispute, certain it was the easiest way to put the matter to rest. Unfortunately"—he frowned—"it did not happen that easily."

Graeme wasn't sure what he'd expected from Gillian's father, but a story about his recent history was not it.

"Instead, the ruling was split. I would retain the title and land, but a large portion of Lyndwood's coin was awarded to the bastard who hasn't stepped foot in this country in two decades."

Graeme tried to understand the implications of Lyndwood's lost wealth. It explained quite a bit—the betrothal to Covington, the bride price the man had charged him.

"And so you raised coin by attempting to collect an overly large dowry for Gillian's hand—"

"Despite the man's age and reputation, yes," Lyndwood finished. Continuing to defend himself, he added, "He's not known to be a cruel man."

Graeme rolled his eyes. "What better candidate for a woman such as Gillian?"

Her father at least had the decency to look embarrassed. They both know Covington did not deserve her. And if her father didn't know that, then he did not know his daughter.

"None of which explains your support of Blackburn." Graeme sat back, crossed his arms again, and waited, more than a bit surprised at Lyndwood's forthrightness, if not his haughty attitude.

For a moment, he thought Lyndwood would not answer him. As if he were more comfortable talking about selling his daughter to the highest bidder than admitting to why he'd supported a man he knew to be guilty.

"He paid me to do so," he finally said.

"Blackburn?" Graeme could not hide his shock.

"Nay. Covington."

"But what does—"

Then, suddenly, it all made sense. The Earl of Covington had a reputation for being one of those men who thrived when disorder reigned at the border. Men of his rank could not profit from blackmail without repercussion, unless the truce day, and terms of the treaty, fell apart. And then he, others like him, and even members of the clergy, could become even richer from the men and women they cheated. Blackburn was another such man, and that they appeared to be working together was at once unsurprising and alarming.

"You understand what these men aim to do?" he ground out.

Lyndwood lowered his chin to his chest. He stared down at his hands and tonelessly answered. "Of course I do."

Graeme stared at him, unsure of what to say.

"How bad is it?" he finally asked. It had to be very bad indeed for the man to have so completely abandoned his principles.

When Lyndwood looked up, he did not meet Graeme's eyes. Instead, he stared off into the distance as if there was something more interesting to be seen beyond him.

"Without Covington's support," he said tonelessly. "We will lose everything." Finally, Lyndwood looked at him. "Whether you believe me or not, Lyndwood is an ally to Clan Scott. So no, I did not want revenge against my son-in-law. I am simply trying to survive."

He didn't doubt the man's words, but Graeme did question his methods.

"By aligning yourself with men such as Covington and Blackburn? You can find no other way?"

Some of the baron's fire returned. "You think I haven't considered every possibility?"

Graeme shook his head. "It will never work." At Lyndwood's confused expression, he continued. "Those men will never be satisfied until the March Law is completely destroyed. They believe it will benefit them if lawlessness returns to the border, and they won't rest until they've destroyed everything our fathers built. Covington will continue to use you, and your influence, for himself."

Lord Lyndwood blinked. "She's not told you then?"

He didn't like the sound of that.

"Told me what?" The identity of the "she" was unquestionably Gillian.

"I'll not need to be beholden to men like Blackburn in the future."

If this had anything to do with his wife . . .

"The banns have just been posted. Covington will be marrying my daughter. My other daughter. Once our debts are paid, Lyndwood will be free once again to take a stand."

Lady Allie.

Lyndwood would use the only other asset available to him. And apparently Gillian already knew . . . and had not said a word about it. He chided himself for forgetting, even for a moment, that his wife had not chosen him.

He stood. "My lord."

Without waiting for a response, he left the increasingly stifling room and went off in search of the woman to whom he was married but hardly knew at all.

20

*G*illian sat in her old room, which had already been stripped of all of her things—the tapestries had been taken down, the hand-stitched coverlet she'd had since girlhood exchanged for a plain cream coverlet suitable for guests. It felt like a stranger's room.

Allie had left to prepare for dinner after helping her to change into her father's favorite of her gowns. Their conversation had not gone quite as she'd hoped. Her sister had been less than enthusiastic about her plan. Gillian had wanted to speak to her father before he locked himself away with Graeme, but it was too late for that. She could only hope he'd still listen to reason.

A foolish hope. Father will never give up Lyndwood. He loves it more than Mother, Allie, and I. More even than himself.

"Gillian?"

She hardly recognized the hesitant voice as her husband's.

"Aye," she called out, jumping from the bed.

Graeme shut the door behind him, none too gently, before crossing his arms and glaring at her as if she'd lied to him. Which, in a way, she had. So he knew . . .

"I take it the meeting with my father went well?"

Her husband wasn't amused. "I believe you failed to mention something to me."

There was no use denying it. "I'd have told you earlier if it were not for what happened at the Day of Truce. But after my father—"

"You are my wife."

She wasn't sure she liked his tone.

"And you are my husband."

Graeme took a deep, dramatic breath before speaking. "You put me at a disadvantage with your father. When he told me of your sister's betrothal—"

"That's why you are upset? That my father had more information than you?" Of course, he was a man, after all. A chief. Power mattered to him, and what greater power than knowledge?

"No, Gillian. I am upset I had to learn of something so important from a man who betrayed me."

"What would you have done had I mentioned it before we left?"

He started speaking, too soon. "I'd have asked what you intended to do."

She waited. "And what would you have done after I told you I planned to talk my father out of it? Appeal to my mother to intervene? And, when both inevitably failed, that I intended to take Allie back to Scotland with us?"

"Take Allie?" His eyes widened. "Are you mad, woman? Take Covington's betrothed to Clan Scott land? And what do you suppose would have happened next?"

She'd thought of that as well, but it hadn't persuaded her from her plan. Her sister shouldn't have to bear the burden of maintaining their family's standing.

"Well, I suppose my father, and Covington, would be a mite upset. And my father might even lose Lyndwood."

He cocked his head to the side, though his expression stayed neutral.

"So my father told you about that?" She'd not have expected him to be so open about his troubles. "My parents would be forced to live at one of their other more modest holdings. And Covington—"

She hadn't thought much about his reaction, preferring instead not to consider the man at all.

"Let me finish for you, my queen." He uncrossed his arms and took a step toward her.

"Covington would challenge me, as chief, forcing my clan to choose between giving back his betrothed or going to war with a powerful border lord, one who would prefer to end the peace that your friends at Kenshire and I are trying to bolster. The March Law would be in more danger than ever."

"I don't think—"

"Exactly. You didn't think."

She blinked back tears. This was why she hadn't told him. She'd fooled herself into thinking Graeme would take her side, but a part of her had feared he would leave her home if she told him the truth. And then her sister would have had no chance at all.

She'd been wrong about him. He didn't love her. Their situation was as he'd described it from the start. They were only open with each other in the bedroom.

Very well.

She sailed past her husband, shoving off his hand when he tried to touch her. Nothing but her sister's safety and happiness mattered. And while she was here, there was still a chance.

HER SISTER WAS DOOMED.

Gillian found her mother before dinner, but their conversation led nowhere. Her mother was, as always, polite, understanding, and completely ineffective. The argument she put forward was a familiar one. Without Allie's dowry, Lyndwood would be lost. It was the very reason she'd agreed to marry Covington herself, only she wouldn't let her sweet, innocent sister bear the sacrificial burden.

In the end, she kissed her mother on the cheek, excused herself, and went in search of the only man who could change her sister's future.

Unfortunately, her father was already seated at the high table, early for the meal as was his custom. Despite their reduced circumstances, Lyndwood continued to boast an impressive staff, including the cupbearer who filled her father's mug with ale. Perhaps if they'd made more adjustments, the alliance with Covington wouldn't have been needed.

"Good evening, Father."

His beard, less closely shaven than usual and now dotted with gray, made him look older. She much preferred him clean-shaven.

"Daughter."

So he was still upset with her. That he'd taken himself away with her husband without hardly a greeting should have told her as much, but it still hurt. This was the man who had betrothed her to the Earl of Covington, aye. But she also remembered him as the father who'd held her on his lap and told her tales of King Arthur. The one who had showed her how to mount a horse and hold a bow.

"I'd hoped to speak with you before the meal," she said, stepping up onto the raised dais and coming around to give him a quick kiss on the cheek. Mayhap if she pretended all was well, it would be. In the end.

"And here I am."

She sat next to him, in the seat that had been hers before she became a Scottish clan chief's wife. Her sister would sit here now, and she and Graeme would move farther down the dais.

"You are still upset with me," she said, lifting her hand to get the attention of the cupbearer. She smiled as the boy filled her goblet with wine and tried not to dwell on her father's dour expression.

"Upset? Indeed not. Lyndwood fares well in your absence."

Oh, Father, please don't do this.

"I am pleased to hear it," she said, folding her hands on her lap. "Although"—she peeked out from under her lashes—"I cannot say I am pleased to hear of Allie's impending nuptials."

No response.

"Father." Since he refused to be reasonable, she might as well speak her mind. "There must be another way. After what happened with Blackburn—"

"You know nothing of such things."

Her temper flared. Gillian had spent a lifetime containing it, and for once, she nearly allowed it to take hold. But that would not do. Not if she wanted her father to listen. He'd always made it quite clear he did not abide emotional women.

"I know only what my husband has told me," she agreed.

"And why would he have told you anything?" her father asked.

"Because she is my wife."

She'd been so intent on studying her father's face, looking for any signs of hope, that she had not noticed Graeme's approach from the side of the hall. Though she was still deeply upset by his casual dismissal of her plan, Gillian would put her disappointment aside for the sake of appearances. After a lifetime with her mother, she found the appearance of civility came easily to her.

Gillian stood, gave her hand to Graeme, who kissed it so lightly she could hardly feel his touch, and allowed herself to be escorted to her seat. She watched as her mother and sister entered the hall.

"You were correct," Graeme said politely. "Your sister is quite lovely."

"And kind," she offered. "Allie thinks more of others than she does of herself."

Graeme stood as the women approached. "Sounds familiar."

She glanced at her husband out of the corner of her eye, only to immediately regret it. Though she was still angry with him, Gillian's heart raced as she watched him greet her mother and sister. Had a more handsome man ever existed? Of course, there were other handsome men, nearly as good-looking as Graeme, who'd never caused her heart to beat at this furious pace. The Waryn men, or so she'd heard beyond Geoffrey, with their black hair and crystal blue eyes, sent women into an absolute frenzy, much to the dismay of Sara and her sister-in-law Catrina. But there was something about Graeme . . . his easy charm and fierce loyalty, his natural leadership, and the way he wielded his eyes as if they were weapons.

She sat and leaned forward to greet her mother, seated on the other side of her sister.

"Good evening, Mother."

"Gillian."

Everyone called her Gill here, except her mother.

"So, my lord, tell us," Allie said to Graeme, "how fares Highgate End and Scotland?"

"Very well now that it has your sister for its lady," he responded.

If only he believed that to be true.

"Has your clan accepted my sister then? Even though she is English?"

Gillian rolled her eyes. "I am sitting between you," she said. "If you were not aware."

"Indeed you are, dear sister," Allie said, feigning surprise. "How did that come to be?"

Gillian tried not to smile but failed when she caught Graeme's expression. His ear-to-ear grin made her want to melt beneath the table. And kick his leg in aggravation.

"Clan Scott has a history of caring more for peace along the border than anything else. Those who would not accept Lady

Gillian because she is English would not be made welcome by me or, indeed, their clansmen."

Graeme's answer was only partially for her sister. Much of it was directed at her father, who seemed more interested in the freshly-served mince pie than in the conversation around him.

"And you, sir? You've accepted Gillian as well?"

"Allie!" She turned to Graeme, prepared to apologize for her sister, but he was already answering.

"I am not a 'sir,' but a simple clan chief," he said, though his words held no malice. "And as for your question . . ."

He looked at her then, his eyes filled with an emotion she couldn't identify.

"I accepted her the moment I handed her that wreath of flowers."

She looked away, her anger at him beginning to dissipate despite her best efforts.

"Then a toast to the happy couple," Allie said, raising her cup. When none but Graeme moved to join her, she prodded them each individually.

"Mother. Father. Gill. A toast."

When each of them had raised their mug or goblet, Allie smiled. "To a happy marriage, to salvation, and to peace."

If she thought it was an odd toast, she wasn't alone. Her father frowned gruffly and said, "Salvation? And whose salvation are we toasting to, my dear?"

Though his tone was softer than it had been with Gillian, he was clearly displeased by Allie's choice of words.

"Why, all of ours, of course."

Allie was up to something. Gillian suddenly knew it in her bones. Earlier, Allie begged, pleaded, for Gillian not to intervene, but she could not possibly want to marry the earl. So why did she seem so unconcerned about pacifying their father?

"Allie?" she whispered into her sister's ear after everyone had finally returned their attention to the meal. "What are you planning?"

Allie grinned. "I told you to trust me, did I not?"

Gillian glanced at Graeme, certain he was listening. But to her dismay, her husband simply smiled.

"It seems you're not the only one here with plans, my dear."

21

"*D*on't you dare tell me something is afoot, Allie." Gillian used the "big sister voice" her sister hated. Deliberately.

"So suspicious. Gill, I believe we should be getting back to the meal. No one, most especially your eagle-eyed husband, believes you suddenly felt faint. In fact, for as long as I've known you—"

"'As long as you've known me' being our entire lives, Allie. Which is exactly why I know you're planning something, and before I have another discussion with Father, I mean to—"

"You spoke with Father?"

Allie pulled her more deeply into the stone alcove. Though most everyone would still be dining in the great hall, the wagging tongues of errant servants had gotten them into trouble more than once before. At least, gotten Allie into trouble. Gillian usually managed to stay out of it.

"Of course I did. Do you honestly believe I will leave Lynd-wood knowing you are still betrothed to that man?"

"Gill, please. Please, I'm begging you. Will you stay out of this?"

She shook her head, not understanding. "No, I will not. It's my fault you're in this mess at all. If it weren't for me, you wouldn't be betrothed to that man. And . . . what? Why are you looking at me that way?"

Allie's face, only partially visible courtesy of the wall torch, fell. She looked miserable. But not, oddly enough, because of Covington. Her sister really didn't want her to intervene on her behalf.

"Because I've never lied to you before today." Allie took her hands. "Look at me."

Gillian did, wishing they could go back to simpler days. Conspiring to get out of their lessons. Walking to mass together, giggling as they tried to predict how long the hymns would be.

"Do you trust me?"

"Of course," she said, automatically.

"Then will you let me handle this on my own?"

"Allie, I—"

"Please, Gill?" Her sister squeezed her hand.

"Will you at least tell me why you're being so secretive? Why you can't tell me what's happening? Because I can't do it, Allie—I can't watch you marry that man—"

"I've asked you to trust me. Does the rest really matter?"

Allie had never looked more serious in her life.

The chill that ran through her had nothing to do with the draft of the empty corridor. Her typically carefree sister appeared so much older suddenly. When had that happened? She was desperate to know the answer to her question, but ultimately it didn't matter. She and her sister were similar in that way—when they gave their word, it meant something. As Gillian had told her so many times, they had precious little else to give.

"Nay, I suppose it doesn't matter," she relented. "But that doesn't mean my heart is whole. Not knowing. Or understanding."

"And not being the one to protect me," Allie finished. "Trust me," she repeated. "It will all be well in the end. Though I do worry for Mother and Father."

"But why should you worry for them?"

"Losing Lyndwood will kill father. I did ask Mother once if it would be so bad to have the title stripped away. To live at Ashwood Manor, with a smaller staff. She admitted that it would suit her just fine if it meant neither you nor I would have to marry such a man as Covington."

Gillian was shocked. "Mother said that outright?"

"Aye, she did." Allie's smile didn't reach her eyes. "And I believe her."

They should be getting back. But Gillian knew she and Graeme would be returning to Highgate in the morning, and the idea of simply leaving her sister here . . .

Allie grabbed both of Gillian's hands once more. "You've protected me our entire lives. We've learned to rely on each other. Can you not trust that meant something? Our late-night discussions under the stars, devising ways to please Father . . . pacify Mother. Understand our place in all of this? Trust me, Gill."

Gillian nodded. "I do."

"I will come to you as soon as I'm able to explain everything."

"Come to me? To Highgate End?"

Allie smiled, this time in truth. "Aye. Now go back to that handsome husband of yours. He must be wondering where you've gone to."

"Not any longer." The booming voice behind them startled both women.

Graeme.

"But I do thank you for the compliment, Lady Allie."

Her sister, never sheepish, simply smiled.

Graeme turned to her. "Are you still hungry, my dear?"

"Hungry? Nay, I've eaten plenty—"

"Good. My lady," he addressed her sister, "will you please give your parents our regrets? We will, unfortunately, be retiring early."

Allie looked back and forth between her and Graeme, her smile understanding. Although *how* it was so Gillian would have to ask her sister later. Beyond the maids' gossip, neither of them had much experience with men.

"My pleasure," Allie responded. And then she disappeared.

Gillian spun toward her husband. "I'm not yet tired, my lord. And would very much like to have finished—"

"Conversing with your parents?" He took a step toward her. "Pacifying your father?"

"How dare you!" Her frustration with the situation, and with the promise she'd made to Allie, bled into the words.

"I dare much, my queen."

When he pulled her toward him, Gillian did not for a moment consider stopping him to resume their conversation. She was angry still, mayhap more so now, but she also craved this man's touch more than she did food and drink.

His arms encircled her, strong and warm. His lips descended, crushing her with their urgency. She met his tongue thrust for thrust, needing to lose herself in the familiar, welcome feel of him.

When he moved down her chest, leaving a trail of kisses and fire behind, Gillian clutched onto him, only vaguely aware of their surroundings.

"We should retire in truth," she managed under his wicked onslaught.

"Mmm." Instead, he continued, his hands reaching forward to cup both breasts. He squeezed gently and then slipped his hands inside her gown.

"Graeme! What are you doing? You can't—"

Her words, cut short by the shock of his next action, stuck in her throat. The man actually reached inside her bodice and managed to free one of her breasts. If anyone walked by them now . . .

If that was not shocking enough, her husband actually touched his tongue to her breast, circling her nipple but never quite touching it. In the corridor!

"Shall I stop?" he asked, circling still.

CECELIA MECCA

"God, no." Was that even her voice?

Chuckling against her breast, he finally took it in his mouth, simultaneously pressing his body against her. The evidence of his desire for her, coupled with the feel of his mouth now alternatively suckling and teasing, made her legs go weak. She could hardly stand.

Graeme must have sensed as much, for he spun them around so that Gillian's back was pressed to the cold stone wall behind her.

If they were caught . . .

But he had resumed his ministrations, and Gillian threw her head back, reveling in the sensations, desperate for him to continue the onslaught. Graeme licked and gently bit on her nipple, his hand holding her breast up as if it were a revered treasure.

When the throbbing began, Gillian tried to stop it. She couldn't allow herself to succumb to her pleasure here. But Graeme had a funny way of reading her. He must have sensed she was close to the edge because he pressed against her in exactly the right place.

"Yes," he whispered.

"Not here," she managed, but it didn't seem to matter. The throbbing came quicker. Intensified. She looked down, grabbed a fistful of his hair and let go.

Somehow she didn't scream, or even make a sound. Her hands clenched around him and then her body went limp. Luckily, Graeme held her up, because Gillian would easily have slipped to the ground and lain there, content, until discovered.

Wouldn't that give them something to talk about?

Realizing she was still clutching Graeme's head, Gillian released him. He stood then, and she looked up into his eyes as he reached inside her gown and pulled the material over her breast. Without speaking, she grabbed her husband's hand and led him into the hall and then toward her bedchamber, marveling all along that she was the kind of woman who would do such a thing. Lead a man through these halls, having just been thoroughly ravished, with the intent of making love to him. She would have giggled at the absurdity of it, but a voice behind them stopped Gillian cold.

22

"Gillian."

She turned slowly. Had he seen them together in the alcove?

"Aye, Father?" Though she tried to steady her voice, Gillian was sure the effort was unsuccessful. Graeme looked at her as if she'd suddenly sprouted wings.

"I hope you're feeling better. You said you wanted to speak to me earlier?"

She wasn't fooled. Her father's calm demeanor was for Graeme's benefit. He was no more amenable now than he'd been since Covington came into their lives.

"I did." What could she say? She doubted she could lie to him, and surely he wouldn't believe her if she said she was content to let the situation unfold.

"I would like to speak to you as well," her father said.

"You would?"

Gillian couldn't hide her shock. Lately, the only time her father wished to speak with her was to admonish her for something. But what could she possibly have done wrong now? Other than marrying Graeme, of course.

"I am not leaving her side," Graeme interjected.

The men glared at one another.

"Father?"

He finally shifted his dark expression to her.

"I'm not angry," her father said. "Your husband hates me. Has a right to, in fact."

Graeme did not disagree.

"But I would not want to think my daughter does as well."

She looked back and forth between the men. Though he struggled to keep his expression neutral, Graeme did indeed appear as if he wanted to murder her father.

"I regret how events have transpired. And I know you don't agree with your sister's betrothal—"

"Father, how could you?" The words burst out of her, regardless of what she'd promised her sister.

"I have no choice."

Gillian broke away from her husband and went to the man who had raised her.

"Of course you do. The title—"

"Title? You think I'd marry your sister off to Covington to retain a title?"

His voice echoed against the stone walls of the corridor.

"You know as well as I do that Lyndwood is on the verge of being lost. And do you know how it came to be in this family?"

"Of course," she replied. "My great-grandfather was granted it on the battlefield—"

"Aye. And do you know what your great-grandfather was before becoming a knight?"

She thought back to her lessons. To the stories her father had told her about the family that had held the borders for three generations. "I don't believe I do."

"He was a blacksmith."

Her mouth dropped open.

"A commoner. Who forged his own sword, practiced with it

day and night. Saved enough coin to purchase armor, though not enough for his own horse. That"—he frowned—"he stole. So I suppose you could say he stole his knighthood, and this land grant, though he never apologized for it."

"A blacksmith?"

She turned back to Graeme to see what he thought of this revelation. But he was gone. Nay, not gone. He'd retreated to give them privacy, but she could see his shadow just ahead.

"I retain a legacy, not a title, Gillian."

"If you're asking for me to condone this marriage, I cannot," she said. "Though I understand your motives, you are condemning Allie to . . ."

She'd almost said, "your life with Mother," but stopped herself.

She watched his face for any hint of understanding. But there was none. Still hard. Still stubborn. Still very much her father.

Gillian sighed.

"I see you will not be convinced. Go," her father said. "We'll speak again in the morning."

Was there anything left to talk about?

"You are really not angry about Graeme?"

He raised his brows. "Are you happy with him?"

She almost said, "I will be." Her deep, dark hope was that Graeme would come to love her. That she had not, after all, been mistaken about the feelings developing between them. But she would not say such a thing aloud. To her father. Or to anyone.

"Aye, Father," she said instead. And had to contend with the fact that even though her father still refused to budge, he'd done something this eve she could not ever recall him doing before.

He'd explained himself.

Which was exactly what she needed her husband to do tonight. An explanation for his dismissive behavior earlier. But she owed him something first.

GRAEME WATCHED HIS WIFE SLEEP, wondering if he should wake her.

She'd said she wanted to talk, but they'd not had much of a chance to do so. After the impromptu visit from her father, his no-longer-so-proper English wife had explained in no uncertain terms that they would have a serious discussion "afterward," and then she'd taken it upon herself to seduce him.

Once Gillian made her intent clear, he was like a man possessed by Eros. It had been the singularly most passionate bout of lovemaking he'd ever experienced. Perhaps it was because Gillian had initiated it. Perhaps it was something more he wasn't willing to examine.

Exhausted, Gillian had promptly fallen asleep, which he should have done long ago. But sleep did not appeal to him. Watching her now, he fought the drab darkness of slumber in favor of seeing the candlelight flicker across her face. He touched the faint freckles on her cheek, perhaps his favorite feature of hers.

Graeme closed his eyes, planning to rest for just a moment, and startled awake to light streaming through a sole arrow slit. So he'd slept after all. A good thing since they would travel back to Highgate this morn.

He rose from the bed as silently as possible and dressed. Before he could leave the room, he heard a small voice behind him.

"Graeme."

Turning, he nearly was brought to his knees by the sight of her. Would he ever be accustomed to watching her rouse from sleep? She lay there with tousled hair and a smile that would make the devil himself grin.

He returned to the bed, sat on its edge, and smoothed Gillian's hair away from her face. "Much better."

"We need to talk."

He braced for whatever was coming next. Their overnight truce had come to an end.

"I don't like being dismissed—"

"Dismissed?" he asked. "What are you speaking of, Gillian?"

She sat up, pulled her hair to the side, and began to braid it.

"When we spoke of my sister. You didn't listen. Or even consider my words. Instead, you insulted me by assuming I am completely ignorant."

That had not been his intention at all. He reached for her hand.

"I am sorry you felt that way. I don't believe you're ignorant."

She frowned.

"You are the lady of Highgate End. My wife. Why would I dismiss you out of hand?"

"Because that is what husbands do."

She looked so sincere, Graeme forced himself not to smile. "So you've been married before?"

Gillian rolled her eyes. He really should not find such a gesture endearing.

"Of course not. But I've witnessed husbands and their wives. I know how it goes between them."

"Your parents?"

"Aye, my parents. Among others."

"Well, my own parents were . . ." He'd almost said in love. ". . . happy together."

"Do you suppose we will be?" she said in a small voice.

"Happy?"

He wanted to say, "Aye, of course." But Graeme also knew his next words would displease her, mayhap even infuriate her.

"I hope so," he said. "But Gillian, we cannot take your sister with us."

He braced himself for the storm that never came. Instead, Gillian stared at him, made a sound very much like, "Hmm," and got up from the bed on the other side, away from him.

And so it began.

"While I do not believe you are ignorant to the situation, neither are you privy to all of the facts. Blackburn and your father set us back. Even now, rumblings of the broken truce are picking up traction. If our allies choose to boycott the next Day of Truce, then Clan Scott will be forced to take sides. And this is without stealing the Earl of Covington's bride from—"

"Very well." Gillian moved to the trunk at the foot of her bed, took out a green riding gown, and shook it.

"I hoped this was still in here. I wonder why Morgan didn't bring it to Highgate," she said to herself, ruining the effect of her body-hugging shift by stepping into the practical gown.

He moved toward her to assist, wondering why he was putting her into the gown rather than taking her out of it. When his hands brushed the sides of her breasts, he considering pulling the gown back down. "Perhaps we should—"

She spun around, nearly knocking herself over since the gown was not fully lifted. "We are in the middle of an argument. This is certainly not the time for—"

"Oh, my dear wife, you've not made a careful study of husbands and wives after all."

She continued to pull the gown up, in the exact wrong direction. They'd left Morgan behind at Highgate. According to Gillian, the poor woman had nearly broken into tears at the prospect of riding south again so soon. Though an adept rider, she'd apparently hoped not to see the backside of a horse for some time.

"During a fight is the perfect time."

"I disagree."

Graeme considered showing her just how enjoyable love-making could be at such a moment. Until he remembered how badly he wanted to get away from Lyndwood. Instead, he heaved a sigh and continued helping Gillian until she was properly dressed.

"I'll have to ask my mother's handmaiden to assist with my hair," she said, lifting a pewter brush from her belongings.

"Let me help."

He took the brush from her and gently nudged his wife to turn around. As he brushed the dark locks, Graeme couldn't resist touching them, lifting them to his face. He breathed in deeply, savoring the scent of lavender. And something else?

"Lemon?"

She shrugged. "Once, father returned from a trip to London and brought lemon-scented soap back with him. A merchant claimed he'd just returned from Greece with it, but Father thought it far more likely 'twas fashioned right there in London. He brought it home to us nonetheless. Now I make sure to get new lemon-scented soaps and sachets every market day."

He resumed brushing. "An interesting man, your father."

Graeme pulled the hair from her front to the back to ensure every strand was as smooth as the others.

"You hate him," she said blandly.

He certainly did not like the man.

"I can understand why he feels compelled to go to desperate measures to save Lyndwood. And yet the choices he's making . . ."

Graeme stopped, realizing something. "But I could never hate that which created you."

He finished, and Gillian turned toward him.

"Thank you." Her eyes glimmered with some emotion.

A dangerous proposition, speaking from the heart. Perhaps he should have kept silent. He'd learned that such openness only ended one way.

With him getting hurt in the end.

Again.

"So tell me, why are we not taking your sister with us back to Highgate?"

She looked so startled, Graeme couldn't resist laughing.

"Because you . . ."

He crossed his arms and waited.

"Well. She's not marrying Covington after all."

"She's not? How does she plan to get out of it?"

"I know not. She refuses to tell me anything more. Only that I must trust her and she has a plan."

"In that case," he said, gathering up his wife's belongings. "God save us from the Lyndwood sisters and their plans. 'Tis time we return to Scotland."

He couldn't get away from this place fast enough.

23

"*G*illian, nay."

They'd entered the doors of The Wild Boar just before sunset. And for some reason, Gillian refused to dine in their room.

"But there are women in the hall. I saw them. Surely—"

"Not the kind of women . . . not like you."

She, of course, refused to listen to reason. And so he found himself following his wife into the rowdy hall, which showed no signs of becoming tamer. While The Wild Boar had a decent reputation as a safe retreat for both Englishmen and Scotsmen, its hall was surely not a place for a gently bred lady such as his wife.

Everyone in the room turned to stare. Gillian garnered attention everywhere she went, even if she didn't seem to notice. He sat with the rest of his men, pulling his wife nearly onto his lap.

"Do move over," she said, pushing him aside.

"You don't care to sit next to your husband?"

"I know what you're doing Graeme, and you can just stop right now." Though she said it in a whispered hush, surely the others could hear. Not that he cared much. But it amused him that Gillian had suddenly shed her usual reservations.

Since leaving Lyndwood, she had been different. Whether it was her father's confession or the hope that her sister might very well be safe from Covington's clutches after all, he couldn't be sure. But the slightly worried, reserved woman he'd married had given way to one who stared brazenly at all The Wild Boar's hall had to offer. And though he liked the change, Graeme wasn't quite sure how to handle it.

"My lady," Malcolm addressed her. "Yer sister's quite beautiful."

All of the others laughed at his nerve as a serving woman dropped mugs of ale on the trestle table. The woman winked at Graeme when he looked at her, so he turned away immediately.

"Aye, Malcolm, she is," Gillian agreed.

Graeme moved one of the mugs in front of her. She looked at it and then up at him.

"Is something wrong?" he asked.

"Nay," she said, her hair falling over her shoulder.

Graeme moved it back.

"'Tis just . . ." She looked from him to the men.

"What is it?"

"My father," she said finally. "He says women don't drink ale."

The men laughed, but Graeme wisely did not join them. "That's enough," he told them. Turning to her, he said, "Gillian, is your father here now?"

She looked around as if making sure. "Nay."

"You asked to eat in the hall for a reason, did you not?"

The others, momentarily distracted by another serving woman, this one with very little clothing to speak of, ignored him and Gillian.

"I did."

Ah. This was not about wanting to eat in some dirty hall. Gillian was finally beginning to move out from under her father's rule, and Graeme could have kicked himself for not seeing it earlier.

And for trying to stop her. He'd been wrong to attempt to shield her from the hall.

In attempting to protect her, he'd taken away her choice . . . which was the same thing her father did. *That* was why she'd been so angry back at Lyndwood. Marriage was a complicated dance, he realized, and he had yet to learn the steps.

"Graeme?"

He wouldn't give Gillian permission to drink the ale. She didn't need it. His wife needed to decide for herself. Instead, he lifted his own mug and drank deeply.

When Gillian took a sip from the mug he'd given her, her reaction was immediate.

She promptly stuck out her tongue. "Ugh, 'tis awful."

Malcolm pushed the mug back toward her. "Try again, my lady. It gets better each time."

Graeme laughed so hard at her expression that his stomach hurt. The others joined him as Gillian lifted the mug again and took the daintiest of sips.

"Not true, Malcolm. 'Tis still awful."

"Drink it down," another yelled, and before long each of the men were chanting.

"Drink. Drink. Drink."

Gillian took a deep breath, raised the mug, and did just that. She drank until the others did the same, all in support of this wee slip of a woman whom he adored.

Careful, Graeme.

He reminded himself of Catrina. And Emma. And the fact that Gillian had been forced to marry him. If not for that, she would likely have spurned him too.

When they pounded their empty mugs on the table, Gillian did the same. Splashes of it escaped her mug because it still contained ale. She seemed to think that quite funny, and soon she was laughing just as hard as the rest of them.

"Enough," he said, waving for their food. "Keep drinking like that, woman, and you'll not feel up to riding back home."

She smiled and Graeme did the same until someone called Graeme's name so loudly from the entrance that all turned to stare.

"Reid," her husband said, turning toward the voice. "You always did enjoy an entrance."

———

GILLIAN ONLY KNEW about the Kerr brothers from reputation. Though her thoughts were hazy from the ale, she remembered that Graeme and the Kerrs had once been bitter enemies but were now allies.

It was because of that enmity that Toren, the clan chief and eldest brother, had refused to honor Graeme's betrothal to Catrina. She'd been afraid to discuss Catrina with her husband, but the end result was that she knew little of her family. Why was the youngest brother so angry?

Gillian raised her arm into the air. She needed another ale.

"Are we ever to meet in Scotland, my friend?" her husband welcomed Reid Kerr, even though the man continued to scowl.

A slight bit shorter than Graeme but just as well built, the newcomer would have been good-looking if not for his smug expression. His face was twisted into a scowl even though his lips curled up on one side. The smirk made him look arrogant and smug, as if he thought quite highly about himself.

"It appears not." He stood before her, waiting for an introduction.

"Reid, this is my wife, Lady Gillian, daughter of John Bowman, Lord Lyndwood."

When she moved to stand, the newcomer indicated she should remain seated.

"Gillian, Reid Kerr, youngest brother of Toren, chief of Clan Kerr."

The newcomer bowed, took her hand, and pressed it to his lips.

Graeme frowned. "I'd ask you to sit, but as you can see, the bench is full."

He sat between them, an obvious insult. "It appears there is plenty of room, de Sowlis."

Ignoring the glares of Graeme's men, the impertinent gentleman . . . if he could be called that . . . turned to her husband. "I heard you were married. Congratulations to you both."

When Gillian's ale arrived, Reid asked for one as well. "And some of that soup."

"Eat," he said to everyone. "Do not starve on account of my arrival."

Gillian was the only one who actually ate. The others, it seemed, did not want to comply with the new arrival's bidding. She cared only for her rumbling stomach.

"Talk, Reid." Graeme was clearly becoming impatient.

"I'd not presume to discuss such matters now."

Gillian addressed him directly. "Because of me?" Though she asked sweetly, there was nothing sweet about her mood. She didn't like this man's attitude, and was not afraid to show it.

"Precisely, my lady. Ahh, many thanks, love," he said to the serving wench who handed him both ale and soup. When she turned, Reid stared at her backside, none too subtly.

"You can say anything you'd like in front of my wife."

Gillian sat up just a bit straighter.

When Reid looked at her and smiled, Gillian did not smile back. He thought to seduce her favor? Poor luck to him. She saw him. Understood his game. Unfortunately, she was the only one. When the serving woman reappeared, she circled the table looking for imaginary items to pick up.

"Very well," he said in a slightly different accent than her husband's. "Word reached Brockberg that you'd traveled to England to speak with one of the men responsible for Blackburn's release."

"Aye, which is exactly what I've done."

"That *man* is my father," she added.

Reid looked at her as if she were daft. "Of course he is." And then he turned back to Graeme.

Ugh. What a despicable man. And this was truly her husband's ally?

"And?" Reid prodded.

"He will not be a problem in the future."

Both men looked at her as if she might have further insight. If her father had truly been paid to speak on Blackburn's behalf, then Graeme was no doubt correct. She just prayed Graeme kept the sordid story to himself.

She sensed everyone watching her.

With nothing left to say, she picked up the mug, forgot that she despised ale, and drank. When Malcolm laughed, she held the mug up in a silent salute.

Clearly confused, Reid turned back to Graeme.

She watched the two men as they stared at each other. Everyone at the table fell silent, all eyes focused on the silent standoff.

Finally, Reid slowly nodded. "Then there appears to be nothing more to discuss on the matter," he said.

With that, they drank.

That was it? Reid would say nothing more about the matter?

Gillian finished her soup in silence. Something had passed between Graeme and the newcomer, something which she didn't fully understand. It had been clear Reid was angered by Clan Scott's lack of action after Blackburn's release, but the attack had been on Scott land. Why should he care enough to challenge her husband about his own affairs? And why did Graeme look so concerned?

"Gillian?"

"Aye, husband?"

"Are you ready to retire?"

Some of the men had already wandered off, though their bowls remained on the table. No doubt the maid intended to wait until more people left so she could use the cleanup as an excuse to get to know Reid Kerr.

"I am," she said, standing. Graeme rushed to her side and held her arm. "What are you doing?"

Reid chuckled, drawing a look from the serving maid. The poor girl looked as if she would swoon at any moment.

"Assisting you abovestairs."

"Kerr," he said. "You're staying the night?"

Reid looked at the maid once more. "I do believe I am," Reid said.

Graeme began to lead her away from the table. "Then we will speak in the morning."

"Graeme?" She suddenly felt quite strange and was glad for her husband's arm.

"I know, you will be well once we get to bed."

"Did I drink too much ale?"

"I believe so, my lady."

She smiled.

"Smile now, my queen," he whispered. "You won't be doing so in the morning."

"*G*raeme, will you please ask the men not to shout?"

They'd stopped to give the horses a rest, which Gillian had been glad for since this morning's ride was easily the most horrific of her life. With every movement, her head hurt more than the last, and no amount of rubbing her temples seemed to help. She longed for chamomile tea and a hot bath. In fact, she could barely stop thinking about how much she needed both.

"I would, if they were shouting," he replied.

He tore off a chunk of the bread Magge had given him before they left. The innkeeper had openly flirted with him, but in a teasing way that hadn't bothered Gillian. Something else had.

Her unfortunate encounter with Reid Kerr.

No sooner had she emerged from her room that morning, preparing to meet Graeme, who had already gone down to the hall to break his fast, than she'd bumped into Reid in the hallway. Literally. Gillian had been walking along, mayhap with her eyes a bit closed due to the sunlight streaming in from a far-off window at the end of the corridor, and slammed straight into his chest. He'd laughed heartily despite her pleas to lower his voice.

"Did the lass have a wee bit too much ale?"

Gillian had not been prepared to spar with him so early. "Perhaps."

"You should be more careful."

She did not need a lecture. "And you should mind your manners."

Now, thinking back, Gillian wasn't exactly sure why she'd said such a thing. He hadn't, in fact, done anything wrong. But she simply didn't care for the man.

Graeme took her hand and whispered to Malcolm, "We will be right back."

She allowed him to lead her into the woods. It was much quieter here. The wet grass, evidence of an earlier rain although they'd been lucky enough to avoid it, drenched her leather boots.

When she heard the sounds of the river, Gillian froze. "Nay, I—"

"This time, I will go to the water's edge with you."

She looked at him and would have laughed if her head had not hurt so badly. "I still can't believe I fell in. On our wedding day."

Graeme pulled her along.

"You saved me."

He didn't respond. Did he realize she spoke of more than just the day she'd tumbled into the river? Likely not.

Although she'd promptly fallen asleep upon returning to their room last night, every other night they'd spent together had been consumed by passion. Gillian had never imagined such wondrous feelings existed.

But she longed for more. She longed to know all there was to know about this great clan chief who treated her so tenderly, this man she'd fallen in love with despite herself.

"Here." He bent down and she with him. At least the water was not raging but instead flowed smoothly, inhibited only by a stray rock or two.

He cupped the water and splashed his face, indicating she

184

should do the same. Gillian looked down at her gown, which was sure to get wet.

"'Tis only water," he said.

Sure enough, when she cupped her own hands, reached down into the icy cold water, and splashed it onto her face, wetness dripped down her neck and onto the neckline of her gown.

Graeme looked as if he would hand her his linen cloth. Instead, he moved closer and began to wipe her face himself.

A surge of emotion shook her. Aye, she loved him. There could be no doubt. But did he love her back? Could he?

"Thank you for not telling Reid Kerr about my father."

He moved the cloth down to her neck. "I'd never betray you Gillian. Surely you know that?"

She did. Or was beginning to.

"Why didn't he question you further?" She thought of the strange look that had passed between them and wanted to understand.

"We are allies."

Gillian waited, but he did not say anything more.

"And?"

"And I asked him to trust me, so he did."

"But you never said—"

"I didn't have to."

"When my sister asked me to trust her, I did not do so immediately," she said, staring into his tawny eyes. What did that mean? Was Graeme just more loyal than she was?

"But you did."

She thought of how many times Allie had begged her. "Aye. Eventually."

When Graeme began to rise, she stayed him with her hand.

"Whenever we speak like this, you leave. Can you not stay?"

The tender look he'd been giving her transformed to his familiar chief look. She had his answer even before he opened his mouth.

"The men are waiting."

"Graeme, why do you do this?"

He stood despite her plea. "Do what? Gillian, we really must—"

"Sometimes you're so open with me, so tender and loving. But at other times, like now ..."

When he didn't respond, she pressed on. "... you might as well be a stranger to me."

Graeme looked as if he were about to say something, but he took her hand instead.

She pulled it back. "Nay, Graeme. Talk to me. Please. Tell me why I'm speaking to the clan chief now, and not my husband."

"Gillian, I don't know what you want me to say."

"I want you to tell me how it's possible that the man who makes love to me so passionately is the same one who walks away every time we speak of anything more than border politics or my family. Won't you let me in?"

Gillian hadn't realized how desperately she wanted to deepen their connection until that moment. She held her breath waiting for his answer.

He dropped her hand.

"I cannot." With that, he turned and walked away.

It took her a moment to realize he wasn't coming back. Part of her wanted to stay, to force him to come back to fetch her. But that wasn't going to help anything. He would simply remind her that she had no choice but to follow. The men were waiting.

So she put one foot in front of the other, the mud conspiring to slow her pace, until the men came into view.

Her husband had already mounted. Sitting straight and tall, his expression grim.

The clan chief.

The man she foolishly loved.

For the remainder of the ride back to Highgate, Graeme thought of Gillian's question.

Won't you let me in?

At dinner, he hardly spoke. The hall had since been cleared of evidence of the meal, and conversation swirled around him as he sat at the hearth. His gaze returned again and again to his brother and Gillian. Aidan was regaling her with stories about their youth over a chessboard. Until now, Graeme hadn't realized she could play chess, though he shouldn't be surprised. Though sheltered, his wife was remarkably intelligent. She listened intently.

It was one of many, many endearing qualities about his English queen.

So why not let her in?

"A commendable move for someone who apparently had quite the headache earlier today," Aidan said to her.

He watched from the corner of his eye, noting Gillian did appear much recovered. They'd arrived with enough time for her to call for a hot bath, which she'd taken in her own chamber. He hadn't said anything, unsure what to say really, and had instead used the time to catch up with his brother.

"Nothing a little rosemary- and lavender-scented bath wasn't able to cure."

So that was what he'd smelled when he escorted her to the hall. Mixed with the scent that was pure Gillian, a heady combination, Graeme had nearly marched her right back to their chamber.

Until he remembered she had reason to be upset with him.

"Ahh, the Englishwoman strikes again."

Graeme ignored them, uncomfortably aware that the dull ache that started in his chest and ran up to his heart was partially self-induced.

Or completely self-induced.

"I must leave you to contemplate your next move. I fear the events of this long day are beginning to take effect."

Gillian stood, so he did the same.

"Stay, Graeme. I fear my headache is returning, so I shall retire for the night."

"I'd like to speak with you anyway," Aidan said to him.

He looked from his wife to his brother and relented. When Fiona appeared from the side of the hall to escort Gillian away, he simply watched her go. His feet, suddenly made of iron, refused to budge.

"Come, drink with me."

When the last bit of her yellow gown disappeared, he turned to Aidan. Joining him, he lifted his mug and his brother did the same.

They drank in companionable silence until Aidan broke it. "You are an arse, you know."

Graeme didn't need to ask what he meant. "I suppose I am."

Staring at the fire, he raised the mug to his lips and drank. "You are also a lucky man, Graeme."

He frowned. "Aye. Lucky indeed."

Aidan looked confused—and well he should. Graeme hardly understood himself. He turned to look at the hall, mostly empty with the exception of a few servants who had begun to push the trestle tables to the side of the room against the walls.

"What is it? What could possibly be wrong? You yourself said Lyndwood will not work against us. Douglas is coming in two days' time to speak to you personally about what happened. All is as well as can be expected for the moment."

He looked up, not wanting to talk about Gillian with his brother, but needing to do so. "It's not the border troubles."

"Then why are you so distant with Gillian? The wife you didn't want but were lucky enough to get anyway?"

"Nay, I didn't want her. Not Gillian nor any wife. Not after Catrina. And then Emma."

There, he'd said it aloud.

But Graeme already wished he could take it back. He didn't

believe he meant it, and surely it wouldn't help matters to voice his insecurity.

"What do either of them have to do with Gillian?"

Was his brother daft?

"You want me to explain it to you?" he asked incredulously.

"Aye, I do."

Graeme shook his head. "I'll not—"

"You were never in love with Catrina. Not in that way."

"We were promised to each other for years—"

"What does that matter? You pledged as children to be together. The foolish actions of our relatives tore the alliance apart, aye, but be thankful it did. Otherwise you would now be married to a woman who is more akin to your sister than—"

"Aidan!"

"I just meant . . . the two of you were friends. Nothing more. You know it as well as I do, brother. And you also know she belongs with Bryce Waryn."

"Of course I know that. She is expecting a child, so I've heard, and I'm happy for them. But that isn't what I meant."

"And Emma." Aidan shrugged. "You cannot say you cared for her?"

He didn't answer.

"She is a beautiful, charming woman, aye. And you, for some unfathomable reason, were looking for a wife. 'To start a family,' as you said. But it was nothing more than that. None of this has shite to do with Gillian."

Graeme looked at Aidan incredulously. "It has everything to do with her. Don't you see, brother? Catrina. Emma. Mother. Even when they care . . ."

She asked for more than he could give.

"As I said earlier. You are an arse."

A sadness descended on Graeme, reminding him of the day he'd learned Catrina had married Bryce Waryn. It was true he didn't love her in that way, but he had imagined her as his wife for many, many years. For some reason, her defection had still hurt.

"That might be true," he finally responded. "But this arse is your brother whether you care for the fact or not. And he is going to bed."

Graeme stood. He and his wife still had matters to sort out between them, but they were perfectly in accord in one way, and at the moment, he needed that. Needed her.

Tonight more than ever.

25

$\mathcal{T}$wo days after Graeme found Gillian sleeping in the lady's chamber, and not his own, he woke in his empty bed to a sound from the wardrobe room. Acting on impulse alone, he jumped up, grabbed his sword, and ran to the door.

Opening it, he discovered Gillian's maid attempting to move a large trunk from the center of the room. She turned to him, gasped, and promptly spun away. He looked down at his nakedness and the sword, closed the door, and went back to his own chamber.

Well, how was he to know the maid would be up earlier than the rest of the household? If he hadn't been sleeping, he may have even been sufficiently able-minded to realize it could easily have been his wife. Graeme dressed and went to the door once again. This time, he opened it without his sword in one hand.

"Mistress Morgan?"

Had she fled already?

The maid stepped out from behind a wooden screen.

"My lord," she bowed.

"My apologies," he said. "I—"

"Nothin' to be sorry for, my lord. I am sorry to have woken

you. But last night Gillian mentioned moving some of her gowns in here, so I thought to tidy it a bit."

"Thank you, Morgan. I will leave you to it."

He closed the door once more and retreated to the empty chamber that had never felt more so. It was unconscionable, to be so close to Gillian and yet so far away.

That first night, he'd wanted to wake her, but she'd suffered from a headache for most of the day. It wouldn't have been right to rouse her for the simple reason that he wanted her in his own bed. After spending the following day hearing complaints and administering justice, he'd assured himself he would speak to Gillian at the evening meal.

When she'd requested that her meal be brought to her chamber, Graeme should have gone to her. Instead, he had spent the evening congratulating himself on being right about his wife all along. It was exactly as he'd thought from the beginning. She wanted nothing to do with him.

As a husband, at least. If she wanted to be with him, to *give her all of himself*, as she'd suggested, then surely she would have come to him by now.

A little voice in his head told him he was being foolish, that she was right to be upset with him, but something had stopped him from going to her. Perhaps pure stubbornness.

He shook his head. He would need to resolve this soon, but not this morn. He needed to find Aidan to ensure they were prepared for today's meeting with Douglas. They had much to discuss with the Lord Warden, namely how to influence March Law revisions and ensure guilty parties were punished and not set free.

As expected, very few were about the castle at this time of day. He greeted those who were and walked through the hall and outside, into the courtyard. The sun had just barely begun its ascent into the sky. Though dampness hung in the air still from a light rain the evening before, the clean, crisp air was just what he needed.

"Morning, brother."

"Aidan," he said, without turning around.

"Have you spoken to Malcolm?"

Graeme thought back to the previous day. "No, why?"

His brother stood next to him, his arms crossed.

"He says the men are becoming anxious."

"As they do whenever we fail to rush headlong into battle after a provocation. I am not surprised."

"Nay, Graeme. It's more than that. Old Ned says the unrest reminds him of just before the first Day of Truce was first negotiated." He paused. "When is the last time you can remember a woman being killed in a raid?"

That was easy. "At Bristol."

"Aye, years ago. And now Grace . . ."

His voice trailed off, but Graeme understood Aidan's concern. He shared it. "This is precisely why Douglas is coming here. He's met with the new English Warden, and it is my understanding there will be another meeting with the English before the next Day of Truce."

"Meetings. That's all we do any longer. Meet. Discuss—"

He was not in the mood for this. "Am I chief or no?"

His brother didn't answer.

"We meet with Douglas. And hope for peace. If it can't be achieved . . ." He shrugged his shoulders. "Then we do exactly what Old Ned and the elders did before us."

"Which is?"

"We go to war with the English."

Although he was quite sure his own English war had already begun.

"Nay, I didn't want her. Not Gillian nor any wife. Not after Catrina. And then Emma."

Get out of my head.

The words intruded on her sleep and during every waking moment. Gillian held a pillow atop her head, trying to rid herself of them for good, but they stubbornly refused to go away.

She could hear Morgan moving about in the adjoining room but was not ready to wake just yet. In fact, Gillian would be content to lay here for the remainder of the day. If only she hadn't gone back for Graeme that night. And to think she'd returned to the hall to ask if he'd be up shortly. She'd still wanted to talk to him. To make things right.

She hadn't meant to listen to the conversation, and was, in fact, surprised neither man had seen or heard her approach. But unfortunately, she *had* heard. And now, no matter what she did, Gillian couldn't unhear the words Graeme had spoken about her.

Well, of course he didn't want to marry you. This marriage was forced upon us both.

True, of course. But though she had known of his former interest in Catrina and Emma, Gillian had not realized how deeply they had hurt him.

Still, ignoring her husband was not a solution to their problems. Though she couldn't do anything to solve her sister's problems or her parents' financial issues, she could surely do something to improve her own life.

Gillian tossed her legs over the side of the bed and called for Morgan. The maid appeared after the second time she called her name.

"Good morn, my lady."

"Good morn, Mor—" She just realized where she'd emerged from. "What in the name of the king were you doing in there?"

When a flush crept up her face, Gillian was even more confused. Surely the maid shouldn't be embarrassed to have been found in the wardrobe.

"You mentioned moving some of the trunks in there, my lady. You know I rise early and so . . ."

Gillian knew Morgan well. Something was amiss.

"Morgan?"

"Aye, my lady?"

"Is there something else you are not telling me?"

"Aye, Lady Gillian."

She waited, but Morgan simply stared at her toes.

"And do you plan to tell me some time this morning?"

Still, nothing.

"I saw your husband," she finally blurted. "But not really! The door to his chamber burst open, and when I looked . . . but I spun around so quickly, I really didn't see much at all."

Gillian was about to tell Morgan not to be so silly, that she'd done nothing wrong, of course. But she decided to tease her maid instead.

"Are you sure you saw nothing at all?"

Morgan swallowed but didn't move otherwise.

"I know my husband does not sleep with any clothing. Did you perhaps—"

"I saw it! But 'twas so quick, I did not get a good look, I swear. I couldn't help it."

Gillian burst out laughing. She just couldn't keep it in. "Your face. I'm so sorry, Morgan. I should not have done that to you."

In truth, she was glad she had. It had given her a moment of pure amusement amidst all the stress and pressure of the last several days.

"Oh, you are evil," Morgan said, shaking her head.

"Come and help me dress. That very fine man you got a peek of is the same one I must now speak to."

Morgan made a quite unladylike sound. "If I had a man as such, I'd not be talkin' to him, and that is the truth."

Gillian chuckled, feeling much better than she had in quite some time. Avoiding Graeme only made her feel worse. It was time for a new strategy, one she should have tried from the start.

$\mathcal{H}$e was nowhere to be found.

Gillian broke her fast alone, joined by neither Graeme nor Aidan. Finally, spying Fiona at the other end of the hall, she made her way toward her.

"Fiona," she called out, "have you seen Graeme this morn?"

Gillian could not have been happier with how well Morgan and Fiona were getting along. In fact, the two had become practically inseparable. Yesterday, when a stableboy was overheard saying that Highgate had become overrun with English, Fiona had taken care of the matter herself. Insisted on it, actually. Gillian wasn't sure what she'd said to the boy, but he'd apologized to both her and Morgan. Begged her not to mention the incident to the chief and promised never to say another bad word against his lady, or her maid, "until the day I die." A long time for such a young lad.

So she wasn't surprised to see Morgan just behind the older woman.

Fiona looked into the air, her nose scrunched in concentration. "I don't believe I have, my lady. Were they not at the morning meal?"

Gillian shook her head. "Nay, they were not."

So much for her idea. It would be difficult to make things right with Graeme if she could not talk to him.

Her shoulders sagged.

"Have you forgotten about Master Timothy, my lady?"

"Who?"

"The merchant I mentioned. He usually stays just a few days, so I thought perhaps—"

She'd nearly forgotten. What a treat it would be to visit him. "Oh aye, Fiona. 'Tis just what I need. Would you two care to accompany me?"

"You youngins go. These old bones don't take kindly to the saddle any longer."

"Then 'tis you and I, Morgan. Come."

The maid followed her into the courtyard and to the stables, and the boy that had made the comment about the English rushed to saddle their horses. The women had ridden just beyond the gatehouse when a rider approached from behind.

"Malcolm?"

"My lady, they say you're headed to the village?"

"Aye," she said, wondering how the captain had learned of it so quickly.

"Allow me to accompany you."

She and Morgan exchanged a glance. And then she realized why he'd made such a request.

"To guard us." Graeme had told her never to leave the castle walls without a guard. And while she thought it a reasonable directive—she'd been expected to travel with a guard back home too—she'd been so distracted she'd completely forgotten.

"Of course, thank you, Malcolm." It occurred to her that Malcolm, who was nearly always at Graeme's side, might know what Fiona had not. "Do you know where my lord is by chance?"

He looked beyond her and pointed, and Gillian turned her horse toward the horizon. Four specks, becoming larger each moment, rode toward them. No, not specks, men. Four men with the rolling green hills of Highgate End behind them.

Graeme.

The man always had an effect on her, whether she saw him from near or afar. As he rode closer with Aidan and two men she didn't recognize, his brown-blond hair catching errant rays of sunlight, her heart thudded in her chest.

"It appears he rode out to meet Douglas," Malcolm said from beside her.

James Douglas, Lord Warden for the Scottish, was one of the most feared men in all of Scotland. She'd known of him even before becoming the lady of Highgate Castle.

The men slowed as they approached. Gillian could immediately tell which of the two strangers was Douglas by the way he sat on his horse. The man was powerful and fearsome, but her husband was even bigger and just as ferocious looking. Especially now, when he did not smile.

They all appeared so serious.

Until she smiled, and one by one the men did the same. All but one. So she addressed him first. "Greetings, my lord," she said to Douglas. And then, "Husband. Aidan."

If Graeme looked at her oddly, it was likely because these were the first civil words she'd said to him in days. Not that she'd said much, of course, but it was an improvement from silence.

"Gillian, may I present James Douglas, Lord Warden of the Eastern Marches, and his man, Darden. This is my wife, Lady Gillian, daughter of John Bowman, Lord Lyndwood—"

"I know her father well," Douglas replied, not very kindly.

"But you've not had the pleasure of meeting his daughter," Graeme said firmly, the rebuke not lost to anyone.

Though Douglas did not reply, he did nod his head to her, a deference to Graeme's retort.

"We are headed to the village for supplies," said Malcolm by way of explanation.

Graeme looked pleased, likely because she'd taken an escort, and she silently reminded herself to thank Malcolm for offering his service.

"Aidan, will you please escort our guests to the keep? I will be along in a moment. I'd like a private word with my wife."

The way he said *wife* sent chills up her arms. It was as if they were alone, and he'd caressed her with the word.

Without further exchange, the men spurred their horses toward the castle. Graeme offered Malcolm a poignant look, and he and Morgan rode ahead, out of earshot.

Gillian's horse was becoming impatient, even more so when Graeme moved closer to her.

"Are you speaking to me then?" he asked.

She'd hurt him. How could she have missed that before? Maybe her husband wasn't prepared to love her, but despite what he'd said the other night, he must care for her. His expression said so as clearly as if he'd spoken the words.

"We need to talk," she said, reminded of the last painful conversation they'd had in the woods. This time, she would not push him so hard. She would not ask for all of him, simply for what he was able to give.

"Gillian, I would be glad to—"

"I have a proposal," she blurted out, before she lost her nerve. This wasn't how she'd planned to share her idea with him, but she would feel so much better after speaking bluntly.

"A proposal," he repeated.

"Aye." She nodded. "Indeed."

His expression did not change.

"What is my favorite meal?" she asked.

Graeme looked at her oddly.

"Spiced pears," she answered. "I adore cinnamon-spiced pears."

"Gillian, I am glad to know it, but—"

"What is the one thing you love above all others?"

When his eyes softened, Gillian thought for one wild moment that he would say her name.

"My brother," he replied instead. "I still do not—"

"We hardly know each other, Graeme. We were married so quickly."

He waited.

"My proposal is that we get to know each other."

He smiled. "I thought we had been doing so already."

"Nay, Graeme. Not in that way. Getting to know each other's pasts. And hopes and fears. Not"—she shrugged—"you know."

Graeme smirked. "I won't make you say it."

"Thank you," she said, belatedly realizing he teased her. "I believe we should make it our first priority. That we should get to know each other better without complicating our courtship."

"Complicating?" Understanding dawned and his eyes widened with alarm. "Nay, not that. No."

"Graeme, do you really think it wise for a man and woman to keep rushing into bed as they are learning about each other?"

Graeme calmed his mount by rubbing him on the head. "Certainly, 'tis better for a marriage to be consummated. If the couple's marriage is arranged, they might not know each other at all."

Oh, sometimes, she really did want to box his ears.

"Graeme?"

He heaved a sigh. "I will play along. Nay, a man and woman do not rush to each other's beds as they are becoming acquainted."

Satisfied, she continued. "So I propose we do not have *relations* for a fortnight and instead take the time to . . . talk."

"Talk?"

"Aye, Graeme, talk." She held her breath, already knowing his response. Her husband was appalled by the idea. And she'd so hoped it would help bring them closer together.

"Define relations?"

Hope sparked in her heart. Might he actually agree?

"You know . . . lovemaking, of course," she said, feeling her cheeks heat. The blasted man. He'd made her say it despite knowing how much it embarrassed her.

"But all else is permitted?"

She suddenly had a vision of his hand inside her, and Gillian belatedly realized *relations* could mean many things.

"Nay, nothing of the sort."

"Nothing?" He raised his brows.

Mayhap she had pushed him too far.

"May I kiss you?" he pressed.

"Nay."

"Two days."

"What?"

His smile was so slow and sensual, Gillian nearly relented altogether. "I will agree," he continued, "but only for two days. It's already been—"

"'Tis ridiculous to think we could learn much of anything in two days."

He stuck out his chin.

"One week," she countered.

"You will sleep in my bed. *Our* bed."

"Done."

With a parting wink, her husband took off in the direction of the castle. And she rejoined Morgan and Malcolm feeling more joyful than she had in days.

GRAEME HAD NEVER BEEN MORE miserable in his life.

It had been three days since his fateful discussion with Gillian, each more painful than the last. He rued most of all his stipulation that she sleep in his bed. Lying next to his wife, knowing he could not touch her, was excruciatingly painful.

For some reason, Gillian had decided this was the single greatest idea in all of Christendom. Admittedly, they'd fallen into a mostly pleasant routine during the days. He would train with the men while she took exceedingly good care of household matters, and each evening he and Gillian would dine together. Their lives had slowly become intertwined in a comforting way. But everything fell together at night. She'd climb into bed, perfectly content to lie next to him and talk, and then fall asleep astonishingly easy. He, on the other hand, hardly slept at all. And when he did, it was a fitful slumber filled with dreams of his wife. His wife the vixen, not the version lying next to him in a shift.

Four more days, he told himself as he ascended the stairs to their chamber. He'd started the countdown after the first painful night. When he entered their chamber this evening, Gillian was already dressed for bed. The trunks she'd wanted moved to the wardrobe sat in the corner of this chamber instead.

Where they would stay.

"Back so soon?" she asked.

Graeme had gone after dinner to speak to one of the elders in the village—a discussion he should have had days earlier, after Douglas's short visit.

"Aye, it went just as I'd expected."

He poured them both a goblet of wine, part of their new routine, and handed one to her. She'd already taken a seat by the hearth, and he sat opposite her before taking a healthy sip from his own goblet.

"They agree that either Aidan or I should attend at least the next Day of Truce, if not each one afterward. Since Douglas has given us leave to insist on Trial by Combat for any future charges of murder or kidnapping, he's advising each of the border clan chiefs that they, or their second, be present in the future rather than sending a consul."

She stopped with the wine halfway to her lips. "Does that mean..."

"It does."

She stared into the fire for a moment. Graeme had learned

his wife adored a fire, even on warm days like today, and wondered if they'd be sitting next to one even during the summer.

"But Graeme, you cannot . . . I cannot lose you."

"And what man, do you suppose, would pose a true challenge to me?"

She considered the question only briefly. "Geoffrey Waryn."

"One man?"

"And his brothers?"

"Even the youngest?" he asked with a smirk.

"Though Neill is yet young, they say he is proving to be the strongest and most powerful of all the Waryn men."

"I've heard as much. But thankfully all three of them are allies to Clan Scott."

"Lord Clave? He appears to be—" Gillian's face whitened as she realized what she'd said.

"Appears to be?"

"I'm sorry, Graeme. I should not have said his name. I was not thinking."

He looked at Gillian, her soft cream shift nearly skimming the ground, her hair pulled back in a braid as it was each night, and tried to quiet his body's response.

"There is no need for you to be sorry."

"But Lord Clave . . . Emma . . ."

Graeme took a drink and sighed, crossing his legs in front of him.

"Emma Waryn is a beautiful woman," he started. "And when I offered for her . . ." He stopped, not really wanting to continue.

"Yes?" she pressed.

He forged ahead.

"I offered for her because she was here. And obviously saddened by Garrick's betrothal. I thought . . ." He couldn't believe he was saying as much aloud. "I thought perhaps she was sad because he was getting married. And unlike my brother, I was prepared to marry. I'd thought of myself as nearly married for years—"

"Being betrothed to Catrina."

"Of sorts. Our families had discussed a betrothal before the rift occurred. After that, she and I remained good friends. We thought to change her brother's mind."

"Which of them was against the marriage?"

"Toren, mostly. Alex and Reid did not seem as impassioned to continue a feud started by our fathers."

Gillian shuddered.

"You don't care for Reid."

"Nay," she said. "Not at all."

Graeme took another sip. "He is actually a good man. Though for some reason he tries hard, successfully at times, to hide it."

"Well, I do believe you are better off without him as a brother-in-law."

Graeme laughed. "Perhaps."

"You were speaking of Emma."

"Indeed." As he talked, it became easier to get the words out. To put the thoughts he'd been mulling over into words. "I thought it would be as good an alliance as any. Although the clan elders may have felt otherwise, I'd never been against marriage to an Englishwoman. Especially one whose ties to the borderlands could provide further inducement to peace."

"Did you love her?"

It was the same question his brother had asked. The answer came easily enough. "Nay, I did not love Emma Waryn. I only admired her."

"Catrina?"

Now that was a more difficult question to answer. Graeme tapped the side of his goblet.

"I did love her." Seeing Gillian's expression, he rushed to finish. "As one would love an old friend. Which is exactly what she is to me. A friend. I am glad she married Bryce."

And he was. He'd been telling himself that for a long while, wondering if it were really true. He'd avoided speaking about the two women who had spurned him, but he meant every word he'd said to Gillian. The rejection still stung, but he *was* happy they'd married other men.

His glass empty, Graeme stood and held out his hand to Gillian. When she simply looked at it, he said, "We cannot break the agreement for such a simple thing? I wish only to hold your hand."

She didn't look convinced.

"That is all, I promise."

Though I very much wish it could be more.

When she put her goblet on the table and took his hand, Graeme set his own goblet aside and led her to their bed. Climbing inside, he lay next to her and thought of their discussion. One of many that had left him feeling . . . exposed.

But not altogether bad. In fact, he enjoyed these intimate moments with her and looked forward to them each day. He looked over to tell her just that, and not surprisingly, his wife was already asleep. The woman really did have an uncanny ability to fall asleep quickly.

He took her hand once more, enjoying its easy warmth, knowing he was in for another long, uncomfortable night.

And not simply because he could not ravish his own wife. But because, when she'd asked if he loved Emma or Catrina, the answer that had almost spilled from him was as frightening as it was exciting.

Nay, he did not love either of those women in that way.

But he did love his wife.

27

"My lady, come quickly."

Gillian had just been prepared to inspect the herb garden when Morgan called to her.

"What is it?" she said, alarmed by her maid's tone. Her cheerful friend had never sounded so morose.

"'Tis Fiona."

Her hands began to tremble as she followed Morgan through the inner ward and toward the granary, the two of them almost running. "She isn't talking or moving, just lyin' there."

A crowd had begun to gather, but Gillian pushed her way through them. Just as Morgan had said, Fiona was lying on the ground. The young stableboy was leaning over her, his eyes wide.

"She's no' yet dead," he said.

Please God, spare this woman. Please.

Gillian knelt at her side and took Fiona's hand. It was warm, but she did not look good. It seemed as if all of the color had drained from her face.

"Did someone send for a physician?" she called, trying her best to remain calm.

By the blank stares, Gillian surmised Highgate had no physician. "A healer then, get—"

That's when it struck her. The healer was dead. Killed on the orders of a man who now roamed as freely as the innocent.

"Is there no one else?"

She should have thought to ask before. Should have made arrangements for another healer to be found. But she'd been so consumed with her own problems she'd never taken the time to fully ingrain herself here. And now it may be too late.

"Where is she?"

Gillian had never heard such a sweet sound before.

"Graeme," she yelled, frantic. "Here. Fiona is here."

"Is she alive?"

The crowd thinned as her husband pushed through them, none too gently. He knelt on the other side of Fiona, taking her other hand and leaning down to feel her breath.

"Aye, but she does not look well, Graeme. Is there no other healer?"

He looked up, his expression both grim and angry. "Grace was a stubborn woman. We'd told her many times she needed to show another her ways, but . . ."

His silence was her answer.

Please, no.

"She must be moved. Graeme, get—"

But he had already begun to lift the rotund woman, fitting her in his arms as if she were as light as a sachet of herbs. Gillian followed them, telling the others they would send word of her condition immediately. Everyone adored Fiona, and their resigned expressions only made Gillian more worried. It was as if they knew something she did not.

Graeme carried her through the hall.

"Bring her to my chamber," she said.

He looked back.

"The lady's chamber," she clarified. Her place was now by Graeme's side, and hopefully that was where it would remain.

She opened the door for him, Morgan and Aidan rushing into the room behind them.

"What happened?" Aidan asked.

Morgan pulled down the coverlet as she answered. "We were walking to the granary when she fell."

"How did she fall?" Graeme asked, feeling her forehead.

"Straight down," Morgan replied. "As if she'd just fallen asleep right there as she walked."

Graeme explored her head with his finger. "No bump," he said, looking at Aidan.

She never wished to see such despair and hopelessness on his face again, but what could she do?

"Go to Donnan," Graeme said to Aidan. "Perhaps he knows who his wife turned to for advice."

"Grace? Ask for advice?"

Graeme's eyes narrowed. "By the time we find another healer—"

"I'll go," Aidan said, apparently realizing he had no other choice.

When he left, Gillian began to pace. Her sister had an interest in the healing arts, but she had never given them much attention. As Graeme and Morgan watched her, Gillian walked back and forth, thinking, praying. Why did they stare at her so?

"What will we do?" she finally blurted. "If no one can be found—"

"Don't say that," Graeme said. "Fiona will be healed."

Typical Graeme. He never wanted to hear a bad word spoken, as if fearing something would make the deed come true. What other choice did they have but to hope and pray? But she would think only good thoughts, for Graeme's sake. *Fiona would be healed. Fiona would be healed. Fiona—*

"Morgan!" She ran to the maid who stood quietly by the old

woman's side, holding her frail hand. "Do you remember the boy at Lyndwood, the one who followed Allie around as if she were his mama?"

"The marshal's nephew?"

"Aye." Gillian started pacing again, excited by the thought.

"Gillian, come here," Graeme said.

When she went to him, her husband merely grabbed her hand. She looked at him in confusion until she realized her walking back and forth worried him. Despite his assurances that all would be well, his face was nearly as pale as Morgan's.

"Graeme," she said with as much confidence as she could muster. "Fiona will not die today."

He didn't look convinced. And neither was she, but if he could will good things, then so could she.

"Fiona will not die today. Do you hear me?" She turned to the woman who had welcomed her from that very first day. "Fiona, you may not leave us. I've much to learn about Highgate. You said yourself Morgan is only passable as lady's maid."

Morgan looked up, and Gillian shrugged. Mayhap she should not have said that. Though Fiona had said it fondly.

"She needs you. Highgate needs you."

"My lady," Morgan pressed, "the boy?"

She'd nearly forgotten. "Oh, aye. Do you remember two summers ago when the boy did much the same as Fiona? Simply dropped as if someone had clunked him on the head?"

Morgan nodded. "I do, but—"

"I saw it happen. Like her, he had no other ailments—"

"But, my lady, he was just a young boy. And Fiona . . ."

She looked at the old woman as if to say the two patients were very different. And while that was true, something told Gillian she was right. She tried to remember what Lyndwood's physician had said. The boy had experienced a similar event before. The first time, his lips had gone blue and his hands had developed a tremor.

They'd called the priest, thinking the boy possessed. Of course, that was not the case, and he'd healed just fine after being treated with . . .

Fiona would do the same.

"Morgan, we need rue."

She and the maid stared at one another before Morgan fled in search of an herb Gillian prayed they grew at Highgate.

Gillian went to Fiona's side and took the maid's place. Graeme joined her there. She was no healer, and Gillian wasn't even sure how to administer the herb. But they had to try. Neither she nor Graeme spoke until Morgan returned in a rush. When she handed her a potent-smelling blue-green herb, Gillian wordlessly crushed a bit of it into the palm of her hand.

At least she knew the bitter smell meant only a small amount should be given. Would Fiona take it in this state? Would it be too much? Too little?

"Open her mouth," she said to no one in particular. When Graeme did so without question, Gillian placed the crushed herb under the maid's tongue, just as she'd seen Lyndwood's healer do many times before.

And then they waited.

After what seemed like days, Fiona's eyes fluttered open.

"Fiona," Graeme said, the relief in his voice making Gillian want to weep.

The woman took a deep breath and opened her eyes fully. "Where am I?"

Gillian looked around at the unused chamber, glanced at her husband and Morgan, and said, "Your bedchamber."

Her husband's tender smile tugged at her heart.

"My . . ." She tried to sit up, but Graeme pressed her back down.

"Aye, your bedchamber. I will not be using it, and 'tis a shame for such a room to remain empty."

Fiona laid her head back down.

"What happened?" she asked.

Fiona shook her head. "I know not. I remember thinking to check on the grain stores, and I was walking." She looked at Morgan. "With you?"

"Aye, Mistress Fiona. And then you fell."

"I did?" She closed her eyes once again. "I don't remember it, lass."

"Does anything hurt?" Graeme asked.

Fiona shook her head. "Nay. My thoughts are unclear, as if I am reaching for something I canna' grasp. But no. Nothing."

Gillian wasn't sure why her hands began to shake again. Fiona appeared to be just fine. She was not going to die on them . . . at least not yet.

"Someone should stay with her through the night," Graeme said.

"I will do it." Both she and Morgan said it at the same time.

Graeme leaned down and placed a kiss on Fiona's forehead "I will go find Aidan. Stay with her, but you will both sleep tonight. I will stay awake to watch her."

"My lord, I can—"

"Thank you, Morgan. But Fiona has been with me since I was a babe. I wish to ensure she is truly well. Besides"—he looked at Gillian—"I am not likely to get much sleep anyway."

They all turned to look at her. Morgan and Fiona both smiled, though they misinterpreted his remark.

With that, Graeme came around to Gillian, reached for her hand, and leaned down to give her a kiss on the cheek.

"But you—" She stopped, aware that she could not publicly reprimand her husband for kissing her. Oh, but he was the devil himself.

EXHAUSTED, Graeme left his men on the lists and walked back toward the castle. Highgate had originally been built without a training yard. Two years before the first Day of Truce, Graeme's father had fortified the castle's defenses against raiders from both sides of the border and designated the east side of the outer bailey for training. Rather than walk toward the gatehouse, Graeme instead made his way to the secret entrance he'd used with Gillian.

That day in the bakehouse. He could remember the look in her eyes when he'd taken her finger into his mouth. He'd wanted so badly to kiss her then, though no more so than he did at this moment. Or every moment, in fact.

Three more days.

Graeme climbed the stairs and made his way to the lady's chamber, intending to check on Fiona. He'd stayed up all night, watching the old woman sleep, thankful to still have one of the only people who'd known him as a babe. He and Aidan had lost their entire family, slowly but surely, over the course of a decade or so. When his brother had returned, unable to find a healer, Graeme wasn't surprised he had nearly wept at the sight of an awake and alert Fiona.

When he opened the door now, Morgan put a finger to her lips and indicated for him to leave. Fiona was sleeping.

He backed out of the room, content for the moment, and went to his own room, intending to close his eyes before dinner. How had he stayed awake for so long during battles? He'd felt so slow in training today.

Graeme opened the door and froze.

Gillian stood in the middle of the room bent over, and it took every bit of will he possessed not to stride over and claim her that very moment.

She stood when she heard him.

"I didn't expect you so soon." Still looking at the floor, Gillian made to bend over once again, but he stopped her.

"Nay," he said, much too sharply. "What are you looking for?"

"A pin," she said. "It fell from my hair and 'tis the one Allie gave me on my naming day last year."

Spotting the pin, he reached down and picked it up.

"Are you still worried for her?" he asked, handing it over. There had been no messages from Lyndwood.

Gillian placed the pin back into her hair. The front was pulled back and piled onto her head, but the back hung in loose waves. She looked lovely, of course, but he preferred her hair down so that he had a reason to reach for it.

"I am. What do you think she plans?"

Graeme looked up.

It was not the first time they'd discussed the matter, and Graeme repeated what he'd said before. "I just don't know her well enough to say. Though I know you worry about her."

"She's just so young . . ."

Graeme shook his head. "When my father died unexpectantly, there were many who worried about my age. They asked, and not very privately, if I possessed enough wisdom to be chief."

Gillian listened as he remembered the doubts he'd had himself. Ones he was determined not to share, with the exception of his brother.

"Those who knew me well, knew my father had sufficiently influenced my training, were not as worried. But the elders took some convincing."

Gillian understood.

"She could not possibly be thinking of a nunnery." She frowned, at least able to accept that her sister was capable, despite her age. "Allie has always enjoyed the attention of young men, though precious few were suitable. But that hardly seemed to matter to—"

"Did you?" Graeme stood dangerously close to his wife.

"Did I what?"

"Enjoy the attention of young men?"

She seemed to consider it. "I believe all young women enjoy

receiving some attention. In fact, young men do too. Who prefers to be ignored? But nay, not like Allie. She even rouged her cheeks once—"

"But not from their husbands?" He moved just a bit closer.

"I do not understand."

"Women enjoy receiving attention, but not from their husbands?" He was close enough to breathe in her sweet scent. To see the blue in her eyes, which shone bright and innocent. At least, much too innocent for his taste. Graeme had so much more to show her.

"I did not say—"

"One kiss, my queen?"

When her lips parted, he knew she would relent.

"No?"

This would not be as easy as he had hoped.

"We have a deal, Graeme. And it has only been—"

"Four days. I know exactly how long it has been, and longer still since you were angry at me."

When her face fell, Graeme knew he'd said something wrong. That he'd reminded her of something she would rather have forgotten.

"Tell me." He wanted to reach for her. To comfort her. But the source of her upset was likely his inability to open himself to her fully. "Gillian, you never did tell me—"

"I heard what you said to your brother."

He didn't understand, and said as much.

She repeated. "'Nay, I didn't want her. Not Gillian nor any wife. Not after Catrina. And then Emma.'"

He thought back to the conversation. "Gillian, did you not hear the rest?"

"Nay, I left and—"

"You did not speak to me afterward. Listen to me." He clenched and unclenched his fists, unsure what else to do with them to keep from reaching for her. "I asked Aidan what either woman had to do with you. 'Tis as I said to you. I was not in love with Catrina or Emma—"

"That's not what upset me."

"Then what is?"

She frowned. "I know you did not want me—"

"Gillian, that is not at all what I meant. Look at the way I'm standing right now, all because I'm desperate to touch you. Do you think I didn't know how wrong it was to kiss you in that garden? I do not ravish innocent women."

"I know that."

"Or make it my custom to find myself alone with them. But you . . ." For a wild moment he thought to tell her the truth. To say, "I love you, Gillian." But what if she did not feel the same?

She was forced to marry you.

He laughed at the absurdity of the thought. His worries were just the same as hers. How had he never thought about it that way before?

I will tell her. On the day we finally make love again, I will tell her. To hell with the consequences.

"I understand why you asked for this agreement, but please, Gillian. Let me out of it for just one kiss."

He needed to touch her or die trying.

She raised her chin, a final defiance, before she nodded.

It was all the agreement he needed.

Graeme pulled her toward him, pouring everything he felt into her. He coaxed open her mouth and slayed her tongue with his own. Their moans mingled as the past days of frustrated desire melted away. In an instant he was hard, ready for an act that could not happen today.

But, by God, he would take whatever she offered and give no quarter in return.

He cupped her face, moving her head in just the right direction for their mouths to fit perfectly together. In the end, neither one pulled back, but a firm knock at the door intruded on what had been the greatest kiss of his life.

"My lord? My lady?"

"Go away," he shouted.

"Lady Gillian?"

Graeme did not recognize the voice, but whoever was on the other side of that door was no longer going to reside at Highgate Castle if he continued shouting their names.

Just as he brought his lips down once more, satisfied the visitor had gone away, the voice called out again.

"I apologize to intrude, my lady. But it's your sister."

Gillian broke away and ran to the door so quickly that it took Graeme a moment to realize she was no longer in his arms. She opened the door with enough force to slam it against the stone wall behind it.

"What is it? What about my sister?"

The young serving boy looked as if he wished to be anywhere but standing in that doorway.

"She's . . . ," he stuttered. "She's here."

"*H*ere?" Gillian asked in bafflement.

"Belowstairs, my lady," the boy said.

It took a moment for the words to fully wash over her. When they did, she lifted her gown and ran toward the hall.

"Gillian," Graeme called after her.

She slowed just enough for him to catch her.

"How is it possible your sister is at Highgate?"

Gillian didn't like the accusation in his voice. Did he think she'd lied to him and sent for her sister despite his concerns? That she'd conjure a story about having the impending marriage under control?

"I do not know," she replied bitterly, moving as fast as she could.

Bursting into the hall with Graeme behind her, Gillian ran to Allie, noticing she had brought at least four men with her.

"Allie!"

Throwing her arms around her sister, Gillian hugged her as if she'd not seen her in years. She'd thought about her every day and night. Indeed, her dreams the evening before had been riddled with weddings and darkness. Nightmares, in fact, though she'd only just remembered them at this moment.

"What are you doing here?"

Graeme reached them and inclined his head in greeting. If he suspected something was awry, there was no sign of either now. He smiled as if Allie were the king of Scotland, come to visit Highgate.

"Greetings, Lady Allie," he said.

"My lord."

"Graeme," he corrected.

Allie smiled, that broad, open smile she'd had even as a babe.

"Then please, Allie." She turned to Gillian. "I will explain everything."

She looked up as Morgan hurried into the room. No doubt she'd just learned about Allie's arrival. The women embraced as Graeme directed the servants to assist the men who'd accompanied Allie. Her father's men.

"I am most anxious to learn how you came to be here," Gillian said. Turning to Graeme out of respect, though she was still peeved by his first reaction to the news of her sister's unexpected visit, she said, "Will you join us?"

"Nay," he said, his expression giving no indication of his earlier mistrust. "Speak in private with your sister."

Allie's smile grew.

One more woman under her husband's spell.

Gillian tugged on her sister's hand and led her to a corridor and up a set of stone stairs. The women emerged on the very same parapet where Graeme had found Gillian, kissed her, and whisked her away to their bedchamber.

The day they'd first made love.

"Oh, Gill, 'tis so beautiful."

It really was a spectacular view. Rolling hills in the distance, one so high it seemed to touch the clouds. She lifted her face to the sun for a brief moment before turning to Allie.

"So?

"You are glowing, Gillian. I've never seen you this relaxed before."

"Allie!"

Her sister expelled a breath. "I suppose you'd like to know why I am here?"

Gillian crossed her arms.

"Are you angry?"

She was about to become so. Allie bit her lip, clearly avoiding the explanation that Gillian was beginning to dread.

"The Earl of Covington is dead."

A sudden bout of dizziness forced Gillian to close her eyes. It was as if Allie had taken a war hammer to her chest.

Dead?

Nay. It was not possible. Allie had claimed to have a plan, yes, but she could not have done such a thing.

"Gill?"

When Gillian opened her eyes, the first thing that struck her was that her sister looked as worried as she felt. "You . . . killed him?" she asked uncertainly.

Allie's eyes widened. "No!" Her mouth dropped open. "You think I . . . how could you think such a thing? *Killed* him?"

"You said all would be well. That you would not be marrying Covington, and then—"

"No, no, silly. Of course not. Goodness."

Her shoulders sagged in relief. Her sister's tone and the look in her eyes both attested that she was telling the truth. When she lied, Allie tended to look down at her feet.

Thank God.

"Wait, then . . . what do you mean dead? And how did you plan to—"

"We received word two days after you left. In fact, it happened while you were visiting us. He apparently rode off a cliff in the midst of a heavy rainstorm. Can you believe it? Gillian, I am the worst person in the world. A man is dead, and I confess, upon hearing it, I felt only relief."

"Then you were still betrothed to him?"

"Well, of course. You know I was."

"But you said . . . you said you would not be marrying the earl. That you had a plan."

She'd been so stupid. How could Gillian not have seen what was so clearly on her sister's face before?

"You were going to marry the earl."

"Please, please, listen to me. I am so sorry. You have no idea how horrible I feel for lying to you. I normally would never do such a thing. You know I love you and—"

Gillian clenched her hands to stop them from shaking.

"You planned to marry him."

"I know you, Gillian. You would not have stopped until something terrible happened. In fact, the moment father told me about the betrothal—"

"Something terrible? Allie, the something terrible would have been you married to that man."

"Father told me everything. How desperate he was to save Lyndwood. The awful lies he told on the last Day of Truce."

Gillian turned from her sister, not wanting to hear it. How could she have been so blind?

A goshawk swooped down in the distance. And though Gillian couldn't see it from here, of course, she could easily imagine the bird's red eyes and white eyebrows were perpetually set in a fierce expression.

Like her father. To be admired but also feared.

She turned back to Allie. "You did this for Father?"

Gillian understood her motives well. She'd spent a lifetime trying to please the man. To prove to him that women could be strong.

"And for you," Allie said. "I knew you'd have no hope of convincing Father to change his mind. And I guessed at your plan too. The implications . . . Gillian, don't you see? I could not let you do that to your husband. Your new clan. To everyone who has a stake in this fight for peace at the border. Even Father."

"What do you mean?"

"Father had been making some very poor decisions—"

She gave her sister a sharp glance. "Such as your betrothal?"

"But I do believe they tore him apart," she continued. "You should see him, Gill. He is not the strong man we know. Mother says she has never seen him this unhappy. He *is* still the man who wants peace, who loves the borderlands. Who loves us."

"He loves Lyndwood more."

Allie shrugged. "Perhaps. Or perhaps he sees Lyndwood as a part of us, necessary for our family's happiness."

"You still haven't told me how you came to be here."

Allie reached for her hands and squeezed them.

"He is ruined, Gill. Father, I mean. When we received word of Covington's demise, the look on his face . . ."

Of course, no wedding meant no dowry.

"Oh, Allie."

"I begged him to let me tell you in person. Of course he said no—"

"You came without his permission?" Her sister had been bold in the past, certainly more so than Gillian herself, but to come to Scotland—

"Nay, of course not. The guards would never have accompanied me without his approval. 'Tis just as I'm saying. I begged and begged . . . I wanted to see you. To get away from it all for just a bit. And he actually said yes. Can you imagine it? The same man who would not allow us to visit the market without a contingent of men large enough to withstand a siege. But he agreed. 'Tis what I've been trying to tell you."

Her poor sister. She'd been through so much. Gillian let go of her hands and embraced her, not wanting to let go. She could feel

Allie's heart beating against her own. Her sister was here. And safe. And would not be wed to Covington.

There would be time enough later to consider her parents and what this meant for them. For now, she just wanted to be with Allie.

And to tell her husband that they would be having a guest.

A very extended stay if I have anything to say about it.

29

*G*raeme had purposefully given Gillian and her sister space, and had instead spent the afternoon with Fiona, who was eager to get out of bed. Though she claimed to feel better, he was taking no chances and had ordered her to rest. That order, and the fact that he was her chief, was the only thing keeping her abed.

He returned to his chamber and changed his clothing to prepare for dinner, waiting for Gillian.

She did not come.

Impatient, he wandered toward the parapet where she and Allie had been standing for some time, but it appeared he'd missed them.

He needed to speak to his wife. She had seen the look of doubt cross his face, he knew it, and while he could not deny that he'd entertained a moment of doubt, the moment had passed just as quickly. Gillian would not have betrayed him. Although Allie's arrival came as a surprise, Gillian was worried about her, and he was pleased she'd come to Highgate. Whatever the explanation, he would have it in good time.

Opening the door to his room, he greeted Morgan, who

appeared to be lacing the back of his wife's gown, relief for having found her washing over him.

"I will finish," he said. Morgan curtsied and scurried from the room.

He took the laces in his hand, explaining before she could even address him.

"Forgive me if I believed the worst for the briefest of moments, Gillian. I know you wouldn't betray me."

She didn't turn, but his declaration must have caught her by surprise. Turning just enough for him to see her profile, she said, "You do not trust me."

"Despite so much that has passed between us, lass, I've known you less than one month. But even so, I do trust you. I know you would not purposefully lie to me."

And surprisingly, it was true. Gillian was not the type of woman to lie.

If he could only show her how he felt . . . he would lean down, move her hair aside, and kiss her neck. Of course, he'd not stop there.

"Covington is dead," she said.

Finished, Graeme dropped his hands, which he hadn't consciously raised, not quite sure what to do with them now. "Dead?"

"Aye. An accident apparently, he rode his horse over a cliff."

Graeme walked toward the chair closest to him. Standing so close to his wife, knowing he wasn't to touch her, physically pained him.

"Good."

Gillian's jaw dropped. "A man is dead—"

"A despicable man."

Gillian frowned, two adorable lines appearing at the creases of her mouth. And what a mouth it was. God, if he could not—

"Graeme? Are you listening?"

Indeed, he had not been. "Nay."

That did not appear to be the right answer.

"I could have lied and said aye," he said. "But just as I know you are truthful to me, I promise to always be honest with you. So nay, I was not listening. I would apologize, but the thoughts I was having about your mouth—"

Gillian's frown deepened. "This is serious," she chided.

"As is my need to feel your lips beneath my own. To coax them open, make love to your—"

"Graeme!"

He was making it worse. Graeme extended and crossed his legs, hoping the activity would help focus his thoughts. "Covington is dead. And Allie no longer betrothed, I assume?"

For a moment, he thought she would punish him by keeping the remainder of the details to herself. But she finally relented.

"She is not. And of course, my father is devastated. They will lose everything, Graeme."

He'd have said, "As he deserves," but he held his tongue.

"I am sorry, lass. But you've done everything you could to prevent it." And then something occurred to him. "What was Allie's plan then?"

Gillian's expression fell, her shoulders shaking ever so slightly. Tears welled in her eyes. Unable to stop himself, he leapt out of the chair and went to her.

"There was no plan," she sobbed out. "She was prepared to marry him."

Graeme took her in his arms, holding her as the tears began to flow. When she wrapped her arms around him too, he tightened his hold.

"She did it for me. For Father. And Mother too. She loves us all so much. But she knew—"

Gillian never did finish her thought. Instead, she sniffled against his chest. He pulled back and wiped her cheeks with the back of his hand.

Perhaps he was getting better at being a husband. For instead of saying, "She knew coming here would be too dangerous," he once again held his tongue.

She pulled back, no longer crying, and looked at him oddly. "Why are you smiling?"

Why indeed?

"I was just thinking that your sister is a remarkable woman. You realized she attempted to sacrifice herself for you. For us."

Gillian nodded.

"You like her then?" she asked, hope in her eyes.

"Very much. Though I know little of her."

And for the first time since he had entered the chamber, Gillian smiled.

"Good," she responded. Appearing satisfied, she blurted, "Because she will be living with us."

GILLIAN SAT between Graeme and Allie, waiting for the final course to be served. After her grand announcement, she hadn't given her husband a chance to respond. But he did not appear to mind. Indeed, he'd accepted her sister so readily, Gillian wanted to reach out and touch him now, just as she'd wanted to do these past few days. Embrace him. Kiss him. Make love to him.

Graeme had accepted her preposterous proposal, and in a way, it had accomplished its intention. But couldn't they get to know each other and be intimate as well? Of course they could. She had just been too afraid to admit it. Afraid they'd married too quickly. Afraid she would fall in love with him, only to find out he was more like her father than she'd thought. She would tell him as much that night.

Everything felt so clear to her, so right, now that Allie was here. Gillian was only sorry Aidan had left that morning to meet with Toren Kerr at Brockberg Castle to discuss Douglas's recent visit. She had no doubt the two would get on splendidly. If it were not for her parents and Lyndwood's fate, she would have been extremely happy.

"Gill, look."

Forced out of her reverie, Gillian followed her sister's glance. "Do we not have a similar tapestry at Lyndwood?"

Both she and Graeme studied the tapestry in question.

"Aye," she said. "'Tis very similar." She'd noticed the same thing soon after her move to Highgate.

Graeme grinned as he looked at the finely-woven piece. "Do you know the story behind the scene?" he asked her sister.

"Nay," she said. "Do you?"

"Aye," he said, taking a drink of ale as a servant placed a tray of nut tarts on the table.

"The unicorn represents the tamed beloved. Though he's tethered to a tree and constrained by a fence, the chain is not secure and the fence is low enough to leap over. The unicorn could escape if he wished. His confinement is a happy one. And do you see the seed-laden pomegranates in the tree?"

"Aye," Allie replied.

"They are a symbol of fertility and marriage, as are the wild orchid, bistort, and thistle."

When Graeme looked at her, Gillian was prepared to smile. When she had spied the tapestry on that first day, her interpretation had been very different. Gillian had assumed the unicorn was trapped. But it was not so.

Was it an omen, perhaps? A symbol of a marriage that had begun out of necessity but grown into so much more.

But his smile had vanished. In fact, Gillian had never seen such an expression on his face before.

"Graeme, is all well?"

Clearly, it was not. Even though he tried to smile, something had changed him.

"Of course," he said, unconvincingly.

"Ours is quite similar," Allie said again, oblivious to Graeme's distress.

"Is it now?" he asked politely. "Tell me of it. Perhaps I can decipher its meaning."

As her sister and her husband spoke amiably, Gillian thought of the sudden change in Graeme's expression. What could possibly have come over him to warrant it?

She looked at the tapestry again.

Was it something there? Another meaning behind it, perhaps?

Well, she would find out soon enough. As soon as the meal was finished, Gillian would make her excuses to Allie so she could learn what exactly had so discomfited her husband. And then she would talk to him about their agreement.

And afterward . . . Gillian smiled in anticipation.

He wasn't coming.

Graeme had said he needed to speak to the armorer after dinner. Allie, tired from her travels, had gone to her bedchamber, and so Gillian had returned to her own room after a quick visit with Fiona. Morgan had assisted her with her gown, and she paced the empty bedchamber now, waiting for Graeme.

How much time had passed? Eventually, she crawled into the empty bed and waited there. When it became evident Graeme would not be returning, Gillian simply could not lie still. She turned on her side, and then her back, and then her other side. She slammed her eyes shut, wishing sleep would take her so that she could stop worrying. It did not heed her.

Finally, unable to lie still, Gillian jumped back out of the bed, grabbed a candle in its stand, and scurried down the corridor to her sister's bedchamber. After tapping on the door, she pushed it open and entered the room.

"Allie?"

The room was dark but for a brazier in the corner of the room. Gillian smiled. Both she and her sister loved to fall asleep by firelight, regardless of the time of year.

"Allie?" she called again.

"Gill, is that you?"

She'd already been asleep.

Gillian put down the candle and made her way to the bed. She felt along the edge and carefully lowered herself onto it.

"I can hardly see you," Allie said. "What's wrong?"

That was the problem. "I don't know."

She told her everything that had happened between her and Graeme, from their first meeting to his odd behavior at dinner.

"He seemed perfectly pleasant, Gill."

"But he has never not come to me at night. We've always had that, from the start. Even when all else seemed so uncertain."

"Then why did you take it away?"

That was the very question she'd been asking herself all evening. "As I told Graeme, we hardly had a chance to get to know each other before we married. I thought perhaps—"

"Being less intimate was a way for you to get to know him better?"

"Aye, at the time it made sense to me." Sighing, she turned onto her side, facing Allie, and adjusted the coverlet. "But I suppose it was not the best of plans."

"So why did you really do it?"

"I am afraid." She could see only the outline of her sister and was glad for it. "I've fallen in love with my husband."

Allie chuckled. "And that is bad?"

"Nay, of course not. But I don't believe he feels the same way. In fact, I know he does not. When I asked him—"

"I know, you told me of that discussion. But have you considered that he doesn't know how to give 'all of himself'? Has he been married before?"

"Of course not."

"Then maybe Graeme feels much the same way you do."

"He's not said so."

"Well, have you?"

"Nay, but—"

"Gillian, you are the kindest, most patient woman in the world. You're an amazing sister and will be an even better wife."

"But?" Her sister had more to say.

"You must stop thinking there's something wrong with you. Father made us feel that way, but I've come to realize Father only pretends to be perfect." Her sister sat up until the side of her face was swathed in the dim light from the candle. "Just like you and I do for him. You do not have to win your husband's approval, Gillian. You already have it. The only wrong you could do is to hold back when you want him to do the opposite."

Silence fell between them for a time.

"Tell him how you feel."

Finally, Gillian smiled in the dark. "How did you come to be so wise? 'Tis I, the older sister, that should be advising you."

"As I'm sure you will one day."

Her sister was right. The time for half measures was over. Gillian would not just tell Graeme why she'd insisted on their forced abstinence. She would tell him that she loved him.

"Do you mind if I sleep in here?" she asked her sister. "I don't know why Graeme hasn't returned, but I'd prefer not to sleep in our bed alone. 'Tis so big and empty."

"Of course I do not mind." Allie leaned over and kissed her on the forehead. "Good night, Gill."

"Good night, Allie."

Gillian closed her eyes, more determined than ever to make things right.

"*I* am leaving for Dunmure to find a new healer."

Graeme had not thought Gillian would return to their bedchamber before he left, but she'd walked in minutes ago, looking poorly rested. When he'd returned to the bedchamber last night, late enough to ensure Gillian would be sleeping, he had been startled to discover that she was not in their bed. With Fiona now occupying the lady's chamber, she would not be there either. A few hastily asked questions and tense moments later, he'd learned his wife had been seen entering Allie's room.

"Oh," Gillian responded, clearly wanting to ask more. Graeme wanted to offer more.

But he didn't.

When she opened the door to the wardrobe chamber, he sat on the bed and put his head in his hands.

What the hell am I doing?

He should tell her now what he'd realized the evening before. Gillian loved him.

Even so, the thought of telling her how he felt was terrifying. He needed to do more than simply tell her. Graeme wanted to show her. But how?

He'd have time to consider it on the way to Dunmure. For as much as he loved his wife, he also loved Highgate and its people. And being consumed with thoughts of Gillian had made him complacent. They needed a new healer before something else terrible happened.

"When do you leave?" She'd returned, already dressed in a simple undertunic and kirtle. His wife, lovely no matter what she wore, stared straight at him.

"As soon as Aidan returns," he clarified. "It could be today. Or tomorrow."

Neither of them said another word.

He should explain why he'd stayed away after the meal. Or why he had refused her when she'd asked him to let her in.

Instead, he watched her walk to the door. Opening it, she made to leave but then turned toward him instead.

"I wanted to speak to you this morn. To tell you something."

His body felt as if it were welded to the bed. He should stand. Go to her. Tell her.

"What is it?" Frustrated by his own uncharacteristic lack of decisiveness, Graeme's tone was harsher than it should have been.

She opened her mouth and then shut it once again. "I don't want to tell you like this."

He tried to soften his tone. "Like what?"

Graeme wasn't trying to frustrate her, but he could tell she was becoming impatient with him.

"You are not like my father," she blurted. And though he had not known what to expect from her, that was certainly not it.

"I should hope not."

"He is, or was, an honorable man. With many qualities worthy of admiration. I love him despite his failings, but I've treated you unfairly, Graeme."

"You've done nothing of the sort, Gillian. It is I—"

"Please, let me finish." Though her hand dropped from the door handle to her side, Gillian made no move to come to him. A good thing since he was liable to forget their agreement if she came too close.

"My father wanted a male child," she said softly. "He never hid the fact."

Most men wanted the same, to continue their family line. Graeme didn't care much about that. Any child was a blessing.

"My mother lived to please him, and Allie and I emulated her. I thought it my duty to keep him happy even though it never appeared to work."

If she was trying to endear her father to him, Gillian was doing a poor job of it.

"But you are not like him," she repeated. "You accepted me, this clan accepted me, from the very first day I arrived in your lives."

He didn't understand. "What is there not to accept? You're a fine woman, Gillian."

When she smiled, a small, faint smile that crinkled her freckles, his heart banged against his chest.

"Thank you, Graeme. And you are a fine man."

"And unlike your father," he finished.

"In the ways that matter."

He still wasn't sure he understood. "And that is what you wanted to tell me?"

When her hand found the iron handle of the door this time, she opened it. "Not precisely."

"Then what is it?"

She looked at him as intently as a skittish deer might regard a hunter. And then turned when a movement outside the door caught her attention.

"Fiona!" she exclaimed. "What are you—"

"I came to see if my lady needed anything."

Graeme did stand then and made his way to the door.

"Are you well, Fiona? Are you sure—"

"Very well, my lord," Fiona replied. "And ready to venture outside."

Gillian looked back at him, blinking, and then turned to the maid.

"Come, Fiona," she said. "I am not certain you should be alone quite yet. Perhaps you should ensure, just for a time, you are accompanied by someone. Or at least in the presence of others."

A good idea, in case the mysterious ailment returned. He had been about to offer his services, but his wife was too quick for him. She'd already reached for Fiona's arm and guided her away from their chamber.

Gillian looked back at him, and Graeme could not decipher her expression. Resolve? Sadness? Regret? What had she wanted to tell him?

And why did I insist on acting like an utter fool?

I need to make this right.

WHY HAD she not told him?

Gillian left Fiona in Morgan and Allie's care and missed the morning meal. She needed to think. To devise a plan. Though she still wanted to know what had become of Graeme last night, she had not found the courage to ask. Something was clearly troubling him, and she thought perhaps it had to do with her.

She'd nearly said the words, "I love you, Graeme," but fear had held her back. She'd spoken instead of her father. Everything she'd shared with him had been true, though it wasn't exactly a blazing declaration of love.

Tonight. She would tell him tonight. She'd ensure he'd come to their chamber to sleep, and she would surprise him by ending the agreement and telling him how she felt.

"I've always wanted a sister."

She spun around, one foot on the steps leading to the door of the main keep.

"What do you say, Gillian. Can I call you sister? It's true enough, is it not?"

"Back so soon, *brother*?"

Aidan bowed as if he'd accomplished a great victory. "You'll find my men along . . . eventually."

Gillian looked across the courtyard but saw no one except a few servants.

"We rose at dawn and raced back," he explained.

"And how goes Brockberg?"

He frowned and looked over her shoulder. "Not as well as expected."

"What's wrong?" she asked, immediately alarmed. Had something else happened to disrupt the peace?

"There was an attack on Kerr land the day before I arrived. No one was injured, but the number of sheep stolen, and the quick retreat of the reivers, has Toren rather upset."

"English?" She almost didn't want the answer.

"Aye," he said.

"Graeme mentioned going to Dunmure when you returned," she said. "To find a new healer." Gillian did not want to explain all that had happened since his departure. At least she could tell him one happy piece of news. "My sister is here!"

"Is she now? Another sister? 'Tis my lucky day." Aidan's expression sobered.

"Something has happened?"

"Her betrothed is dead," she said. When she saw the look on his face, Gillian said quickly, "She can tell you what happened."

Aidan's eyebrows drew together. "It seems I missed much. I saw Graeme on my way inside, but he dodged my questions about you."

She frowned.

"Gillian?"

Though she adored Aidan, Gillian did not want to talk with

him about it. Especially here, out in the open, where anyone could hear.

"We will speak later." She turned to leave, wanting a bit of privacy. Aidan stopped her with a gentle hand on the shoulder.

"Gillian," he said, looking around them. "Don't give up on him."

She turned back around. "I will not. But he does not make it easy, Aidan."

When she met his gaze, Aidan's eyes widened. "You love him."

She nodded. How could his brother so clearly see what he could not?

"He's been through quite a lot, sister."

She smiled at the endearment.

"Is that all that's bothering you?"

Her brother-in-law was quite astute.

"'Tis my parents. And Lyndwood. I worry what will happen now."

"You don't have to share more now." Aidan must have sensed her unease. "But know you have a family here now too. And Gillian . . . please be patient with Graeme. I promise you will not regret it."

Gillian wrapped her arms around him "Thank you, Aidan."

She would not wait for that night. No, Gillian would find Graeme right now. She changed course and made her way to the stables.

A question occurred to her, so she called out to her brother-in-law, "How do you come to be so wise in the ways of love?"

Aidan smirked. "Practice, my dear sister. Lots and lots of practice."

Gillian laughed and walked toward the stables, greeting the groom and looking in every stall for Graeme. She had seen him walk this way.

"If you're looking for your husband, my lady, he is gone."

"Gone?" She looked toward the large double doors. "Where?"

"Dunmure, my lady. He said he would be back in two days' time."

It could not be. Graeme wouldn't leave for that long without saying goodbye. But looking at Aidan's expression, she knew it was true.

Graeme was gone.

*G*illian went about her day as normal. With Aidan as Graeme's second in command, she was not needed to settle disputes, although the castle accounts had fallen to her, and Gillian was glad for it. The numbers had distracted her from the fact that Graeme had simply left Highgate without a word to anyone.

She pushed the ledgers away and looked around the solar, a small room hidden behind the great hall where Graeme conducted much of his daily business. Aidan despised the small space, preferring to sit in the hall instead. And while the candlelit room was dark, with no inside windows or arrow slits to speak of, she rather liked it.

"Gill, are you in there?" her sister called from behind the partially open door.

"Aye," she replied, sitting back, apparently finished for the day. It was just as well. She could not concentrate any longer.

A vision in pale blue, Allie sat in the only other chair in the room and looked around. "Do you not feel confined in here?"

"Nay." She shook her head. "Not yet."

Allie attempted to smile. "I'm sure there is a perfectly reasonable explanation for it."

The *it* was, of course, Graeme's disappearance. Even Aidan, who had been attempting to mollify her just that morning, telling her not to give up on his brother, was shocked by it. Graeme had never done such a thing before, Aidan insisted. Which did not make Gillian feel any better.

"I'm sure there is one," she said, the tightness in her chest making itself known again.

"Tell me again, what was the last thing he said to you?"

"We spoke very little this morn, but we did speak about Father, and I thought it would help matters. I didn't expect . . . this."

"Nothing else?"

Gillian shook her head. "Nay."

She'd thought about that conversation, and last evening's, so many times. There was just nothing to explain his actions.

"Aidan is none too happy with him," Allie said.

She'd introduced Allie to him earlier that day, and to her sheer delight, the two did indeed get along splendidly. Not surprising since they were very similar.

"He's come in to check on me more than once. He is very sweet."

"Sweet?" Aidan said from the door. "That is a word I can say with assurance has never been used to describe me before."

Aidan entered the room and looked around, his gaze settling on the ledgers in front of her.

"Busy today?"

Gillian leaned forward, putting her elbow on the table and her chin in her hand. "I suppose 'tis time to oversee the meal?"

Aidan and Allie exchanged glances. She'd said it without attempting to move.

"Gill," Allie ventured.

She just wanted to be alone. "I will be along in a bit. You two—"

"Will speak to Fiona," Allie said. "Do not worry about tonight's meal. Shall I see if cinnamon-spiced pears can make their way onto the menu?"

"If only someone here would eat such a dish," Aidan offered good-naturedly.

"I appreciate what you are trying to do," she said to them both. "But—"

"No 'buts.'" Allie came around and pulled her out of the seat. "I was going to let you wallow for a bit, but—"

"I do not wallow."

"I believe you were wallowing," Aidan said. When she gave him a sharp glance, he amended, "just a smidgeon, my lady—"

"'Tis enough," she said, standing up. "You are both relentless."

"That sounds more like me," Aidan said. "Sweet? If anyone heard you say such a thing . . ."

Gillian chuckled despite herself. "My sweet brother," she mocked. "If I am to forget, even for a moment, my husband had abandoned me, then I suppose cinnamon pears are our best hope." She tried to make her voice light for Allie and Aidan's benefit. Her movements did not match her tone, however. As she followed the two into the hall, Gillian resisted the urge to turn back around and lock herself back inside the small room. Putting one foot in front of the other, and a rueful smile on her face, Gillian prepared for a long, long night ahead.

"MANY THANKS FOR YOUR HOSPITALITY, KERR," Graeme said to Alex, preparing to mount his horse. They stood in the courtyard at Dunmure Tower. "And for your assistance."

"If you meet up with Reid again before I do, show the boy some manners," he added.

Of all the Kerr holdings, Alex was closest to Highgate, so it had taken only a few hours for Graeme and his men to reach

Dunmure the previous evening. They met after dinner to discuss all that had occurred recently, and Graeme had mentioned seeing Reid at The Wild Boar. Alex insisted his hothead brother did not speak for the Kerr family, at least not in this instance. In fact, Alex agreed with Graeme's decision and was pleased with Douglas's decree. Even after the recent raid. Only the survival of March Law would ensure the borderlands the peace they all desperately wanted.

"My pleasure," Alex said, and meant it.

"Prayers for your wife," Graeme said. Alex's wife Clara was due to give birth for the first time any moment.

Alex smiled broadly. "And greetings to your own."

Graeme had told him about Gillian, leaving out many of the details, including the nagging thought that he did not deserve such a woman.

He nodded, anxious to be back on the road. Then Graeme rode through the gatehouse and onto the muddy road. It had rained earlier in the day, and if the clouds were any indication, it would do so again. His men followed, speaking to each other but not to him. They knew him well enough to detect his mood.

If he'd had any rational thoughts at all, Graeme would have at least told Gillian, or Aidan, that he was leaving. But since he'd planned on visiting Alex anyway, as soon as Aidan returned, he had not stopped to consider anything other than the desire to be left alone with his thoughts. After promptly finding two men to escort him, as was their clan's custom whenever the chief traveled, he'd had his horse saddled. He'd left without packing a single bag.

She loves you.

He knew well the difference between desire and love. Knew it because he'd desired a number of women before Gillian. And now he also knew what it meant to love—to think of someone every waking moment. To crave their touch and affection. To want nothing more than to see that person smile.

Graeme continued to stew in these same thoughts for hours.

Rain threatened, but they pressed on, passing a small manor house that belonged to one of their clan and then Highgate's small village.

No sooner had they come through the castle gates than the skies opened up, soaking them all. His men quickly took shelter in the stables, but Graeme dismounted and walked toward the keep as if it were a bright, sunny day. He watched the puddles around him fill with water. His feet sank into the mud as he came to a decision. This predicament was his fault. He'd dared too much. He'd thought he and Gillian could be intimate without forming a deeper attachment, but such a thing wasn't possible.

He handed the reins to the stableboy and made his way to the keep. Though it was only midday, the sky had gone dark. As he made his way abovestairs, servants lit candles all around him.

"Graeme!"

His brother.

"Not now, Aidan." He kept walking.

Aidan stopped him with a hand on his shoulder. "I don't think so."

Without any other recourse, he turned to face him.

"You leave without a word and think you can walk in here—"

"I said," he ground out, "not now."

They stared at one another, neither willing to be the first to break, until a voice behind Aidan decided the standoff for them.

"Aidan," Gillian said. "I'd like to speak to my husband, please."

With a final glare, his brother spun away and stalked back toward the great hall.

He wasn't ready. She was so lovely, and strong. Could she truly love him?

"Gillian, I can't—"

"You can," she said. "And you will. I was worried, Graeme. To leave like that—"

"I'm sorry, Gillian. I need to see Fiona."

With that, he took his leave. Graeme knocked on the chamber door not far from his own. He opened it just slightly. "Fiona?"

Nothing.

Fear gripped him as he opened it wider. The bed was empty. Surely if something had happened to her, Aidan or Gillian would have—

"Are you lookin' for someone, my lord?"

The relief almost toppled him to his knees.

"You're looking well," he said, trying to act as if he hadn't worried.

But Fiona was not fooled. She'd spent too much time with his grandmother, knew him too well.

The maid put her hands on her hips. "So you thought me dead, did ya?"

He didn't deny it.

"You're wet," she said, looking him up and down.

"Caught in a rainstorm on the way back from Dunmure."

Fiona's eyes brightened, and Graeme remembered she held a special affection for Alex Kerr.

"He's doing well," he said before she could ask.

"And Lady Clara?"

Though Fiona had not met the lady, he was not surprised that her affection for the man would extend to his wife. He smiled. "Is also doing well considering she's prepared to give birth at any moment."

"Glad to hear it," she said, pushing her way past him. "Can't say the same for your wife."

He should not, would not ask. "What do you mean?"

She stopped, turned, and gave him a look that told him exactly where her new loyalties lay. "You should not have left as you did."

Only Fiona would say such a thing to her chief, though right now, he was not anxious to speak to anyone about his wife.

"I had my reasons," he said.

"But do they matter?" With that, she turned and left.

Graeme shook his head. Sometimes he wondered if his own grandmother possessed Fiona's body, so similar were their words and mannerisms.

As he stepped into his bedchamber, which smelled maddeningly like Gillian, he had the first inkling of an idea. He had planned to send an envoy to Kenshire to inform the earl that Douglas had proposed a private meeting between Clan Scott, the Kerrs, Kenshire, Clave, and the English Warden. Or . . .

This time, he did gather some belongings. England was not a half-day's ride like Dunmure. Raining or no, he could be at the abbey by nightfall if he left now. Though he did not like it, Graeme had to find Aidan and Gillian to tell them this time. He looked longingly at the bed he'd once happily slept in alone. What would happen when he returned?

Graeme pushed away the thought as he changed his clothes. Fear would not serve him well now. Graeme would show his wife just how much she meant to him.

our days had passed since Graeme had announced he was once again leaving. Gillian had given up feeling sad about it. This time, she was good and angry.

She'd spent the first two days trying to determine what he'd meant when he said, "There's something I must do." The more she thought about it, the angrier she became. Gillian had practically thrown herself at him again and again. She'd tried to reach out to him, understand him. And true, she'd suggested they not be intimate for a time, but that had only been to mend their broken relationship. To bring them closer together.

Perhaps she'd been wrong about him all along. Gillian had thought she'd married a loyal and courageous clan chief. And there was no denying he was courageous, but loyal? Not to his English *queen*. He'd dismissed her without a thought; his announcement that he was leaving had been cold and emotionless.

But she was done. Everything in her life felt like it was on hold. Graeme was gone. No word had come from Lyndwood. Gillian had begun to pull away from daily life at Highgate, living instead in her thoughts. She spent so much time with the ledgers that Allie had finally recruited Aidan to rescue her. The three of them had taken a ride through the countryside yesterday, Aidan showing them each the various properties, telling stories of his childhood.

When Gillian had approached Allie about staying at Highgate indefinitely, her sister had hesitated at first, not wanting to abandon their parents. But Gillian had promised they would visit their mother and father often, wherever they ended up moving. In the end, Aidan was the one who convinced her. She and her brother-in-law had formed a bond almost instantly, an easy thing to do with Aidan. If the looks they gave each other did not always appear so innocent, Gillian shrugged them off. Her sister had agreed to stay.

Feeling listless, Gillian made her way to the garden. The cook had asked for her advice on additional herbs to plant, something she couldn't help with until she looked at the garden. Though this garden bore little resemblance to the one at Kenshire, she found herself thinking about it nonetheless. Thinking about him.

A lad with a curly mop of hair ran toward her. "My lady, do you know when the chief will be returning? I asked him—"

"Nay, I'm sorry wee one."

The boy turned to walk away, his shoulders slumped. At Lyndwood, very few people had approached her, perhaps because she looked so inapproachable—or so her sister had always told her. She'd developed a tendency to fold her arms and look away, habits that had proven difficult to break. At Highgate, however, Gillian was stopped nearly every moment of the day. She answered questions, sought counsel when needed, and was overjoyed with her new role as the lady of the keep.

"What did you need to ask my lord?" she asked, calling the boy back. "Perhaps I can help?"

He turned back toward her. "Ya think so?"

She smiled, hoping she could. "Of course!"

"I asked if he could find my ma." He said it so solemnly that Gillian didn't have to ask if she'd heard correctly.

"Did you lose her?"

He shook his head. "My pa did."

Gillian pretended to consider that. "I see. Your pa lost her. And how did he manage such a thing?"

The boy pointed to the sky. "He said she's up there, but I don't understand. She's not got wings. So I asked my lord if he could find her."

Gillian's heart broke for the boy. Much too young to have lost a mother. "And what did my lord say to you?"

The boy looked up to the sky again. "He said he didn't need ta find her. That she was already here." He pointed to his heart.

Gillian smiled, glad Graeme had not given him false hope.

"I agree with my lord," she said. "But why are you waiting for him to return, then?"

The boy shrugged. "He told me I could find him whenever I did not feel her here." He pointed to his heart again. "His ma was in the same place, y'see, and he said we could look for them together."

Gillian opened her arms and the boy came right into them.

"What is your name?" she asked as she held him to her, his heart beating rapidly beneath her own.

"Gordie, my lady."

She waited until Gordie pulled away from her.

"My pa is the blacksmith," he said proudly.

Gillian looked toward the smithy, sure she had not seen the boy here before. "And do you not come to work with your father?"

He shook his head. "He says it's much too dangerous, but someday—" His chest swelled with pride.

"Someday you will make the most magnificent blacksmith," she said.

"And someday you'll make a mag . . . mag . . . pretty mama." He smiled, and as quickly as he'd appeared, Gordie ran away.

Gillian sank down to the ground, the boy's words weighing on her.

"He said he didn't need ta find her. That she was already here."

That sounded like the Graeme she'd learned to love. The one she'd tried to make love her back. Had all hope for them died?

Gillian sat in the garden, looking at the herbs but not seeing them, until the sun began to set.

Like it or not, she finally concluded, Graeme was in her heart just as surely as Gordie's mother was in his. But the question now was, what should she do about it?

THE SOUND of a baby's cry woke Graeme from deep slumber. He'd slept so little on his mad dash to England. After his meeting with Geoffrey and Sara the evening before, after explaining that Douglas had proposed a private meeting between Clan Scott, the Kerrs, Kenshire, Clave, and the English Warden, which they set for the day before the next Day of Truce, he'd immediately retired to his chamber—and fallen asleep the moment his head hit the feather pillow.

His dream came back to him in pieces. Gillian wearing a May Day crown. Her eyes wide as she spied on him in the garden. The kiss that had set them on a new path.

He sat up, his eyes adjusting to the dim light that spilled in from the arrow slits in the wall. The sun was up, but just barely if his guess was correct. Graeme rubbed his eyes. He'd leave for home as soon as he broke his fast.

Graeme dressed and began to make his way toward the great hall. Unlike Highgate, Kenshire's corridors remain lit at all times, candlelight flickering against the whitewashed stone walls.

Another cry.

Graeme slowed, unable to look away from an open door where the sound originated.

"Come on then," a woman called from inside.

Gillian was apparently not the only one to favor having a fire on warm nights, for Sara's maid was cradling the baby in her arms by the hearth. The past two days had been unusually warm, and though that warmth did not make its way completely into the castle, the rooms were much warmer at this time of year.

"I did not mean to disturb you, Mistress Faye."

The lady's maid squinted, looking at him from head to toe. "Good morn to you, Chief."

He moved closer. He'd met Geoffrey and Sara's baby just once before.

"Hayden?" he asked, hoping he got the baby's name correct.

Faye looked down at the boy, his eyes wide and his black hair standing straight up in the air. She smiled, clearly in love with the wee bundle.

"Aye," she said, finally looking up at him. "You'll be havin' one of your own soon."

He shook his head. "I'm married only—"

"I know how long ye've been married," she cut in. "The wedding would be hard to forget."

Of course it would be. He and Gillian had been married at Kenshire, which would always make this place special to him.

Where had that come from?

"It must be difficult, that?"

Hayden looked as if he were about to cry again, but Faye tapped his nose and made a face. The baby smiled instead.

"Pardon?" he said.

"Marryin' under those circumstances."

Graeme looked at the woman. Her kindly but stern expression put him in mind of Fiona, though Faye was younger than his grandmother's—nay, Gillian's—maid.

"More than I thought possible," he found himself saying. "Her father has proven to be difficult. And Gillian . . ." He shrugged, wishing he had not said anything.

"Aye? Lady Gillian?" Faye prompted.

Something about the woman forced his mouth open once again. "Married me because she had no choice."

Even he did not believe that anymore. So why did he say it?

"Ha!" Faye promptly began to rock Hayden again, for her robust response had startled a cry from him. "You forget, Chief, I've known Lady Gillian nearly since the day she was born."

Indeed, he had forgotten that fact. Though he didn't see how—

"If ye think she found herself in that garden by chance, then you don't deserve such a fine woman."

"I did not mean to imply—"

"I know what you meant. But Faye is tellin' you she ain't never seen Lady Gillian in such a state over a man. An' we've had some fine young knights strutting around Kenshire. In fact," she grinned, "I remember one time—"

"If it pleases you, let's not discuss the fine men Gillian has met at Kenshire."

He should want to leave, but something about Faye rooted his feet to the spot.

"An' as for that father of hers," Faye said. "I know he promised Allie to Covington before the earl passed along." Faye shook her head. "He wasn't always like that."

"Lord Lyndwood?"

"Now don't mistake me, he didn't coddle those poor girls. But he's done himself a disservice these last years, allying himself with the likes of the Earl of Covington, God rest his soul."

Hayden began to cry in earnest then and Faye stood up, moving him to the front of her chest.

"'Tis time for his feedin'."

"Of course." Graeme stepped aside as the maid walked past him.

"And give Gillian my love," she said on her way out of the room.

He agreed to do so, but did not follow Faye out. Instead, he thought of all she'd said to him.

Would she have wed you had you not been found in that garden?

The truth was, they had not met under different circumstances. But it no longer mattered. His true purpose for visiting England lay ahead of him. He'd get the deed done quickly and return home to the woman he loved.

*S*he hated him.

No, that was not true. She loved him.

Gillian looked back at the guard riding behind her. Still there, still stoic. His expression never changed. She couldn't force a smile from him no matter how hard she tried. She'd even resorted to making faces at him every time she turned around to see if he was still there.

Nothing.

She lifted her face to the sun, slowing as they approached a ridge that gave her a sweeping view past Scott property. They weren't close enough to the border for her to see England, but on clear days, Gillian could spot a tall mountaintop far enough away that perhaps, just perhaps, it could be English.

The borders moved, she knew, even after having been "established" thirty years earlier in March Law. The raids by which manors changed hands—one day English, the next day Scottish—would likely never cease. Or not in her lifetime, at least. But she supposed she should be happy. According to her father, the situation had once been much, much worse.

When Gillian met someone from the south, they nearly always

asked the same question. "Why do you stay?" Her answer . . . her parent's answer . . . was the only one they had to give.

The border was home.

She'd never expected to live this far north. But she'd come to realize the people here were the same as back home. Resilient. Fierce. Borderers were the only kind of people she'd ever want to live amongst.

She looked back, and her protector, still there, stared out into the countryside as well. He was too far away for her to speak to without shouting.

Scotland. Her home, where she'd been accepted by everyone except the one whose acceptance mattered most to her.

Gillian still did not know how she would react when Graeme returned. Part of her wanted to rail at him for hurting her. But another part of her, the one that understood this arrangement had been difficult for him to accept, wanted to open up to him completely. Tell him, as she'd planned to do before, how she felt.

And if he does not accept you?

"My lady!"

The shout was so loud and unexpected that it sent a rush of fear to her very core.

Gillian turned to find a lone rider approaching from her left. Her guard moved his horse in front of her and addressed the English knight, who clearly did not belong here.

"Who are you?" he asked.

Much of the knight's face was hidden by his nasal helm. He looked from Alban to Gillian, and though he did not reach for his sword, Gillian worried this would not end well. Like her protector, the stranger was not a small man. She gripped her reins tightly, expecting the need to flee.

"I am no one," he said. "Just an Englishman on my way to—"
He looked at her then.

"The Isle of Skye," he finished.

"You are a long way from there," Alban said, none too kindly.

"I know," he said, clearly disappointed.

Relaxing—he did not appear to be a threat—Gillian added more gently, "I am not from here, so I cannot help you, sir."

The knight nodded and saluted them both.

"Then I apologize for trespassing. Good day to you both." And with that, he rode away.

"We should return to the castle," the Scotsman said.

Gillian smiled. "What a very mysterious Englishman," she said. "Thank you," she added, "for the warning."

Her only reply was a grunt and something that sounded like "duty."

"Well, I thank you even so. You are a very fine protector."

And though Gillian could not swear it, she thought she may have spied a slight upturn in his lips. A smile? Not quite. But maybe the beginnings of one.

It would have to do for now.

Gillian led them back, lighter than she'd felt in days. And as they approached the gatehouse, she knew exactly how to handle Graeme. No more thinking. No more hesitating.

34

"He's coming."

Gillian had been about to sit for the midday meal. But at Aidan's announcement, she immediately stood back up.

"Sit, Gillian. He isn't walking through the castle doors any moment. I only meant he's on his way home."

She shot her brother-in-law a curious glance. "How could you possibly—"

"Spies," he said, narrowing his eyes conspiratorially. "I have them everywhere. In fact—"

Allie giggled. Gillian shot her a look as she lowered herself back into her seat.

"Malcolm arrived just moments ago. Graeme sent him ahead to let us know he was not far behind. A day at most," Aidan said.

"Gill, are you drinking ale?"

Gillian placed her mug back onto the table. "Indeed."

"Should she not drink ale?" Aidan asked her sister. "The English are strange, I will admit. But—"

"You were saying Malcolm brought word of Graeme?" Gillian was impatient to hear the rest of it. "I thought the chief traveled with two clansmen at all times?"

Aidan did not appear concerned. "This would not be the first time my brother ignored the edict. Though why he sent someone ahead, I can't be sure. Malcolm said Graeme sent him here straightaway to let us know he would be delayed, but by no more than a day."

"Us?" Gillian held her breath. "As in—"

"You and I," he replied.

When she continued to look at him, Aidan replaced his mug and placated her. "He said, 'Tell Aidan and Gillian that I will be delayed, no more than a day behind.'"

He picked up the mug once more. "You can stop staring at me now. He said nothing more."

"I'm not staring," she protested.

"You were staring."

"This"—she widened her eyes and made a face at him—"is staring. I was simply—"

"Who," her sister interrupted, "are you?"

Gillian didn't understand the question.

"If Father or Mother could hear such an exchange, they would surely be aghast."

Gillian sat up straighter in her seat. "It seems my *brother* brings out a different side of me than you are used to seeing."

In fact, both of the de Sowlis brothers had that effect on her, Graeme even more so than Aidan.

"It will happen to you as well, Lady Allie, if you do indeed stay here."

"What will happen?" she asked, her expression innocent.

Aidan scrunched up his face to make it appear more menacing. "We'll rid you of your English," he said in a thick brogue not typically found this far south. "And turn you into a true Scottish lass."

Allie looked at Gillian, who shrugged. "And what, pray tell, do your Scottish lasses do differently that we should be given such a fate?"

The two of them bantered for the remainder of the meal while

Gillian thought about Malcolm's return. When Graeme had left for Dunmure, he'd done so without a word. And though he'd bid her goodbye before taking his more extended journey to Kenshire, he'd appeared almost reluctant to do so. Had something changed?

Either way, she was ready for him.

Gillian would tell him everything the moment they were alone. She loved him, and if it took a day, a fortnight, or a lifetime, she would do everything she could to make him love her too. For the simple fact that she could not help it.

"Gill?"

Allie brought her back to the conversation. Though she hadn't seen him get up, Aidan stood talking with a messenger at the entrance to the hall.

"Do you miss them?"

"Mother and Father?" Somehow she knew who *them* referred to. "Of course," she said. "What do you think has happened?"

She hated to consider it. Gillian wasn't sure her father would survive the loss.

"I do not know," she said. "Do you think they've come already? To take it all away? With the king out of the country—"

"Covington was a powerful man," Gillian said.

Allie shuddered. "Aye, he was."

They fell silent, and Gillian looked across the room at the tapestry Allie and Graeme had spoken of the night before he left.

Gillian, lost in thought over her parents' fate and that of her marriage, hardly tasted the food in front of her. When she looked at Allie and saw a single tear run down her sister's cheek, Gillian reached over and wiped it away. She brushed the hair from her shoulder and moved it to her back, attempting a smile for her sister's sake.

They finished the meal in silence.

GRAEME only now realized how late it had become. Though darkness had fallen some time ago, he'd insisted on continuing until they reached their destination. When the torchlights of Highgate Castle finally shone in the distance, he urged his mount to an alarming speed.

Slow down. You are of no use to anyone dead.

He did, though just slightly, noticing he was far ahead of his companion. His clansman must think him mad.

Finally arriving at the gates, he called to the guard above, who raised the portcullis. The courtyard, empty at this late hour, appeared as it should, though he saw it in a different light—as if the wonder he'd felt as a child had been restored.

He woke the stable master, who took his mount, and ran to the entrance of the keep. Before he could bound up the stairs to make his way to the second floor, a voice behind him stopped him.

"Going somewhere?"

Aidan sat in front of the hearth at the far end of the hall. Mug in hand, his legs stretched out in front of him, he looked very much like their father. Graeme had seen him many times in this sort of repose when all was quiet and the rest of the castle inhabitants had gone to bed.

He walked toward Aidan, who looked rather displeased with him.

"To see my wife."

"Ahh," Aidan said. "You've remembered her."

He was in no mood for games.

"I've remembered her," he ground out, "and have come to my senses."

"Glad to hear it."

Graeme gripped the top of the wooden chair on which his brother sat. Not willing to say more about Gillian, he gave Aidan an account of his visit with the earl and his wife.

"It is arranged," he said. "Geoffrey Waryn will meet with Douglas and the clan chiefs the day before the Day of Truce. We are of the same mind about the changes necessary to March Law and must make it official before a petition to the king is made."

"What about Clave? And Hedford?"

"He assured me Lord Clave and the English Warden would be there as well."

Aidan looked skeptical. "Does that not please you?" he asked, already knowing the answer.

"None of this pleases me very well. But I suppose the plan has *some* merit."

More so than avenging the offenders themselves and risking an all-out war, but he did not care to debate those issues now.

"It seems your visit went well then," Aidan allowed.

Graeme smiled. "Very well."

His brother's head jerked up. But Graeme would not get into the rest of it now. His wife should be the first to know, and he was anxious to see her.

"What is it?" Aidan asked.

But he was already walking away.

35

*G*illian turned to the other side, propping the pillow behind her for support. Her bare arms were cool, so she pulled up the coverlet as well. It was the darkest time of night, but something had woken her. The fire that had died out? The chill she so despised?

The door clicked.

Although Gillian couldn't see Graeme, she knew immediately her husband was back. An odd time of day to return to Highgate, but his actions had ceased to surprise her.

She kept her eyes closed, waiting, and wasn't disappointed. He sat on the edge of the bed, close enough that his warmth filtered to her. Gillian turned and opened her eyes.

Graeme was looking at her with such intensity the hairs on her arms stood up despite being covered. He didn't say a word or make a move to touch her. But his gaze, initially curious, had heated with desire.

The same wicked-hot desire that had been between them from the start, from the first time their eyes had met in that garden.

He looked at her like that now, but he didn't make a move to touch her. "You're awake?"

"Aye . . . You're back very late," she offered.

"We returned in haste."

She did not take her eyes from his.

"I wanted to be with you," he said.

Gillian had so many questions, but she found herself saying, "You left without a word."

Out with it all, Gillian. 'Tis no time to lose your tongue.

"You acted peculiarly at dinner and then left the next day . . . without even a simple goodbye." She couldn't keep the bitterness from her voice. "And then again on an errand that could have easily been run by another messenger. Do not deny it."

The corners of Graeme's mouth turned down before he spoke. "When your sister asked about the tapestry, I saw the look in your eyes. And it occurred to me finally . . . I realized how you truly felt about me."

Gillian sat up, now completely awake. His gaze burned a path to her heart. When a swath of unkempt hair fell into his eyes, she reached out and moved it away.

"I left that night, not ready to accept that I deserved you."

There was more. Gillian was sure of it.

He reached for her, and when their hands touched, her entire body tingled. His hand, always so warm and protective . . . she would be content to simply lie here and hold it for hours. Days.

"I needed to do something to make it right. So I traveled to Kenshire, spoke to Waryn, had our meeting, and spent each night since tormented with thoughts of telling you. Showing you."

He took a deep breath. "I love you, Gillian."

She froze. "What did you say?"

"I love you. I am glad to have been caught in the garden with you. Overjoyed, in fact, that we were forced to marry. Because it brought a proper English queen into my life, one whose kindness and curiosity compelled me since the day we met. If you wish to explore what we have first, get to know each other, and someday—"

He abruptly let go of her hand and stood, crossing his arms and watching her reaction.

Scared. She'd never have imagined it possible, but her husband was scared. Gillian jumped out of the bed and laid her hands on his crossed arms.

"I love you, Graeme. I love your loyalty and passion, your gentleness and . . ."

That she could not say aloud.

Did he believe her? If he would not listen to her words, then perhaps . . .

Gillian turned away, walked to the bed, finding its edge thanks to the sole candle that was still lit, and crawled inside. She really should have disrobed first, but no matter. It was not overly difficult to remove her shift and the braid that held her hair together while lying down. Finally, when finished, she looked to her husband.

HE STARED AT THE BED, the woman he'd dreamt of every night lying completely exposed and vulnerable. Because he knew Gillian. She was not yet completely comfortable with their intimacy, which made the gesture more meaningful.

I love you, Graeme.

Gillian loved him, and by all the saints in Scotland, he loved her too. He tore off his clothes as he approached the bed, needing to bury himself inside her, sealing the pact they'd made with their words.

But not yet.

He spread her legs wide as he crawled between them. Turning his head, he kissed her smooth calf and then edged his lips up toward her thigh. Higher still. Graeme held her legs open with his hands while he placed a soft kiss on her inner thigh.

He looked up at his English queen holding court in their bed.

Shaking off any remaining vestiges of doubt, he told her exactly how their night would end.

"I am going to prove my love for you with every touch of my lips." He kissed the sensitive flesh on the underside of each slightly bent knee. "I will revere you as the queen you are." He splayed his hands wide on her thighs. "And when I enter you," he finished as he glided toward her, "each thrust will give you a piece of me, my love and my eternal devotion to you, Gillian."

She licked her lips, tempting him to take them. But he fulfilled his promise and made his way toward her mouth slowly, each touch of his lips on her skin an apology. For not accepting her the first time she asked for more. For leaving, twice. By the time he reached her breasts, he partially covered her, the feel of her skin against his hardening him even more. Her softness and acceptance touched his very soul.

He gave each breast the attention it deserved, kissing one while teasing the other with his hand, and then finally made his way to her mouth. He captured her lips beneath his own, unrelenting in his message: he loved her, worshiped her, and would prove it this night. His tongue tussled with hers, a soft moan escaping from her lips. Graeme's skin burned everywhere it touched hers. And when she pressed into him, it was an invitation he could not ignore.

He reached down and guided himself into her. But once her tightness enveloped him, his urge to go slowly was overwhelmed by the desire to fit so deeply into his wife that neither of them would have any remaining doubts about where they belonged —together.

Guiding her legs up on either side of him, he whispered into her ear, "Wrap your legs around me."

When she did, Graeme took full advantage of the new position and thrust and circled and thrust until her uneven breathing became louder. He kissed her ear, her neck, his tongue flicking Gillian's skin as he gave her everything he had, waiting . . .

For that. Her legs tightened around his back as she grabbed his hair, groaning. The small spasms intensified, and he finally let go. Spilling himself into her, Graeme captured her lips once more, a silent promise that he would give as much as she offered.

She was his wife in truth, and the thought of it filled him with so much pride that he could not get close enough. He rolled her atop him, their bodies still joined, and held on tight. Her hair covered his face, their limbs indistinguishable.

Graeme could stay this way forever.

Unfortunately, she eventually lifted her head, and he reached up to move her hair to the side.

He opened his mouth to tell her all that he'd been thinking, but words seemed to pale in comparison to what they'd just experienced. Instead, he lifted his head and kissed her.

Her broad smile was the only response he needed.

36

"Move against me like that one more time, and you'll know exactly how I'd like to wake up to you every morning for the rest of our lives."

Gillian chuckled and pressed her backside against him, taunting him. Teasing him. Well, he had not been teasing her. He was already hard and more than ready for his wife. Reaching around to ensure she was also ready for him, Graeme moved over her so quickly Gillian had time for nothing more than a widening of her eyes before he entered her.

Unlike the night before, he did not take his time. She met his every thrust with one of her own, and it took only a change of pace, from fast to slow and back again, before his English queen tipped her head back and thrust her hips up to meet him.

Graeme covered her hands, which gripped the coverlet on both side of them, and found his release with her. Collapsing on top of her, supporting his weight in order to not crush her, Graeme placed a kiss on her nose.

"Good morn, wife."

Gillian glanced at the single beam of sunlight streaming into the chamber and sighed. When she looked back at him, she voiced her thoughts aloud. "A glorious morn to be sure."

Reluctantly pulling himself away, Graeme began to move about the room, cleaning himself and preparing for the day. When he glanced back, Gillian was sitting up. Seeing the look on his face, she immediately dropped the coverlet from her breasts, and it took every bit of Graeme's strength of will for him not to take advantage of the two round, full mounds that stared back at him.

He groaned, his well-used cock responding as it should.

"Nay," he said, more to himself than Gillian, who in fact had not said a word. What he had planned was just too important.

"I have something to tell you," he blurted, glancing back at her glorious body. Now fully dressed, he sat on the side of the bed, giving in to temptation for just one moment. He reached out to fondle Gillian's breasts, sliding closer to her for just one more taste. But rather than pull her nipple into his mouth, he pulled away.

"I will never accomplish anything from this day forward," he murmured.

He tried to focus again, this time walking toward the door before turning to speak to her. Amused, Gillian cocked her head to the side and waited.

"So what is it you have to tell me?" she asked.

He could very happily forget every duty, rip off his clothes, and climb back into bed with the woman he loved. But it was because of that love that he would not.

At least not yet.

"Aye, but not until we find Allie."

"My sister?"

"The very same one." He flicked the iron lock and opened the door, though not too wide, lest anyone get a glimpse of the May Day beauty languishing in his bed.

Their bed.

"Hurry down," he said, excited now. "I will find your sister."

Before she could ask further questions, he left to do just that. Sure enough, she and Aidan already sat at the head table with their heads tipped together, speaking of something they clearly did not want others to hear.

"Good morn," he said, smiling.

Aidan and Allie exchanged glances, both greeting him with wary expressions.

"I see you haven't yet broken your fast?" he said to Allie.

She shook her head.

"Then can I have a private word first?"

While he waited, his sister-in-law stood and followed him from the hall. He led the way to his private chamber at the back of the hall, the windowless one that made him feel as if he couldn't breathe.

Spotting Fiona and Morgan, he gestured to them. "Will you please send Gillian back here when she arrives?"

As he walked by his brother, Aidan gave him a curious glance. He indicated, without speaking, that he would explain later.

"Please sit," he told Allie. She very delicately placed herself on a cushioned chair.

"Why am I here, Graeme?"

"Indeed," a voice behind him added. "Why are we both here?"

Though he'd been elated before, excited to speak to them and hopeful they would approve, when faced with both Gillian and her sister, Graeme began to doubt himself. But the deed had been done, and there was nothing more to do than explain himself.

"If you'd like to sit—"

"Nay, Graeme, just tell me what is happening. You're making my stomach do little flips in anticipation."

His eyelids lowered, for he savored the thought of how else he might elicit that reaction. That would have to wait.

"I've given your father an . . . expanded dowry."

The women exchanged glances, so he hurried to finish.

"On the way back from Kenshire, I stopped at Lyndwood."

267

"You saw my father?" Gillian asked. "Alone?"

"Saw him, spoke to him. Offered him the same amount of coin Covington would have given him had he married—well, either one of you."

Awareness washed over both of their faces at once.

"But you'd already paid a dowry. Did he take it?"

"Do you have such coin?"

"What will happen to Lyndwood?"

The ladies asked their questions so quickly he didn't know who to respond to first.

"Highgate End is a wealthy property, but the fur trade isn't quite that lucrative. Covington offered a substantial sum, one that would indeed have allowed your father to retain Lyndwood for generations to come."

"Then how—"

"Highgate End," he began. "Clan Kerr. Your friend Sara."

Before Gillian could panic, he went to her and grasped her hands, intertwining her fingers with his own. "It is as I told you. Here in Scotland, allies do what is needed to protect their own and those who've pledged loyalty to them. Besides, if your father lost Lyndwood, its next lord may have proven unsympathetic to our cause."

He studied her face. Was she happy? Surprised?

"I know you did not wish to tell Sara, but after all that's happened, with the Scots pledging their support . . . It was not a very large sum, and your friend was happy to help. Indeed . . ." He winked. ". . . I do believe she is wroth with you for not explaining the situation in the first place."

"But I didn't want to burden her," Gillian protested.

"Friends . . . allies . . . husbands and wives . . . they do not burden each other with their troubles. A burden is unwanted, and I can assure you, all involved very much wanted to help."

Graeme nearly fell into his wife when Allie stood and hugged him from the side.

"Graeme, thank you!" She squeezed even harder, her tears wetting his tunic.

He put his arm around her, still holding his wife's hand. Though Gillian didn't say a word, her smile allowed Graeme to breathe normally again. When a tear fell down her cheek, he released her hand to wipe it away. By then Allie had disengaged herself.

Standing in that small, confined room, crowded with two women he'd not known just a short time ago, Graeme silently thanked every saint he could think of for such blessings. For no matter what battles may lie ahead, he'd face them with this magnificent English queen by his side.

EPILOGUE

*G*illian paced the parapet, watching . . . waiting . . . for any sign of her husband. Though he had attempted to convince her otherwise, she knew this Day of Truce would be dangerous. Much had been at stake, but her husband had gone to great pains to ensure that peace had a chance. If only they could find a way to handle those who would benefit from disorder. Who would take advantage of the situation for their own gain.

Like Father.

She shrugged off the traitorous thought, telling herself he'd done what he needed to do. Now, at least, he was back on the right side. For better or worse, she loved her parents, and it was a relief they no longer had to worry about losing Lyndwood. Her father's missive, which had arrived just the day before, had been brief, but he'd never been an effusive sort. He'd wished Gillian well, and her husband too, pleading that she and Allie visit soon.

It was a start.

She stared at the horizon, as if not doing so would delay his arrival. The beauty of this land still humbled her. She spun toward the keep and peered at the spot where their chamber was located.

Smiling, she remembered the last night before his departure. Graeme had not been jesting when he'd told her the bedchamber was not a place for shyness. Indeed, she'd allowed her curiosity free rein, and that night—

When a pair of arms slipped around her waist from the back, she remembered the last time he'd done that very same thing.

Graeme moved her hair to the side and kissed her neck.

"You're safe," Gillian said. Her shoulders relaxed. "How did it go?"

Graeme continued to tease her with his lips. "As well as can be expected."

"But what does that mean? Did the wardens agree—"

"Not entirely," he said, spinning her around. "But it's a start, and all agree that the law needs to change. That what happened with Blackburn cannot be allowed to happen again. I'll gladly share all with you later, but it's been two nights since—"

"You've pleased me," she said boldly.

"And you, me," he said, just as brazenly. "And I don't care to wait any longer."

He claimed her lips and Gillian kissed him back with the fervor of a woman who'd worried for three days about the man she loved. And, just as she'd taken to doing a hundred times a day whenever they were together, Gillian pulled back and said, "I love you, Graeme."

His gaze never wavered. "And I love you, my May Day Queen."

"May Day? I thought I was your queen every day?"

He backed away, bowed deeply, and stood so tall she had to look up to see his face.

"Every day." He smiled. A wicked, sensual smile. "And night."

ALSO BY CECELIA MECCA

The Border Series

BECOME AN INSIDER

Become a CM Insider to receive a bonus chapter of 'The Thief's Countess,' plus other exclusive content including family trees, chapter upgrades and sneak peeks of upcoming books.

CeceliaMecca.com/Insider

ABOUT THE AUTHOR

Cecelia Mecca is the author of medieval romance, including the Border Series, and sometimes wishes she could be transported back in time to the days of knights and castles. Although the former English teacher's actual home is in Northeast Pennsylvania where she lives with her husband and two children, her online home can be found at CeceliaMecca.com. She would love to hear from you.

Stay in touch:
info@ceceliamecca.com

Made in the USA
Middletown, DE
06 October 2018